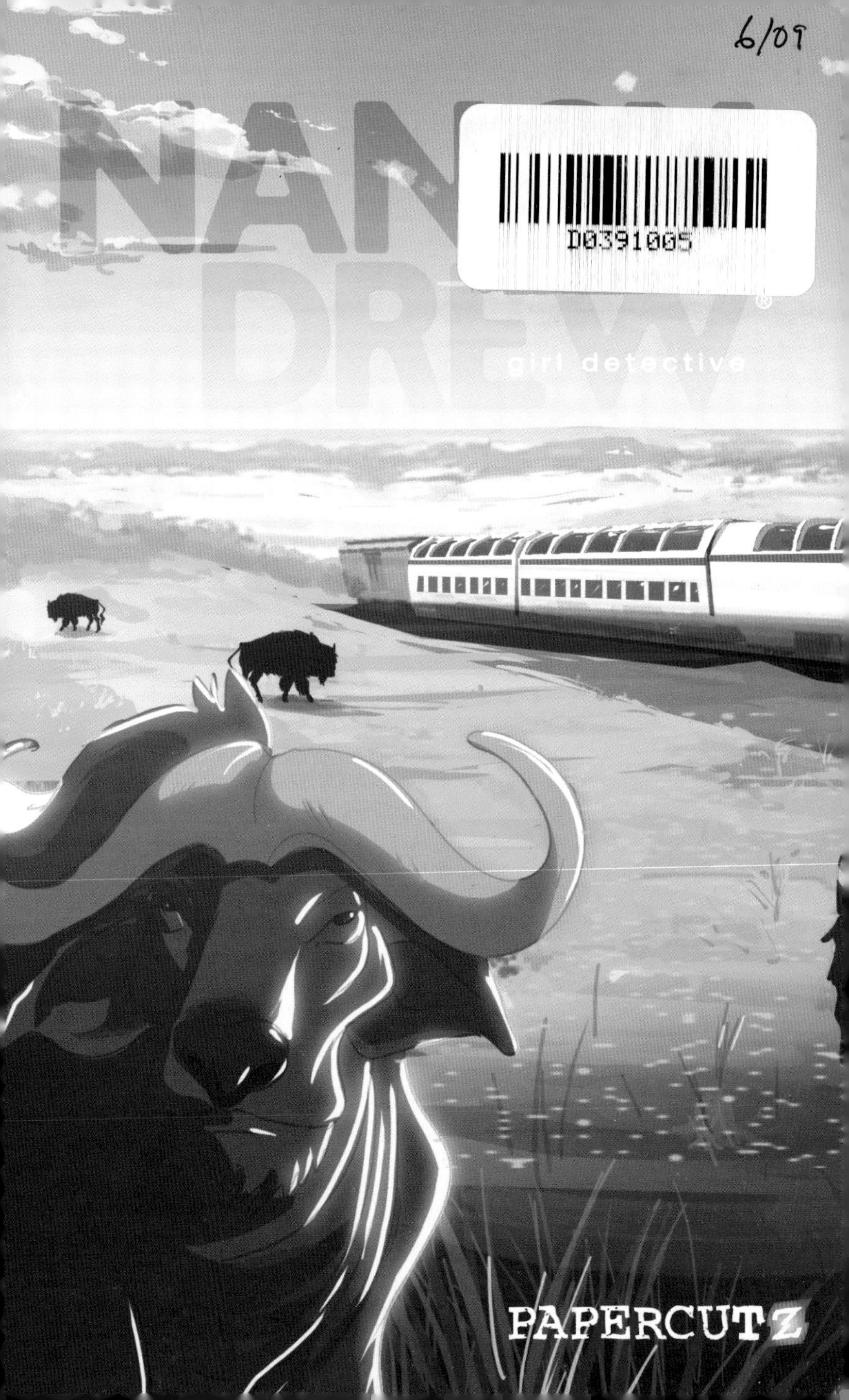
6/09
D0391005
NAN
DREW®
girl detective
PAPERCUTZ

NANCY DREW GRAPHIC NOVELS AVAILABLE FROM PAPERCUTZ

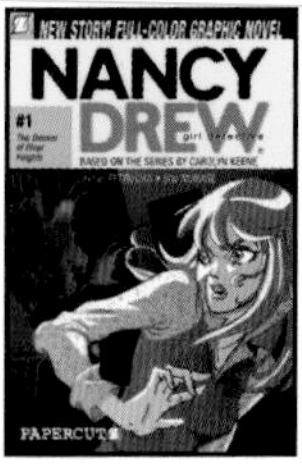
NEW STORY! FULL-COLOR GRAPHIC NOVEL
NANCY DREW
#1
BASED ON THE SERIES BY CAROLYN KEENE
PAPERCUTZ
#1 "The Demon of River Heights"

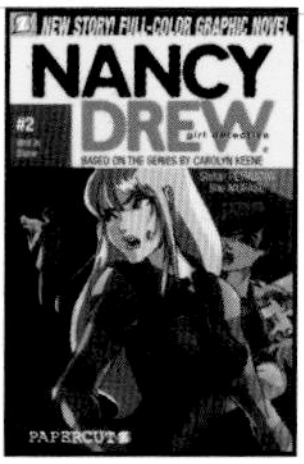
NEW STORY! FULL-COLOR GRAPHIC NOVEL
NANCY DREW
#2
BASED ON THE SERIES BY CAROLYN KEENE
PAPERCUTZ
#2 "Writ In Stone"

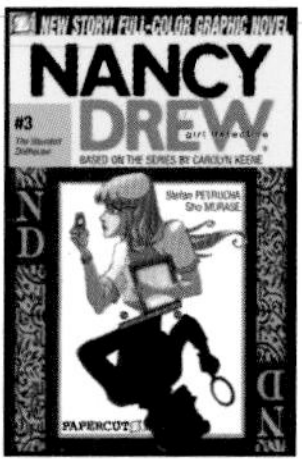
NEW STORY! FULL-COLOR GRAPHIC NOVEL
NANCY DREW
#3
BASED ON THE SERIES BY CAROLYN KEENE
Stefan PETRUCHA
Sho MURASE
PAPERCUTZ
#3 "The Haunted Dollhouse"

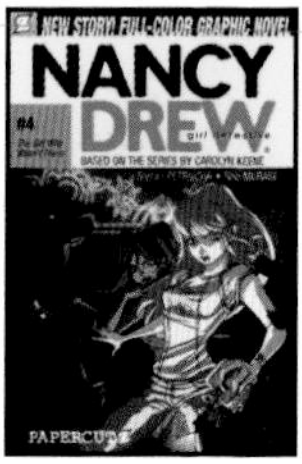
NEW STORY! FULL-COLOR GRAPHIC NOVEL
NANCY DREW
#4
BASED ON THE SERIES BY CAROLYN KEENE
PAPERCUTZ
#4 "The Girl Who Wasn't There"

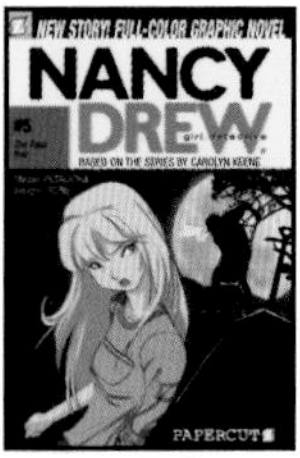
NEW STORY! FULL-COLOR GRAPHIC NOVEL
NANCY DREW
#5
BASED ON THE SERIES BY CAROLYN KEENE
PAPERCUTZ
#5 "The Fake Heir"

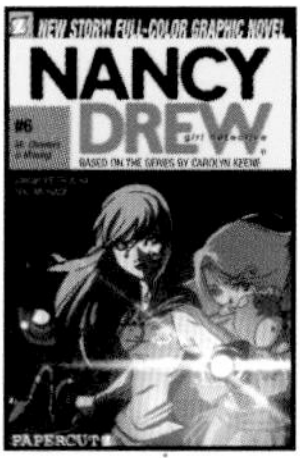
NEW STORY! FULL-COLOR GRAPHIC NOVEL
NANCY DREW
#6
BASED ON THE SERIES BY CAROLYN KEENE
PAPERCUTZ
#6 "Mr. Cheeters Is Missing"

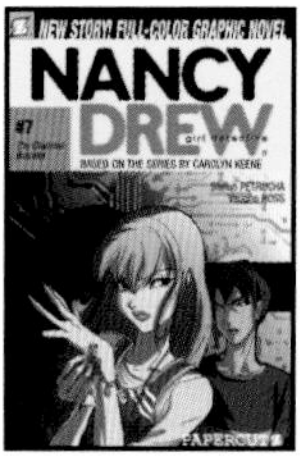
NEW STORY! FULL-COLOR GRAPHIC NOVEL
NANCY DREW
#7
BASED ON THE SERIES BY CAROLYN KEENE
PAPERCUTZ
#7 "The Charmed Bracelet"

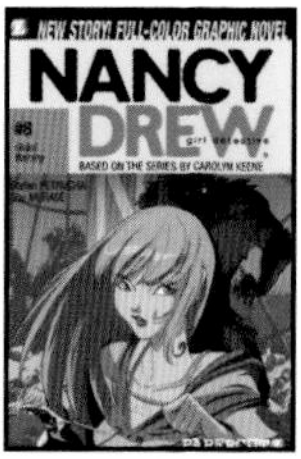
NEW STORY! FULL-COLOR GRAPHIC NOVEL
NANCY DREW
#8
BASED ON THE SERIES BY CAROLYN KEENE
#8 "Global Warning"

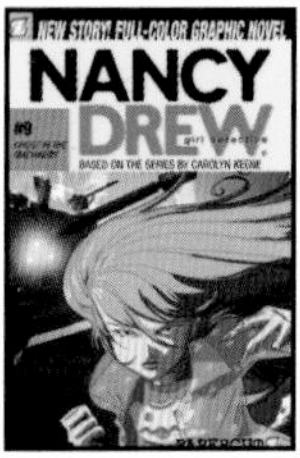
NEW STORY! FULL-COLOR GRAPHIC NOVEL
NANCY DREW
#9
BASED ON THE SERIES BY CAROLYN KEENE
#9 "Ghost In The Machinery"

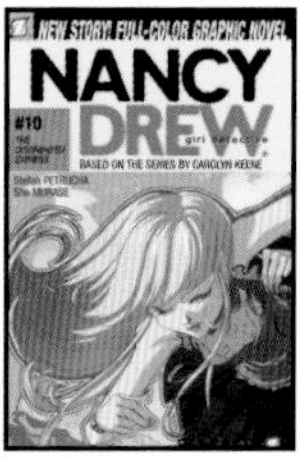
NEW STORY! FULL-COLOR GRAPHIC NOVEL
NANCY DREW
#10
BASED ON THE SERIES BY CAROLYN KEENE
#10 "The Disoriented Express"

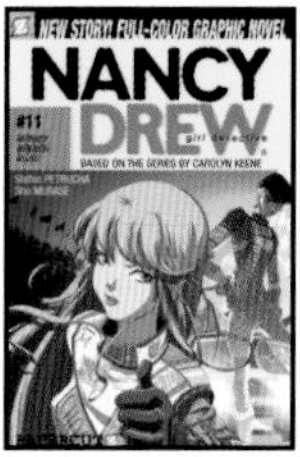
NEW STORY! FULL-COLOR GRAPHIC NOVEL
NANCY DREW
#11
BASED ON THE SERIES BY CAROLYN KEENE
#11 "Monkey Wrench Blues"

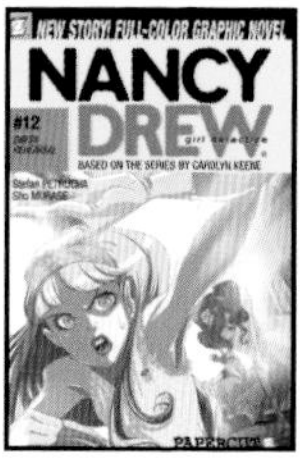
NEW STORY! FULL-COLOR GRAPHIC NOVEL
NANCY DREW
#12
BASED ON THE SERIES BY CAROLYN KEENE
#12 "Dress Reversal"

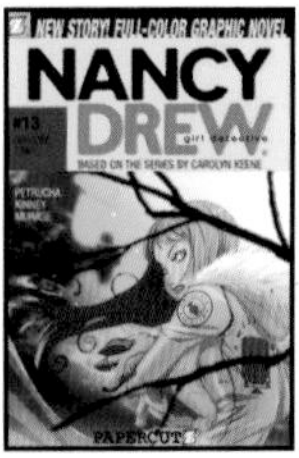
NEW STORY! FULL-COLOR GRAPHIC NOVEL
NANCY DREW
#13
BASED ON THE SERIES BY CAROLYN KEENE
PAPERCUTZ
#13 "Doggone Town"

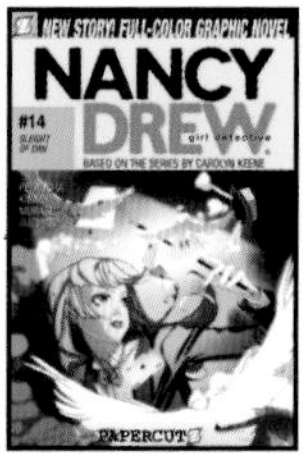
NEW STORY! FULL-COLOR GRAPHIC NOVEL
NANCY DREW
#14
BASED ON THE SERIES BY CAROLYN KEENE
PAPERCUTZ
#14 "Sleight of Dan"

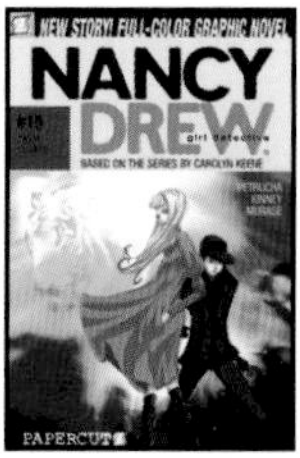
NEW STORY! FULL-COLOR GRAPHIC NOVEL
NANCY DREW
BASED ON THE SERIES BY CAROLYN KEENE
PAPERCUTZ
Coming November '08
#15 "Tiger Counter"

$7.95 each in paperback, $12.95 each in hardcover.
Please add $4.00 for postage and handling for the first book, add $1.00 for each additional book.

Please make check payable to NBM Publishing. Send to:
Papercutz, 40 Exchange Place, Suite 1308 New York, NY 10005, 1-800-886-1223
www.papercutz.com

NANCY
DREW
#10   girl detective ®

The Disoriented Express

STEFAN PETRUCHA & SARAH KINNEY • Writers
SHO MURASE • Artist
with 3D CG elements and color by CARLOS JOSE GUZMAN
Based on the series by
CAROLYN KEENE

New York

The Disoriented Express
STEFAN PETRUCHA & SARAH KINNEY – Writers
SHO MURASE – Artist
with 3D CG elements and color by CARLOS JOSE GUZMAN
BRYAN SENKA – Letterer
JIM SALICRUP
Editor-in-Chief

ISBN 10: 1-59707-066-1 paperback edition
ISBN 13: 978-1-59707-066-9 paperback edition
ISBN 10: 1-59707-067-X hardcover edition
ISBN 13: 978-1-59707-067-6 hardcover edition

6-11-09

Printed in China.
Distributed by Macmillan.

10 9 8 7 6 5 4 3 2

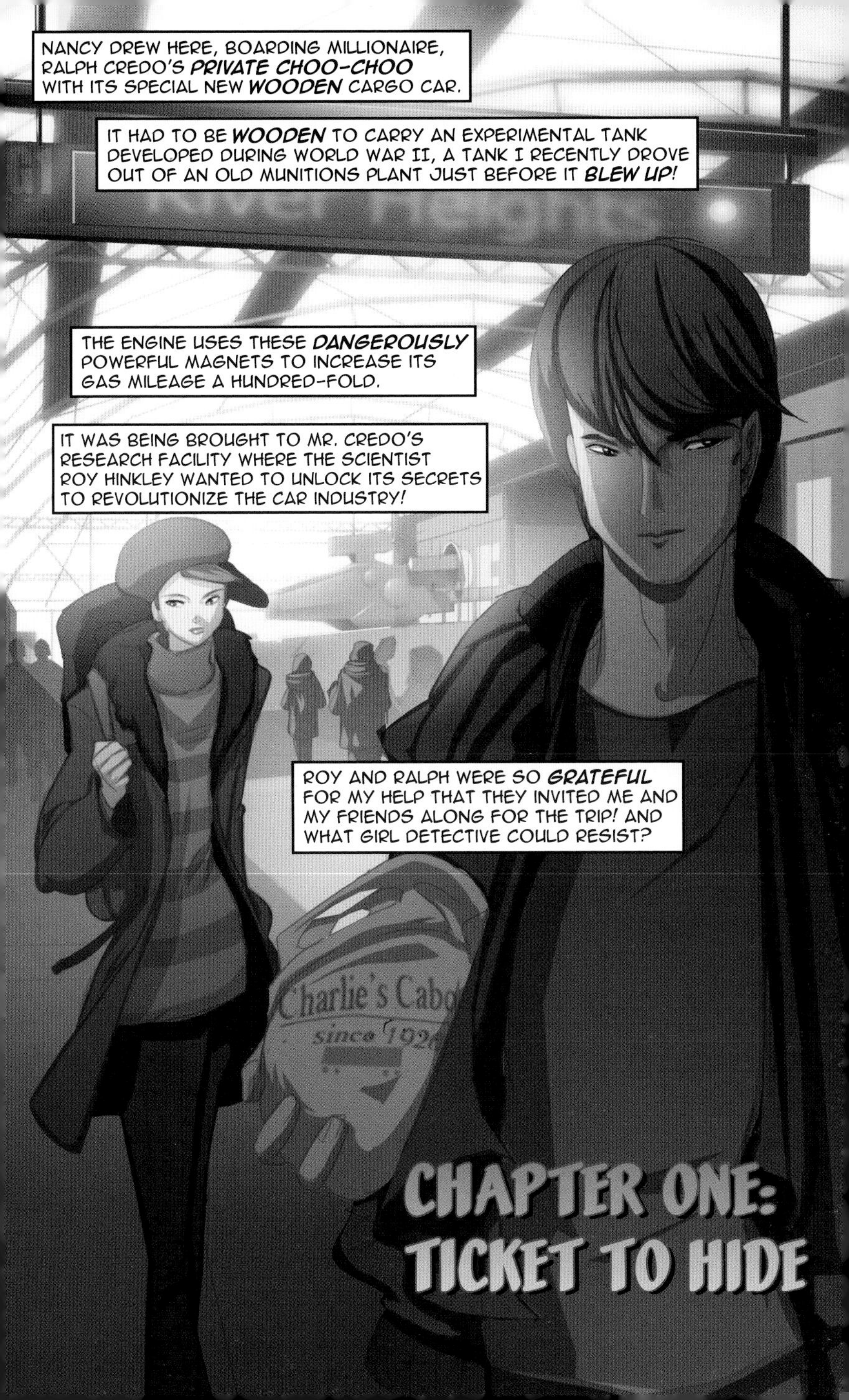

NANCY DREW HERE, BOARDING MILLIONAIRE, RALPH CREDO'S PRIVATE CHOO-CHOO WITH ITS SPECIAL NEW WOODEN CARGO CAR.
IT HAD TO BE WOODEN TO CARRY AN EXPERIMENTAL TANK DEVELOPED DURING WORLD WAR II, A TANK I RECENTLY DROVE OUT OF AN OLD MUNITIONS PLANT JUST BEFORE IT BLEW UP!
THE ENGINE USES THESE DANGEROUSLY POWERFUL MAGNETS TO INCREASE ITS GAS MILEAGE A HUNDRED-FOLD.
IT WAS BEING BROUGHT TO MR. CREDO'S RESEARCH FACILITY WHERE THE SCIENTIST ROY HINKLEY WANTED TO UNLOCK ITS SECRETS TO REVOLUTIONIZE THE CAR INDUSTRY!
ROY AND RALPH WERE SO GRATEFUL FOR MY HELP THAT THEY INVITED ME AND MY FRIENDS ALONG FOR THE TRIP! AND WHAT GIRL DETECTIVE COULD RESIST?
CHAPTER ONE: TICKET TO HIDE

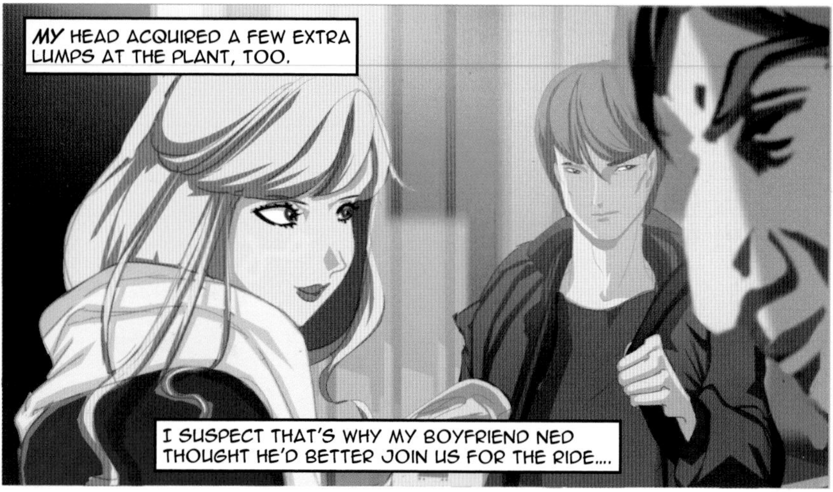
MY HEAD ACQUIRED A FEW EXTRA LUMPS AT THE PLANT, TOO.
I SUSPECT THAT'S WHY MY BOYFRIEND NED THOUGHT HE'D BETTER JOIN US FOR THE RIDE....

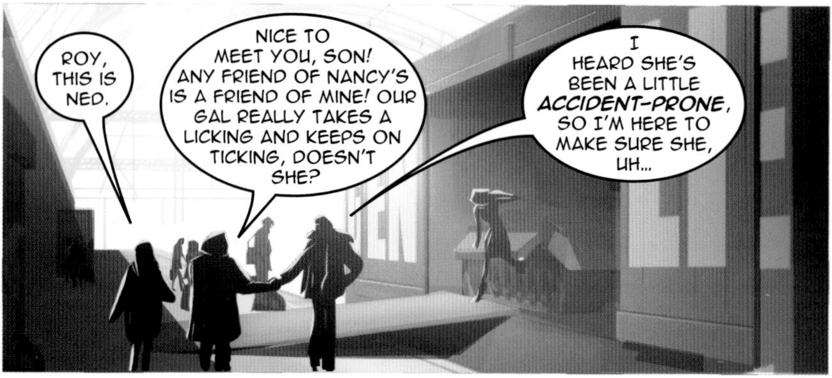
ROY, THIS IS NED.
NICE TO MEET YOU, SON! ANY FRIEND OF NANCY'S IS A FRIEND OF MINE! OUR GAL REALLY TAKES A LICKING AND KEEPS ON TICKING, DOESN'T SHE?
I HEARD SHE'S BEEN A LITTLE ACCIDENT-PRONE, SO I'M HERE TO MAKE SURE SHE, UH...

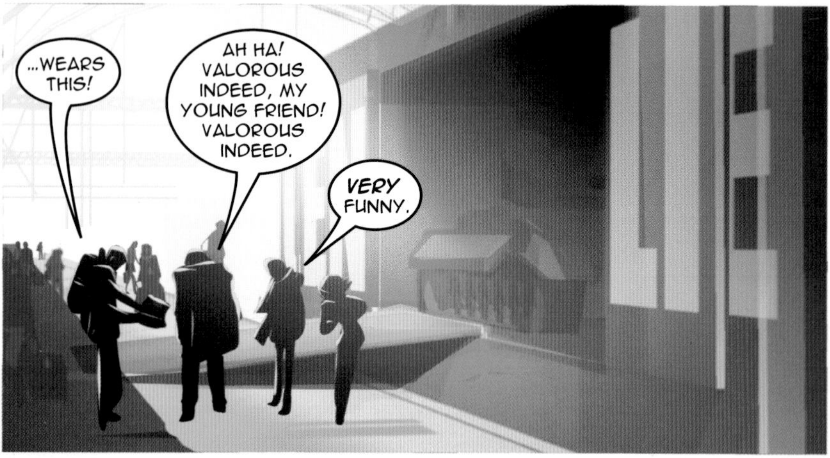
...WEARS THIS!
AH HA! VALOROUS INDEED, MY YOUNG FRIEND! VALOROUS INDEED.
VERY FUNNY.

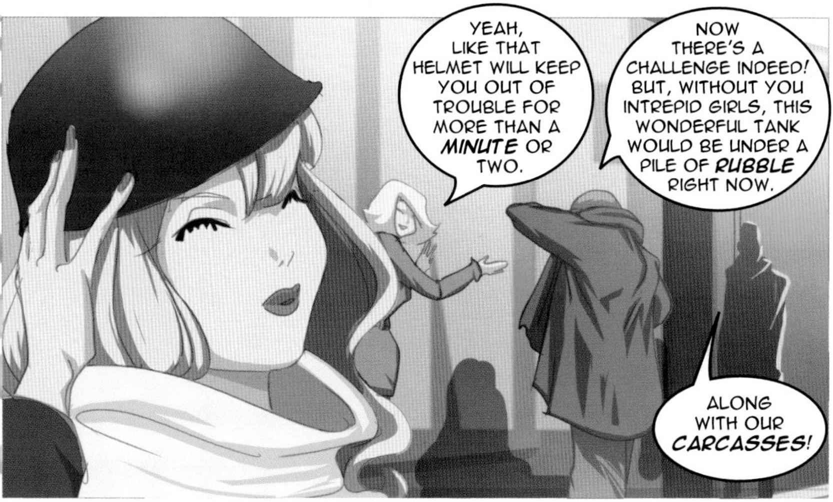
YEAH, LIKE THAT HELMET WILL KEEP YOU OUT OF TROUBLE FOR MORE THAN A *MINUTE* OR TWO.
NOW THERE'S A CHALLENGE INDEED! BUT, WITHOUT YOU INTREPID GIRLS, THIS WONDERFUL TANK WOULD BE UNDER A PILE OF ***RUBBLE*** RIGHT NOW.
ALONG WITH OUR ***CARCASSES***!

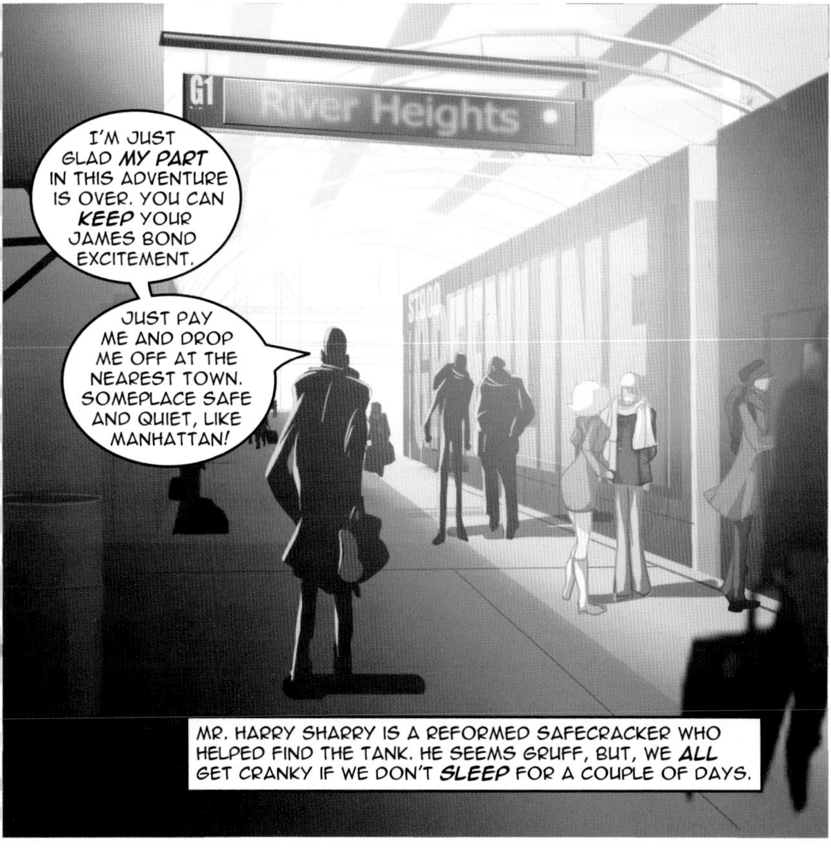
G1
River Heights
I'M JUST GLAD *MY PART* IN THIS ADVENTURE IS OVER. YOU CAN ***KEEP*** YOUR JAMES BOND EXCITEMENT.
JUST PAY ME AND DROP ME OFF AT THE NEAREST TOWN. SOMEPLACE SAFE AND QUIET, LIKE MANHATTAN!
MR. HARRY SHARRY IS A REFORMED SAFECRACKER WHO HELPED FIND THE TANK. HE SEEMS GRUFF, BUT, WE ***ALL*** GET CRANKY IF WE DON'T ***SLEEP*** FOR A COUPLE OF DAYS.

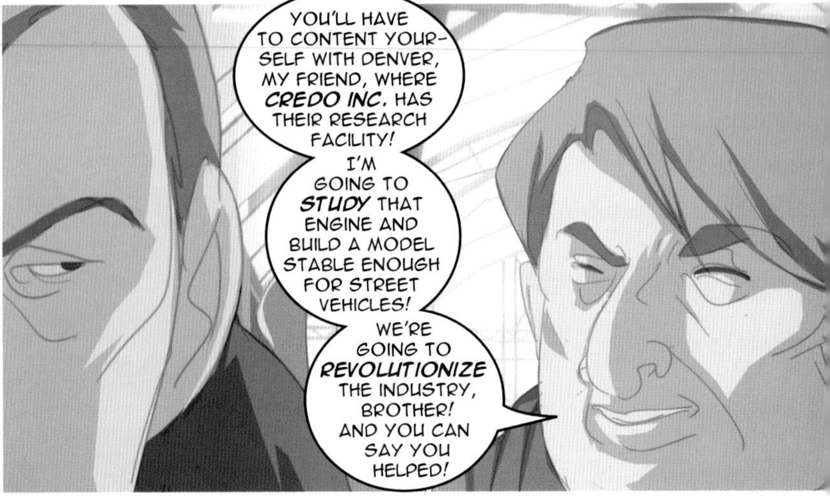
YOU'LL HAVE TO CONTENT YOURSELF WITH DENVER, MY FRIEND, WHERE CREDO INC. HAS THEIR RESEARCH FACILITY!
I'M GOING TO STUDY THAT ENGINE AND BUILD A MODEL STABLE ENOUGH FOR STREET VEHICLES!
WE'RE GOING TO REVOLUTIONIZE THE INDUSTRY, BROTHER! AND YOU CAN SAY YOU HELPED!

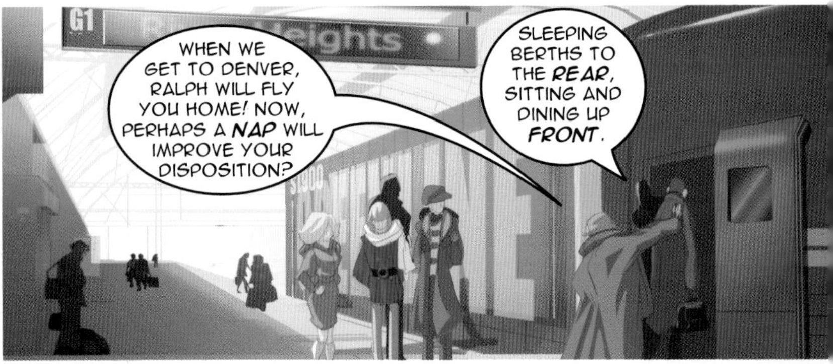
G1
WHEN WE GET TO DENVER, RALPH WILL FLY YOU HOME! NOW, PERHAPS A NAP WILL IMPROVE YOUR DISPOSITION?
SLEEPING BERTHS TO THE REAR, SITTING AND DINING UP FRONT.

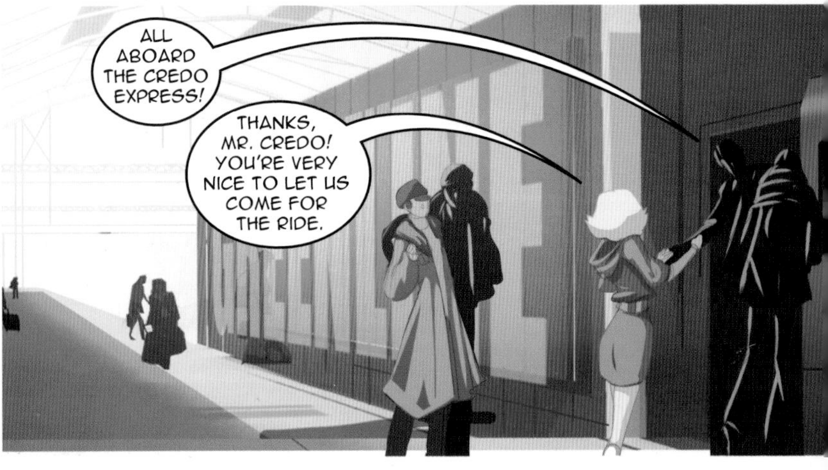
ALL ABOARD THE CREDO EXPRESS!
THANKS, MR. CREDO! YOU'RE VERY NICE TO LET US COME FOR THE RIDE.

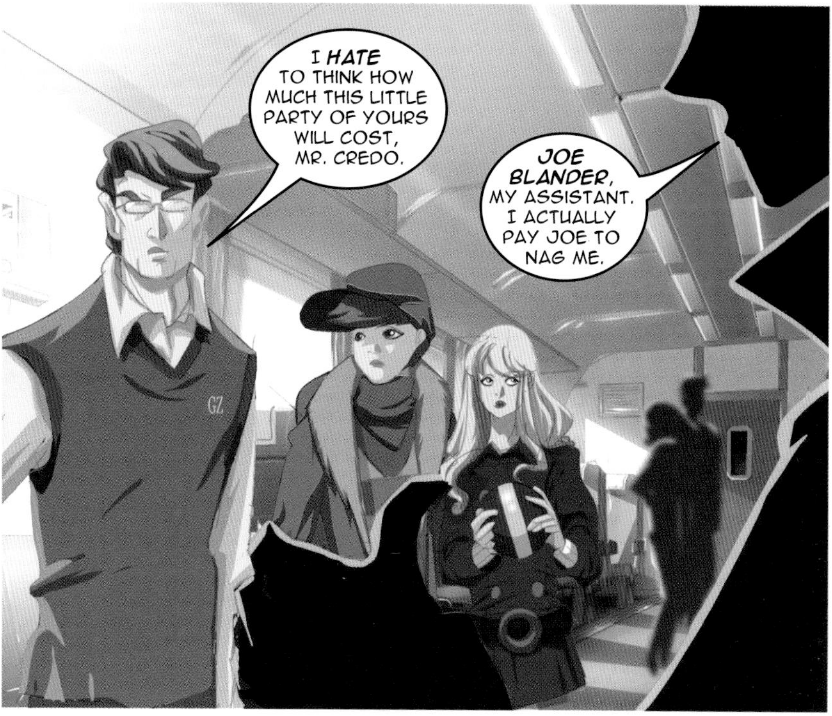
I HATE TO THINK HOW MUCH THIS LITTLE PARTY OF YOURS WILL COST, MR. CREDO.
JOE BLANDER, MY ASSISTANT. I ACTUALLY PAY JOE TO NAG ME.

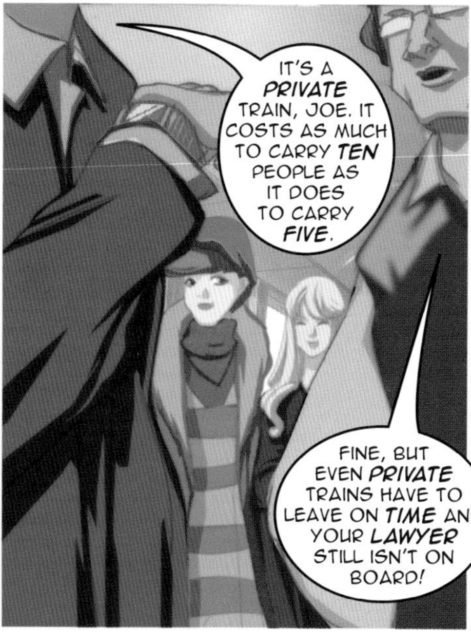
IT'S A PRIVATE TRAIN, JOE. IT COSTS AS MUCH TO CARRY TEN PEOPLE AS IT DOES TO CARRY FIVE.
FINE, BUT EVEN PRIVATE TRAINS HAVE TO LEAVE ON TIME AND YOUR LAWYER STILL ISN'T ON BOARD!

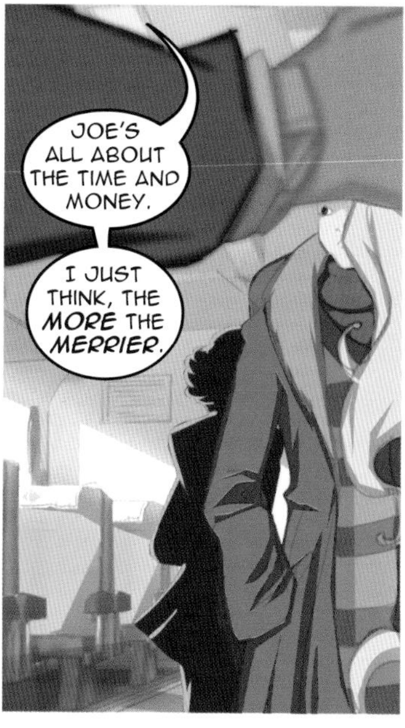
JOE'S ALL ABOUT THE TIME AND MONEY.
I JUST THINK, THE MORE THE MERRIER.

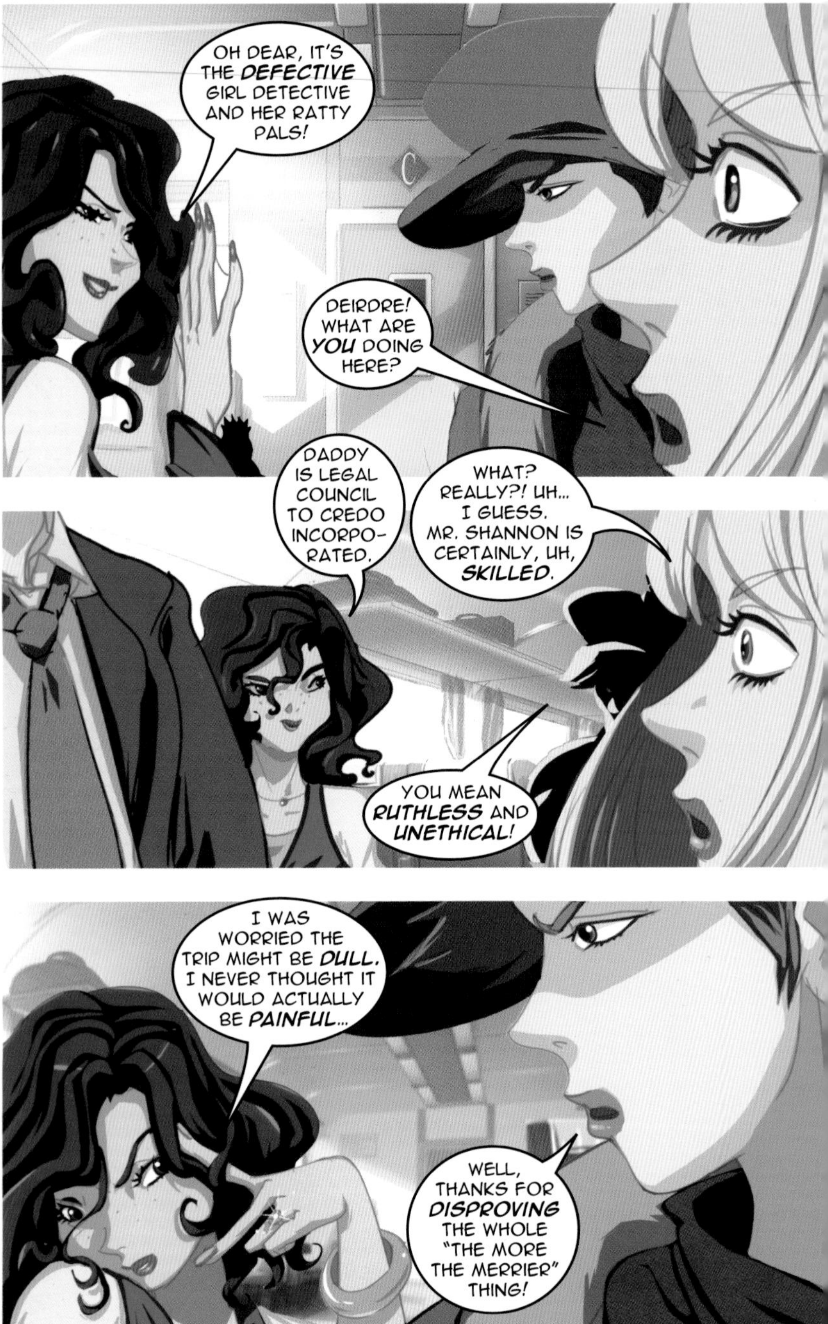
OH DEAR, IT'S THE *DEFECTIVE* GIRL DETECTIVE AND HER RATTY PALS!
DEIRDRE! WHAT ARE *YOU* DOING HERE?
DADDY IS LEGAL COUNCIL TO CREDO INCORPO-RATED.
WHAT? REALLY?! UH... I GUESS. MR. SHANNON IS CERTAINLY, UH, *SKILLED*.
YOU MEAN *RUTHLESS* AND *UNETHICAL*!
I WAS WORRIED THE TRIP MIGHT BE *DULL*. I NEVER THOUGHT IT WOULD ACTUALLY BE *PAINFUL*...
WELL, THANKS FOR *DISPROVING* THE WHOLE "THE MORE THE MERRIER" THING!

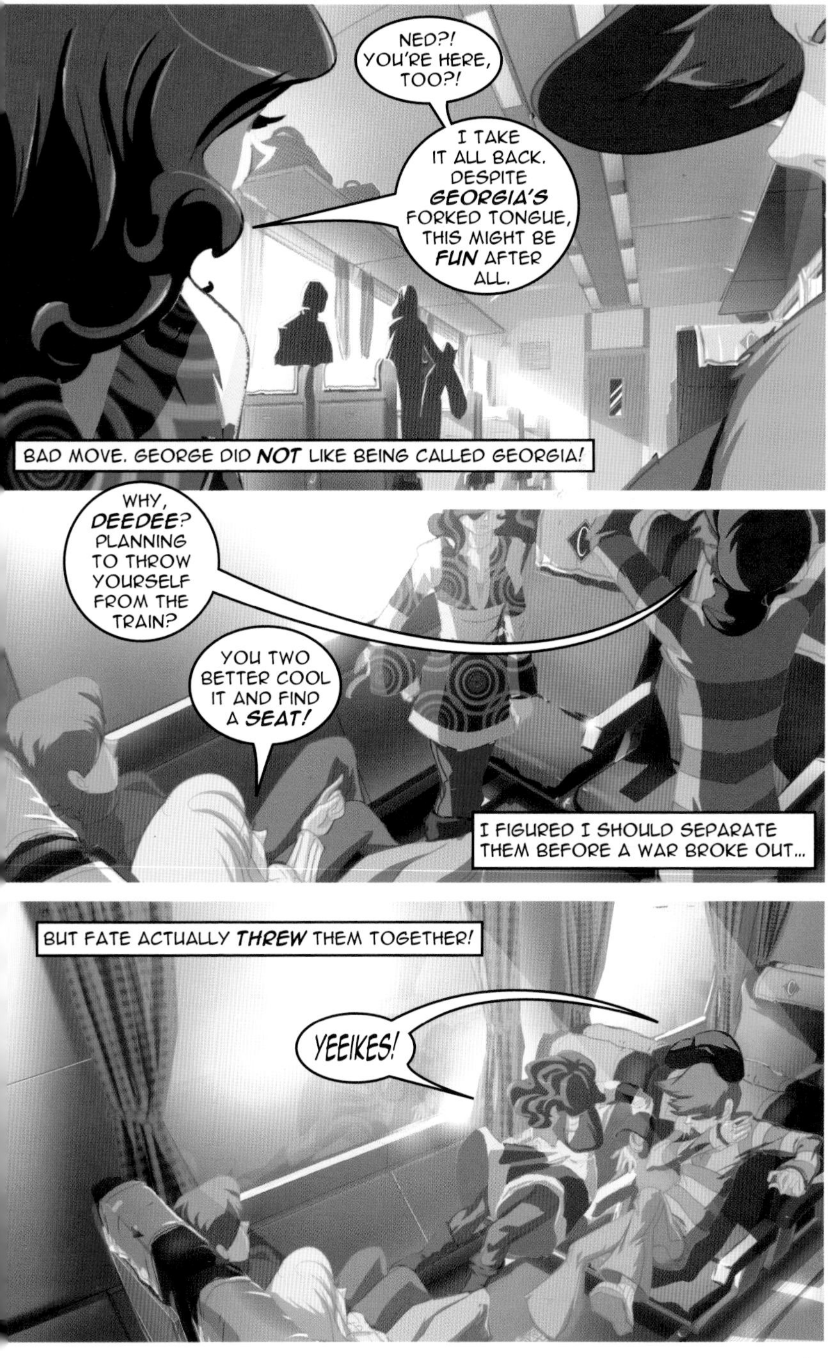
NED?! YOU'RE HERE, TOO?!
I TAKE IT ALL BACK. DESPITE ***GEORGIA'S*** FORKED TONGUE, THIS MIGHT BE ***FUN*** AFTER ALL.
BAD MOVE. GEORGE DID ***NOT*** LIKE BEING CALLED GEORGIA!
WHY, ***DEEDEE***? PLANNING TO THROW YOURSELF FROM THE TRAIN?
YOU TWO BETTER COOL IT AND FIND A ***SEAT!***
I FIGURED I SHOULD SEPARATE THEM BEFORE A WAR BROKE OUT...
BUT FATE ACTUALLY ***THREW*** THEM TOGETHER!
YEEIKES!

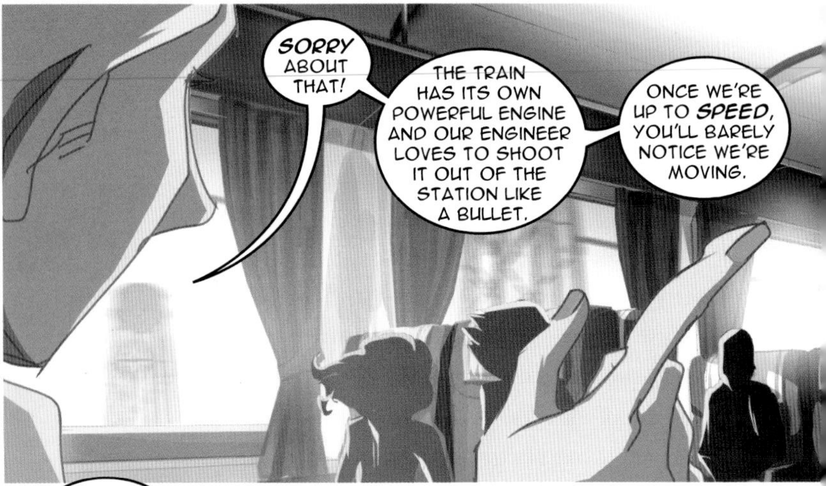
SORRY ABOUT THAT!
THE TRAIN HAS ITS OWN POWERFUL ENGINE AND OUR ENGINEER LOVES TO SHOOT IT OUT OF THE STATION LIKE A BULLET.
ONCE WE'RE UP TO SPEED, YOU'LL BARELY NOTICE WE'RE MOVING.
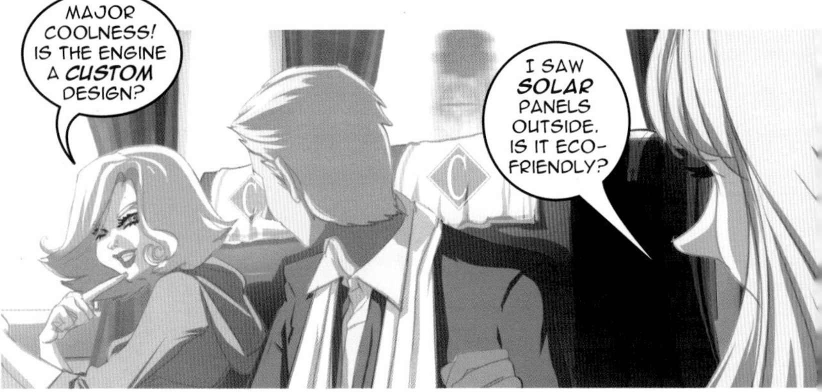
MAJOR COOLNESS! IS THE ENGINE A CUSTOM DESIGN?
I SAW SOLAR PANELS OUTSIDE. IS IT ECO-FRIENDLY?
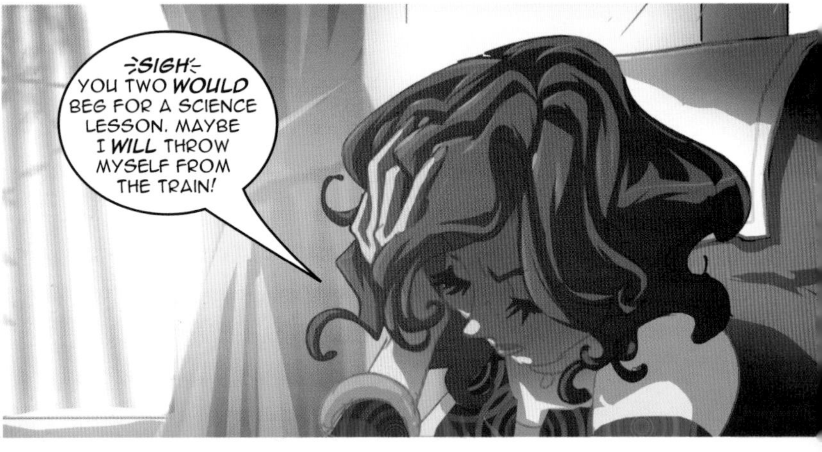
SIGH
YOU TWO WOULD BEG FOR A SCIENCE LESSON. MAYBE I WILL THROW MYSELF FROM THE TRAIN!

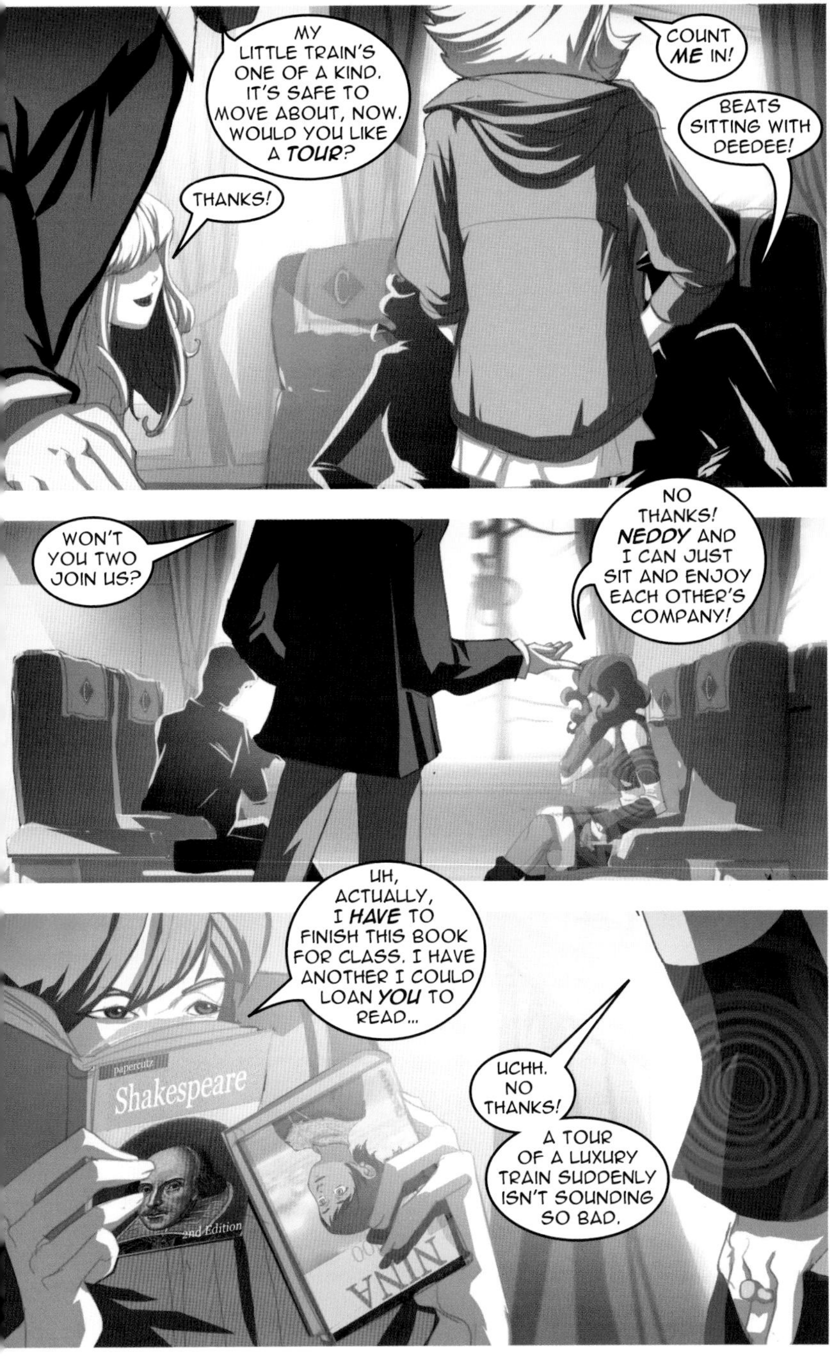
MY LITTLE TRAIN'S ONE OF A KIND. IT'S SAFE TO MOVE ABOUT, NOW. WOULD YOU LIKE A *TOUR*?
THANKS!
COUNT *ME* IN!
BEATS SITTING WITH DEEDEE!
WON'T YOU TWO JOIN US?
NO THANKS! *NEDDY* AND I CAN JUST SIT AND ENJOY EACH OTHER'S COMPANY!
UH, ACTUALLY, I *HAVE* TO FINISH THIS BOOK FOR CLASS. I HAVE ANOTHER I COULD LOAN *YOU* TO READ...
papercutz
Shakespeare
2nd Edition
NINA
UCHH. NO THANKS!
A TOUR OF A LUXURY TRAIN SUDDENLY ISN'T SOUNDING SO BAD.

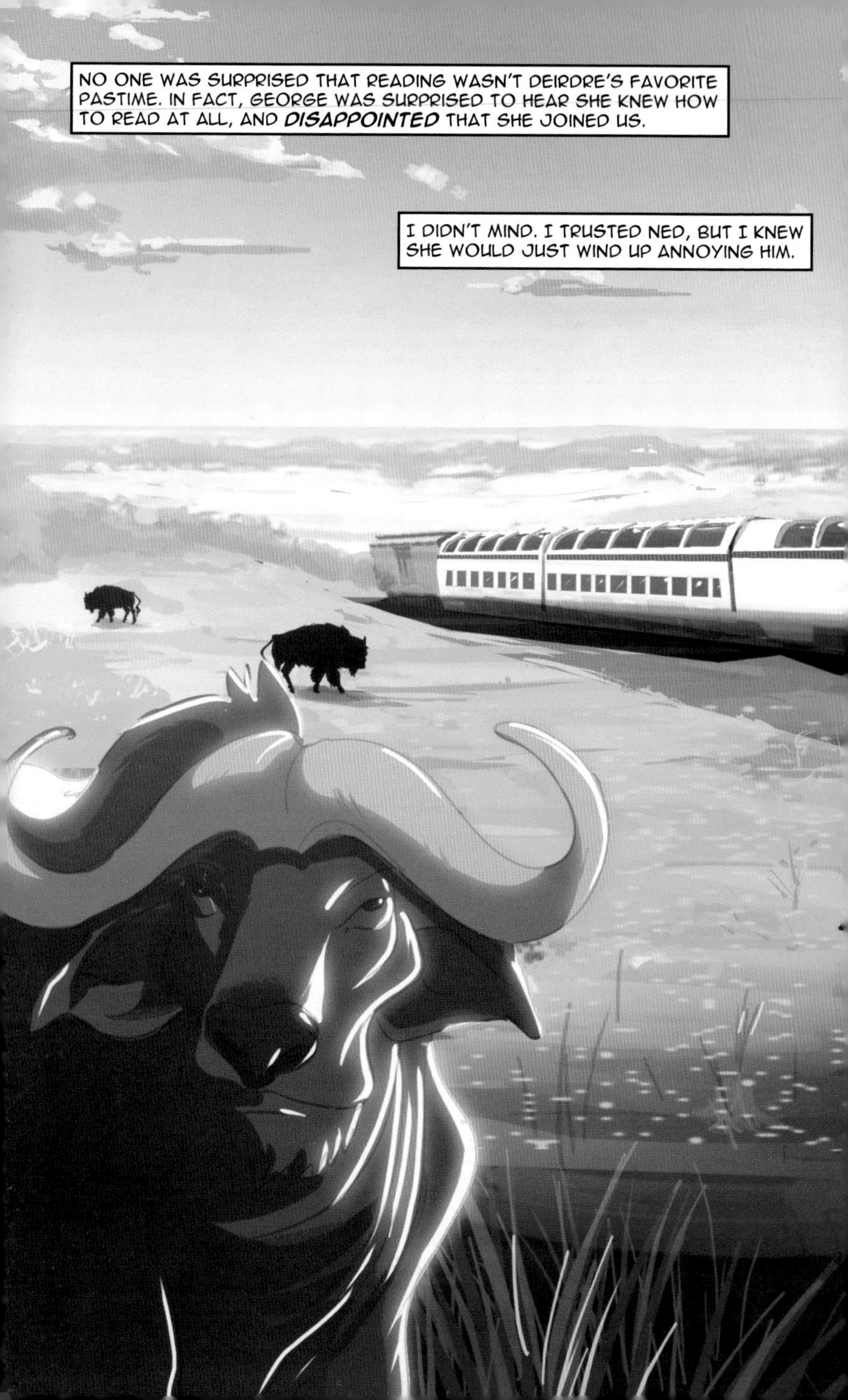
NO ONE WAS SURPRISED THAT READING WASN'T DEIRDRE'S FAVORITE PASTIME. IN FACT, GEORGE WAS SURPRISED TO HEAR SHE KNEW HOW TO READ AT ALL, AND *DISAPPOINTED* THAT SHE JOINED US.
I DIDN'T MIND. I TRUSTED NED, BUT I KNEW SHE WOULD JUST WIND UP ANNOYING HIM.

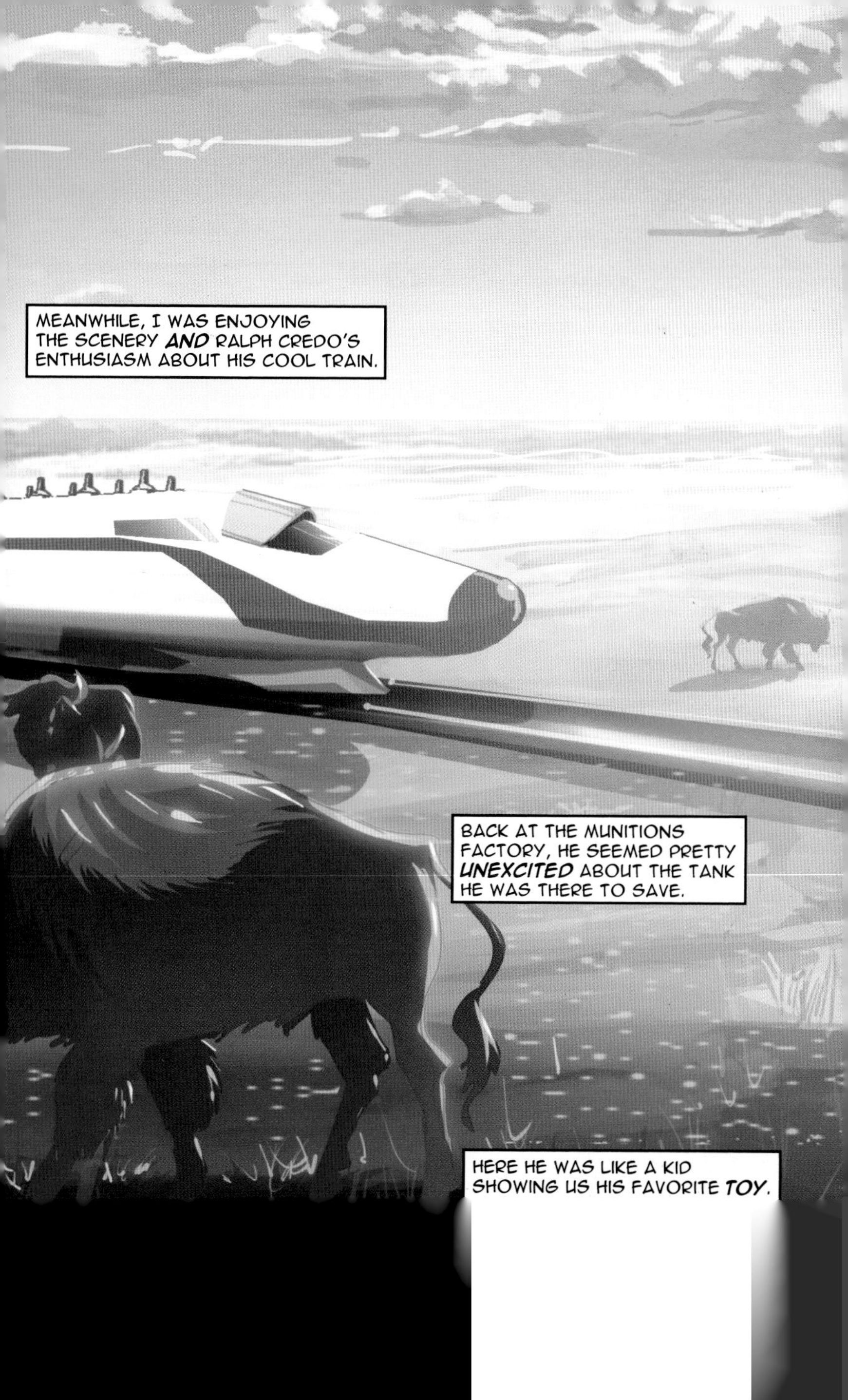
MEANWHILE, I WAS ENJOYING THE SCENERY AND RALPH CREDO'S ENTHUSIASM ABOUT HIS COOL TRAIN.
BACK AT THE MUNITIONS FACTORY, HE SEEMED PRETTY UNEXCITED ABOUT THE TANK HE WAS THERE TO SAVE.
HERE HE WAS LIKE A KID SHOWING US HIS FAVORITE TOY.

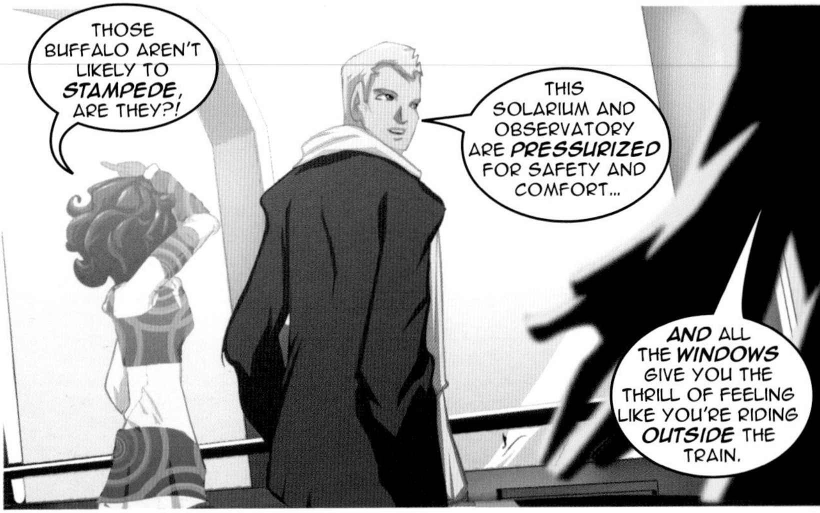
THOSE BUFFALO AREN'T LIKELY TO *STAMPEDE*, ARE THEY?!
THIS SOLARIUM AND OBSERVATORY ARE *PRESSURIZED* FOR SAFETY AND COMFORT...
AND ALL THE *WINDOWS* GIVE YOU THE THRILL OF FEELING LIKE YOU'RE RIDING *OUTSIDE* THE TRAIN.

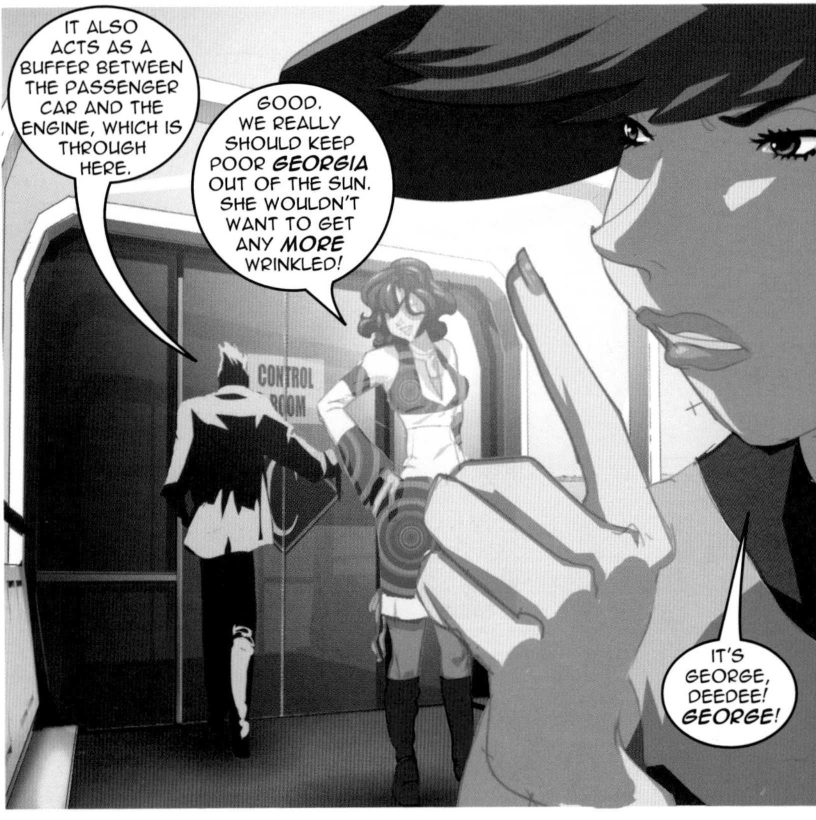
IT ALSO ACTS AS A BUFFER BETWEEN THE PASSENGER CAR AND THE ENGINE, WHICH IS THROUGH HERE.
GOOD. WE REALLY SHOULD KEEP POOR *GEORGIA* OUT OF THE SUN. SHE WOULDN'T WANT TO GET ANY *MORE* WRINKLED!
CONTROL ROOM
IT'S GEORGE, DEEDEE! *GEORGE!*

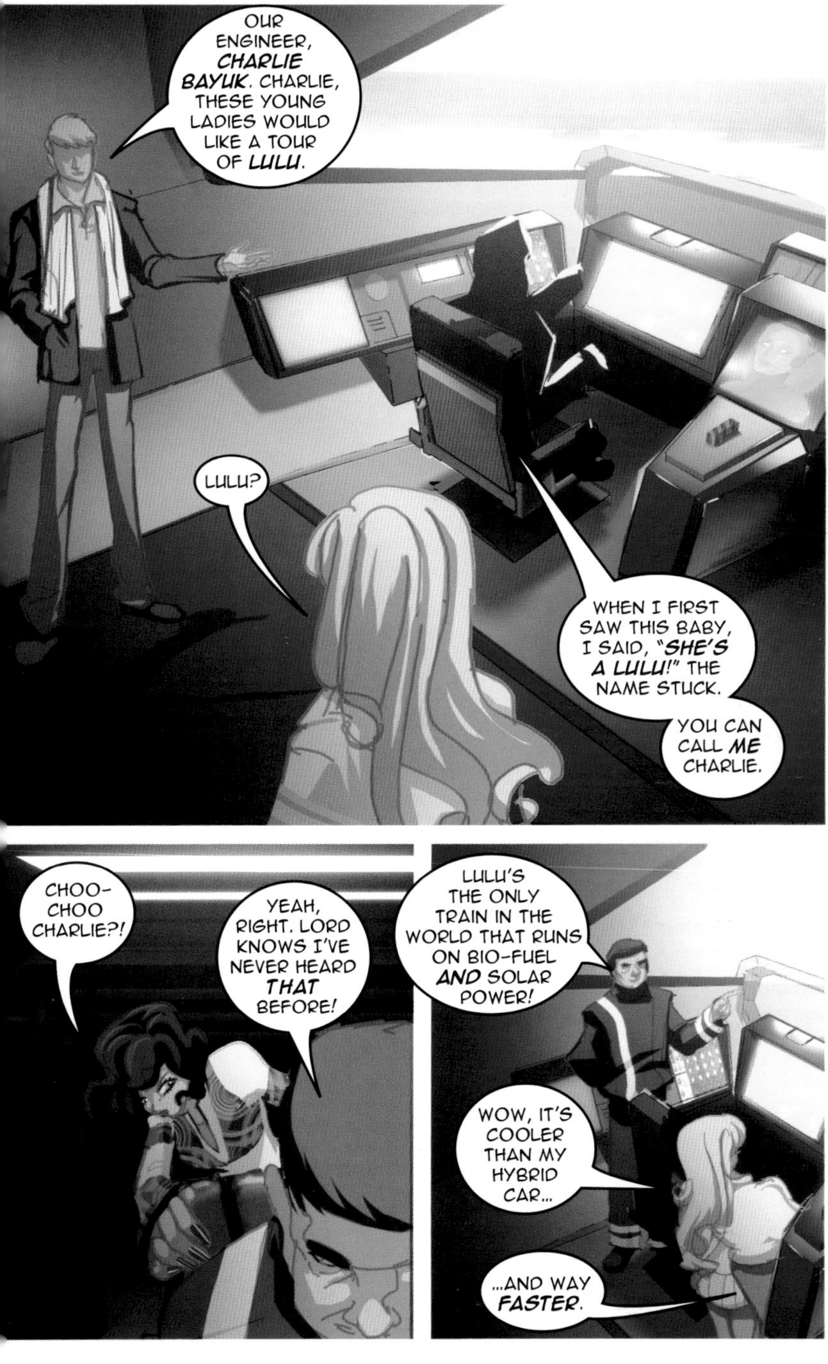
OUR ENGINEER, CHARLIE BAYUK. CHARLIE, THESE YOUNG LADIES WOULD LIKE A TOUR OF LULU.
LULU?
WHEN I FIRST SAW THIS BABY, I SAID, "SHE'S A LULU!" THE NAME STUCK.
YOU CAN CALL ME CHARLIE.
CHOO-CHOO CHARLIE?!
YEAH, RIGHT. LORD KNOWS I'VE NEVER HEARD THAT BEFORE!
LULU'S THE ONLY TRAIN IN THE WORLD THAT RUNS ON BIO-FUEL AND SOLAR POWER!
WOW, IT'S COOLER THAN MY HYBRID CAR...
...AND WAY FASTER.

SIGH

HEY! DON'T SIT ON *THAT*!

NO SWEAT! LULU'S GOT A COMPUTER *OVER-RIDE* FOR PILOTING, TO PREVENT ANY POSSIBLE *HUMAN* ERRORS.

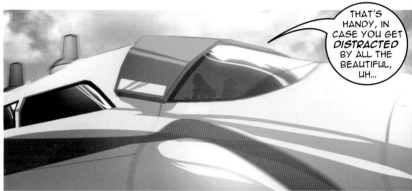

THAT'S HANDY, IN CASE YOU GET *DISTRACTED* BY ALL THE BEAUTIFUL, UH...

...BUFFALO.

THE FACT WAS, OTHER THAN TINY ANIMALS, THERE WASN'T MUCH TO LOOK AT!

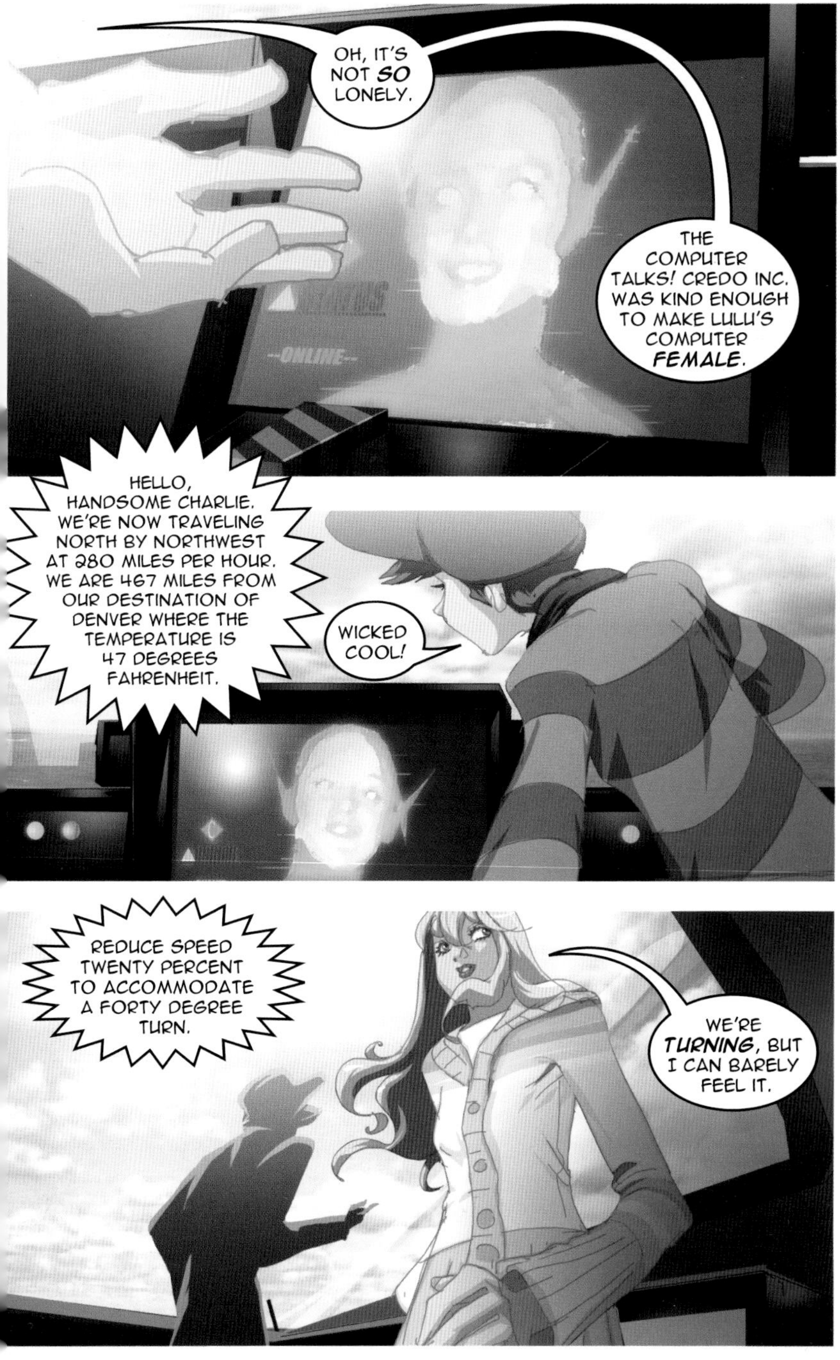
OH, IT'S NOT SO LONELY.
THE COMPUTER TALKS! CREDO INC. WAS KIND ENOUGH TO MAKE LULU'S COMPUTER FEMALE.
--ONLINE--
HELLO, HANDSOME CHARLIE. WE'RE NOW TRAVELING NORTH BY NORTHWEST AT 280 MILES PER HOUR. WE ARE 467 MILES FROM OUR DESTINATION OF DENVER WHERE THE TEMPERATURE IS 47 DEGREES FAHRENHEIT.
WICKED COOL!
REDUCE SPEED TWENTY PERCENT TO ACCOMMODATE A FORTY DEGREE TURN.
WE'RE TURNING, BUT I CAN BARELY FEEL IT.

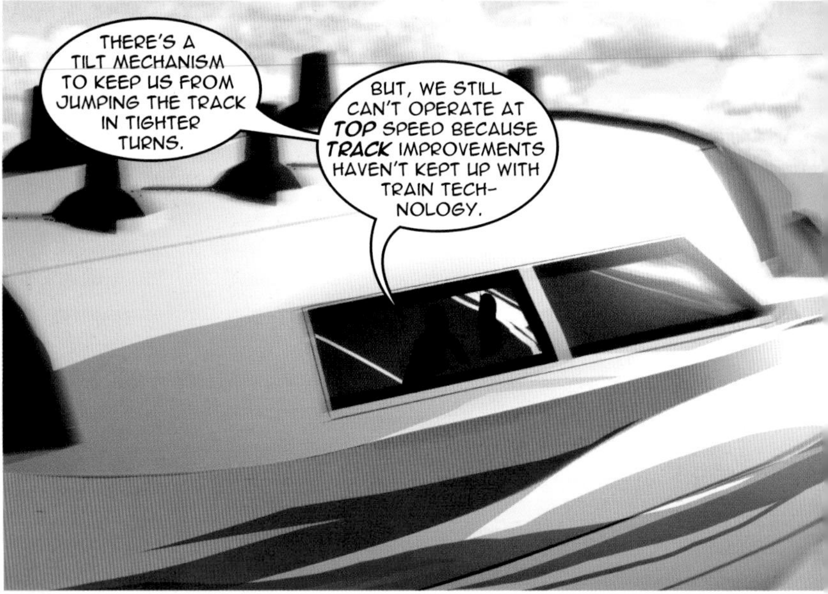
THERE'S A TILT MECHANISM TO KEEP US FROM JUMPING THE TRACK IN TIGHTER TURNS.
BUT, WE STILL CAN'T OPERATE AT **TOP** SPEED BECAUSE **TRACK** IMPROVEMENTS HAVEN'T KEPT UP WITH TRAIN TECH-NOLOGY.

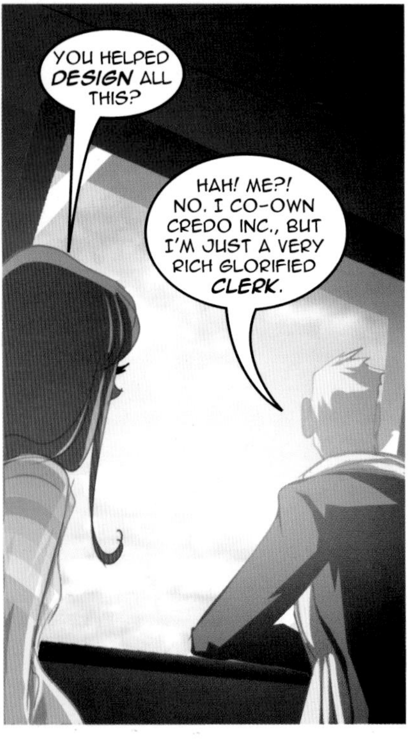
YOU HELPED **DESIGN** ALL THIS?
HAH! ME?! NO. I CO-OWN CREDO INC., BUT I'M JUST A VERY RICH GLORIFIED **CLERK**.

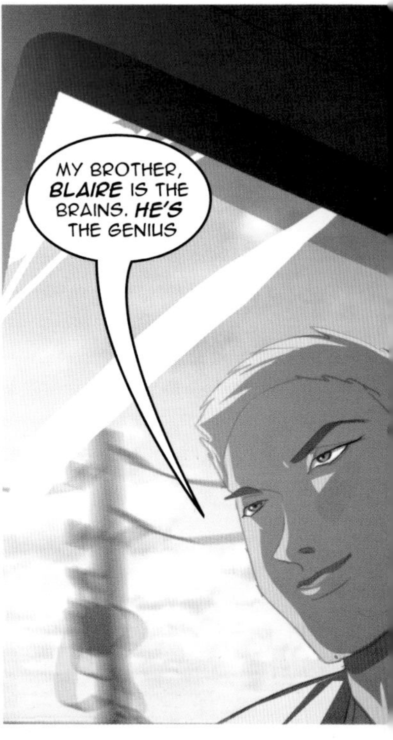
MY BROTHER, **BLAIRE** IS THE BRAINS. **HE'S** THE GENIUS

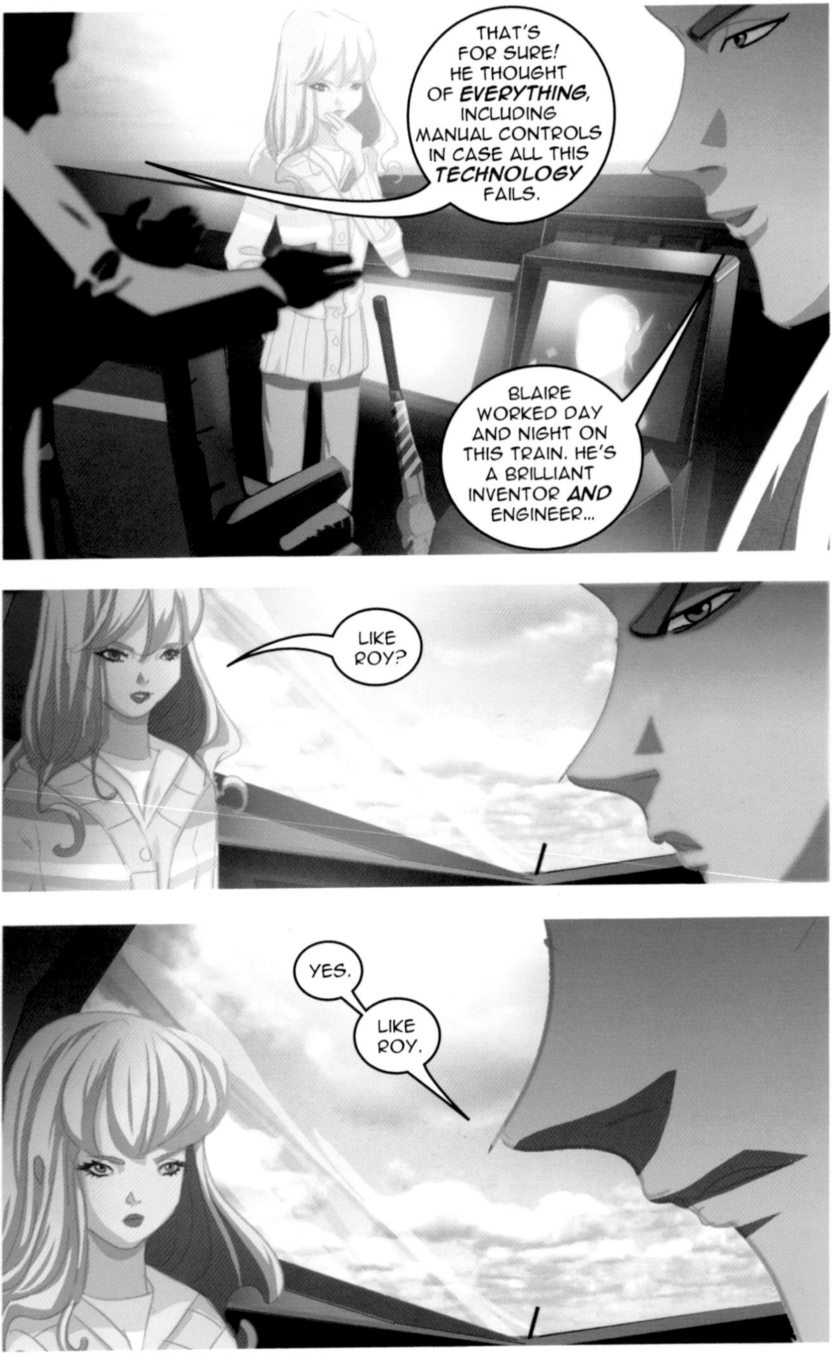
THAT'S FOR SURE! HE THOUGHT OF EVERYTHING, INCLUDING MANUAL CONTROLS IN CASE ALL THIS TECHNOLOGY FAILS.
BLAIRE WORKED DAY AND NIGHT ON THIS TRAIN. HE'S A BRILLIANT INVENTOR AND ENGINEER...
LIKE ROY?
YES.
LIKE ROY.

ANYWAY! LET'S GET BACK TO THE *OTHERS*, SHALL WE?

YES! *LET'S!* I MEAN, CHOO-CHOO CHARLIE NEEDS TO CONCENTRATE ON HIS DRIVING.

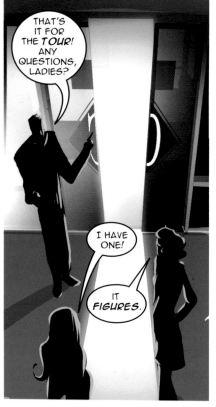

THAT'S IT FOR THE *TOUR!* ANY QUESTIONS, LADIES?

I HAVE ONE!

IT *FIGURES.*

IF THIS TRAIN IS SO EFFICIENT AND FAST, WHY IS IT ONE OF A KIND? I MEAN WHY AREN'T *OTHER* TRAIN BUILDERS USING THIS TECHNOLOGY?!

DEVELOPING PUBLIC TRANSPORTATION IS *VERY* EXPENSIVE.

MY BROTHER *ALMOST* LANDED A BIG GOVERNMENT CONTRACT, BUT THEY TURNED US DOWN.

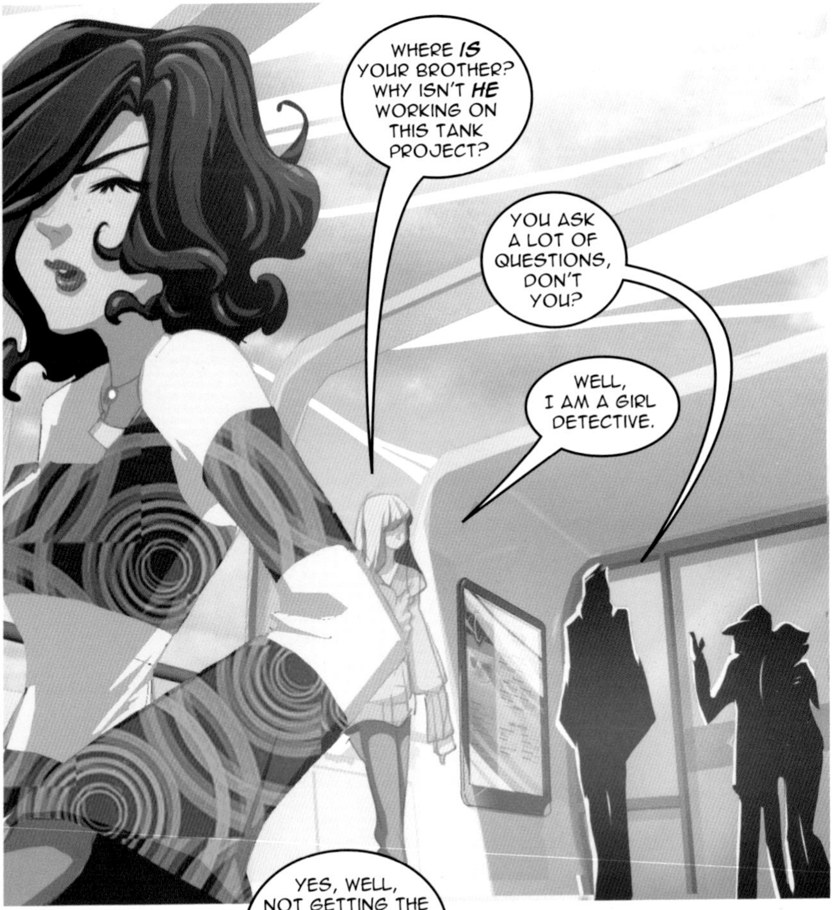
WHERE *IS* YOUR BROTHER? WHY ISN'T *HE* WORKING ON THIS TANK PROJECT?
YOU ASK A LOT OF QUESTIONS, DON'T YOU?
WELL, I AM A GIRL DETECTIVE.

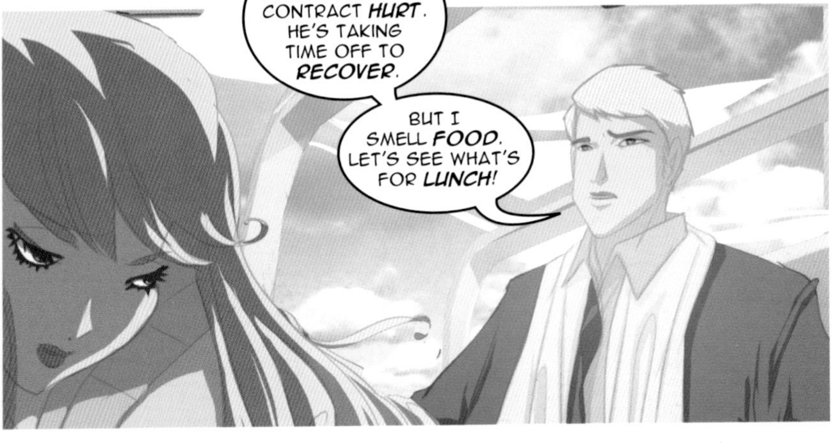
YES, WELL, NOT GETTING THE CONTRACT *HURT*. HE'S TAKING TIME OFF TO *RECOVER*.
BUT I SMELL *FOOD*. LET'S SEE WHAT'S FOR *LUNCH*!

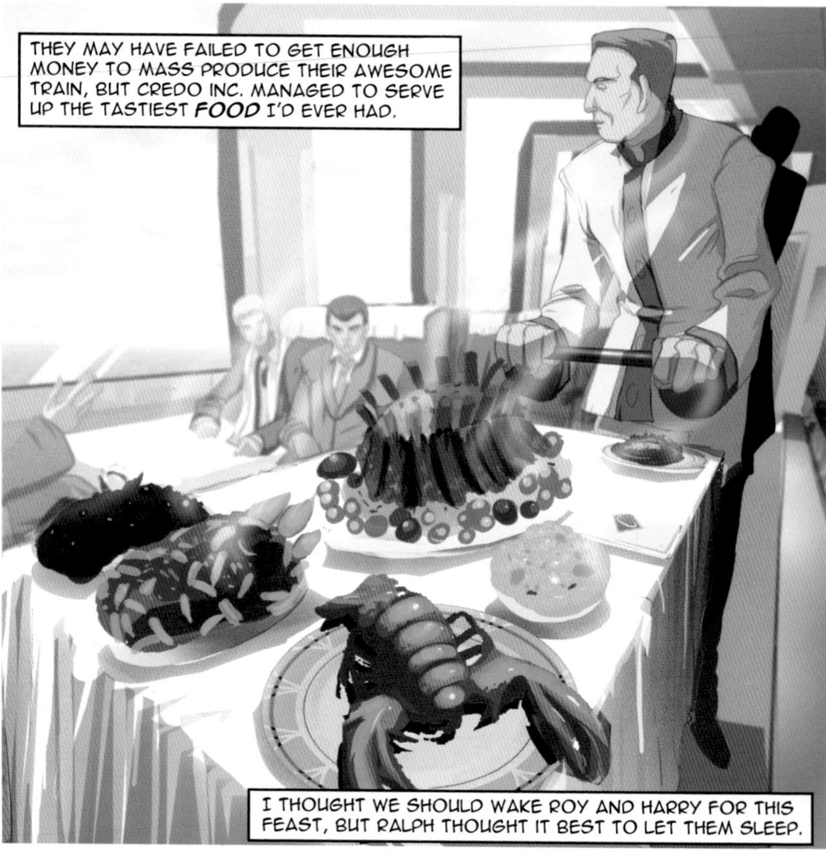
THEY MAY HAVE FAILED TO GET ENOUGH MONEY TO MASS PRODUCE THEIR AWESOME TRAIN, BUT CREDO INC. MANAGED TO SERVE UP THE TASTIEST ***FOOD*** I'D EVER HAD.
I THOUGHT WE SHOULD WAKE ROY AND HARRY FOR THIS FEAST, BUT RALPH THOUGHT IT BEST TO LET THEM SLEEP.

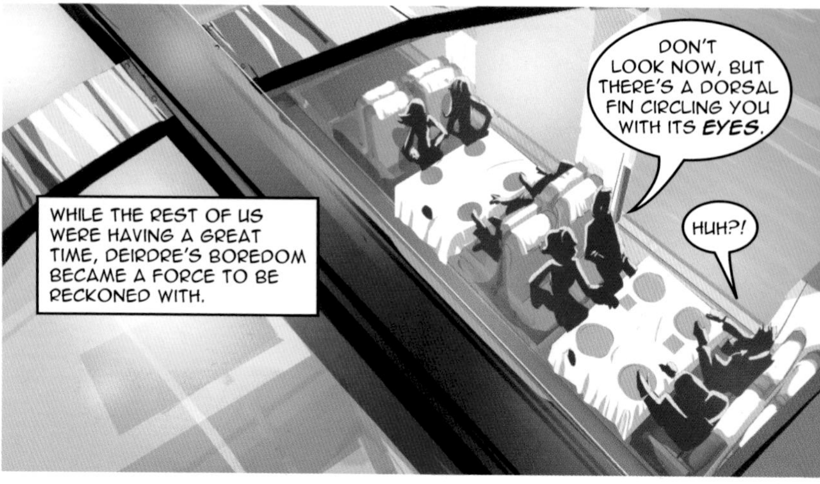
WHILE THE REST OF US WERE HAVING A GREAT TIME, DEIRDRE'S BOREDOM BECAME A FORCE TO BE RECKONED WITH.
DON'T LOOK NOW, BUT THERE'S A DORSAL FIN CIRCLING YOU WITH ITS ***EYES***.
HUH?!

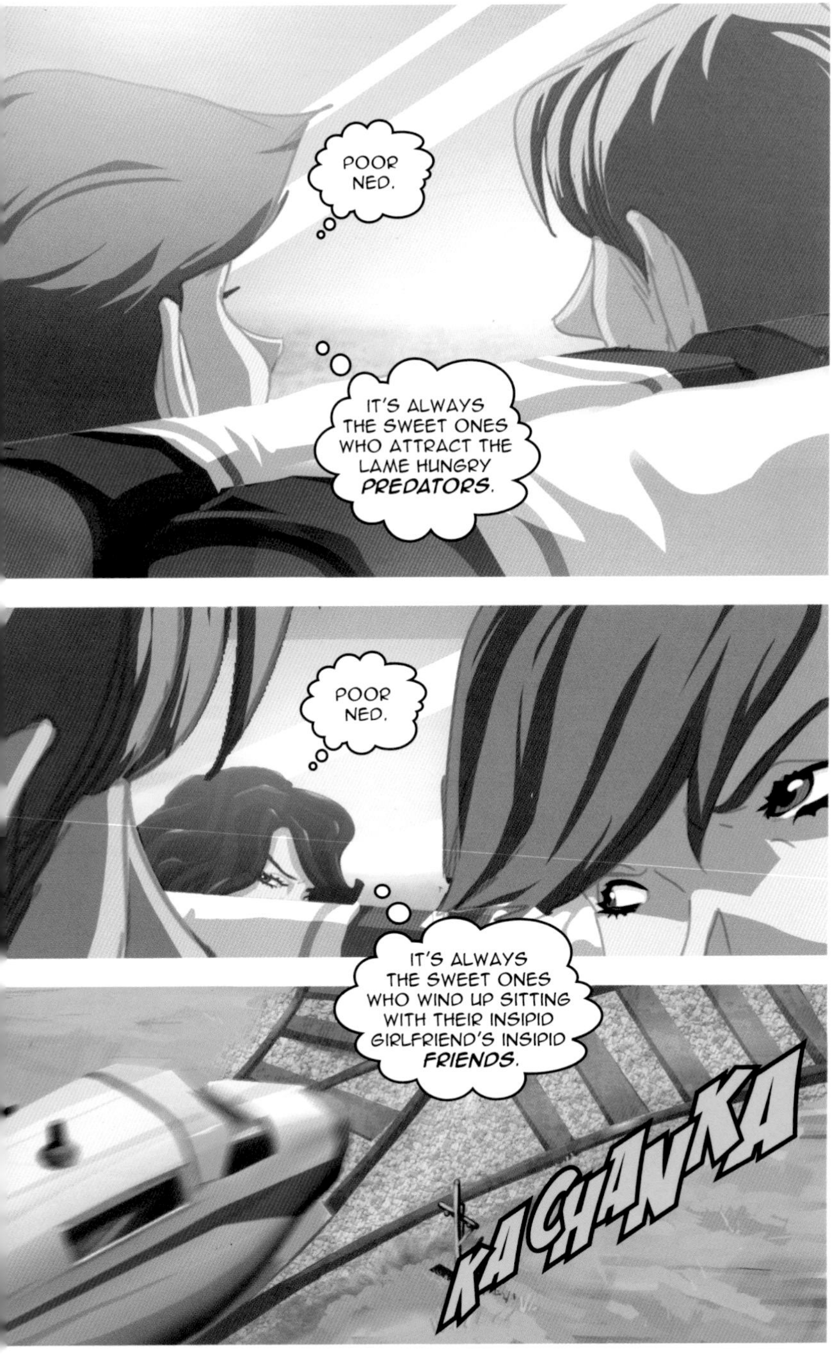
POOR NED.
IT'S ALWAYS THE SWEET ONES WHO ATTRACT THE LAME HUNGRY *PREDATORS*.
POOR NED.
IT'S ALWAYS THE SWEET ONES WHO WIND UP SITTING WITH THEIR INSIPID GIRLFRIEND'S INSIPID *FRIENDS*.
KA CHAN KA

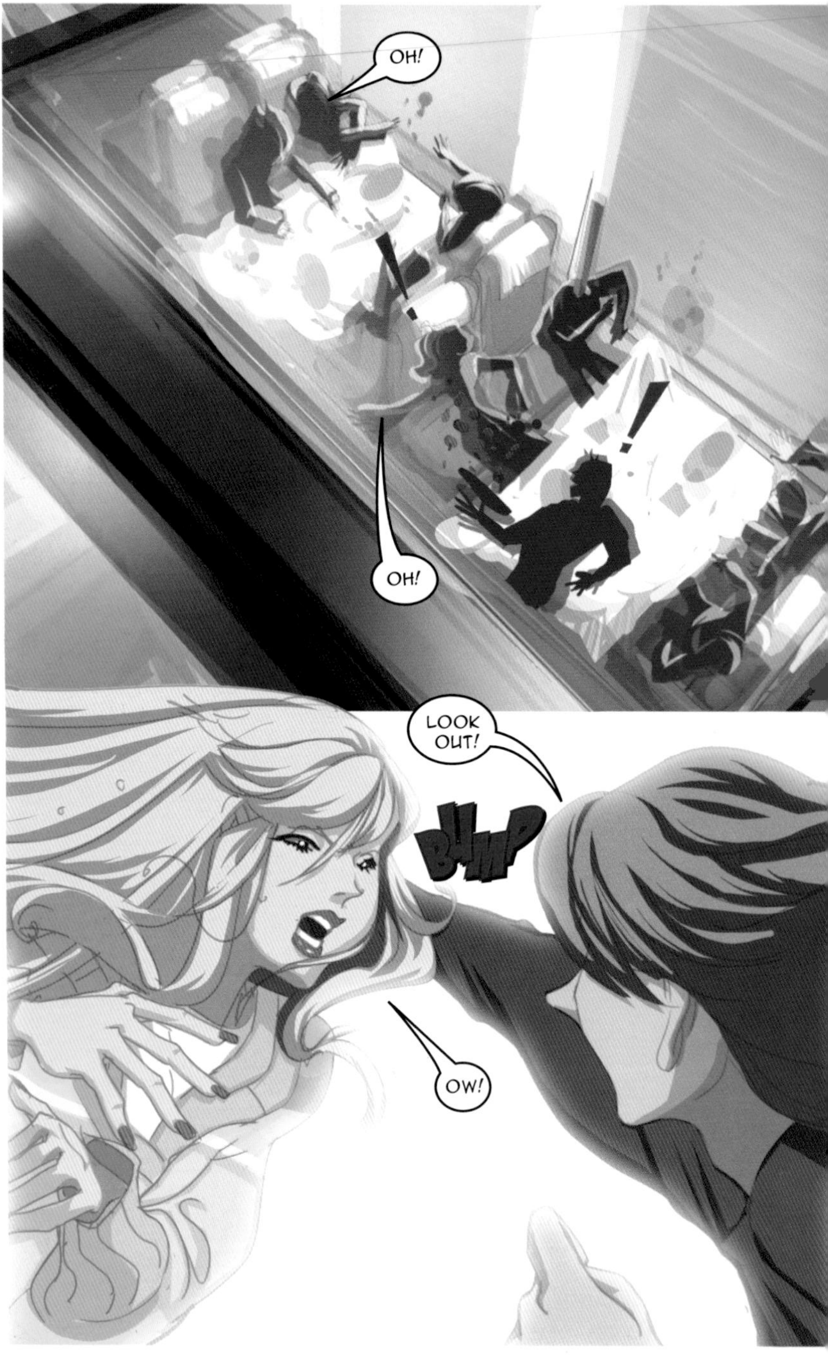
OH!
OH!
LOOK OUT!
BUMP
OW!

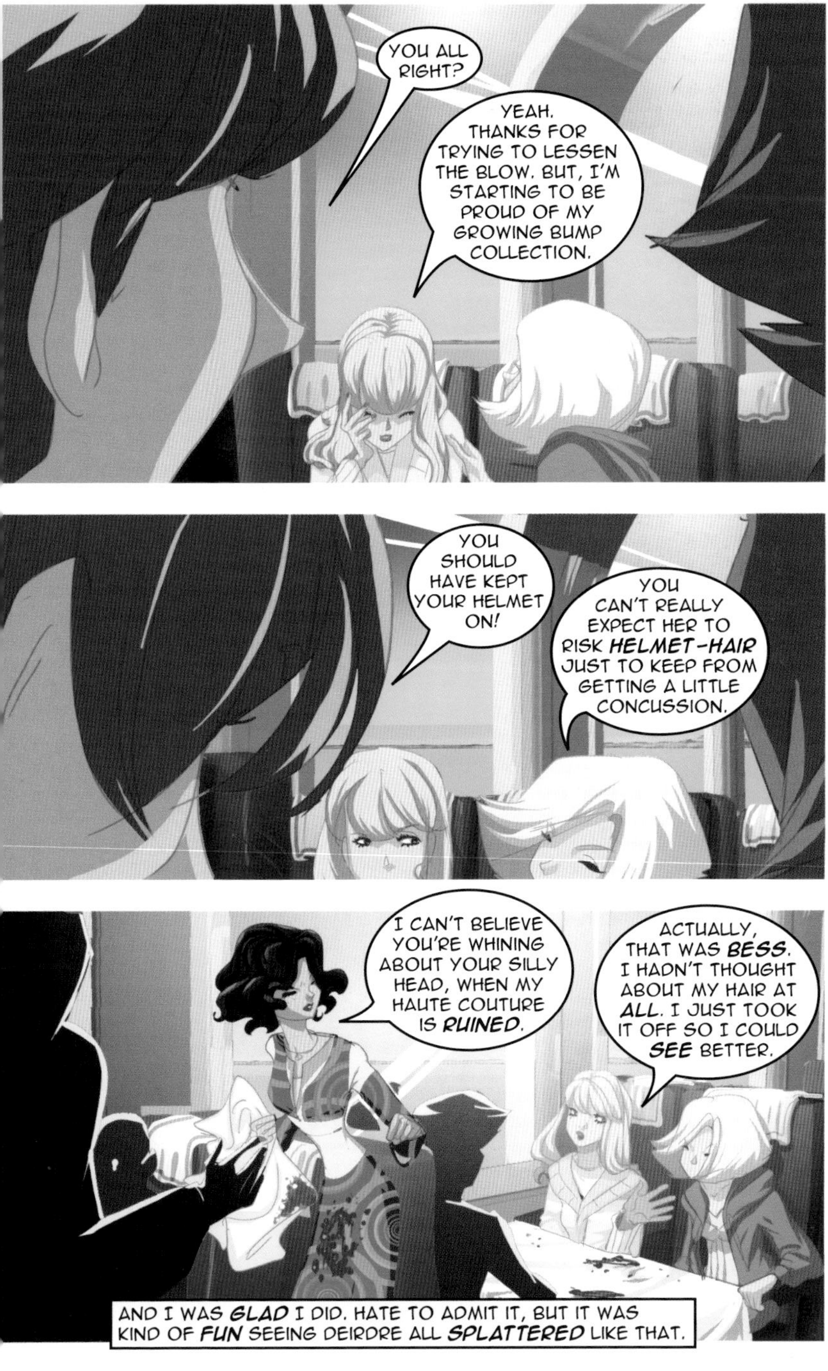
YOU ALL RIGHT?
YEAH. THANKS FOR TRYING TO LESSEN THE BLOW. BUT, I'M STARTING TO BE PROUD OF MY GROWING BUMP COLLECTION.
YOU SHOULD HAVE KEPT YOUR HELMET ON!
YOU CAN'T REALLY EXPECT HER TO RISK HELMET-HAIR JUST TO KEEP FROM GETTING A LITTLE CONCUSSION.
I CAN'T BELIEVE YOU'RE WHINING ABOUT YOUR SILLY HEAD, WHEN MY HAUTE COUTURE IS RUINED.
ACTUALLY, THAT WAS BESS. I HADN'T THOUGHT ABOUT MY HAIR AT ALL. I JUST TOOK IT OFF SO I COULD SEE BETTER.
AND I WAS GLAD I DID. HATE TO ADMIT IT, BUT IT WAS KIND OF FUN SEEING DEIRDRE ALL SPLATTERED LIKE THAT.

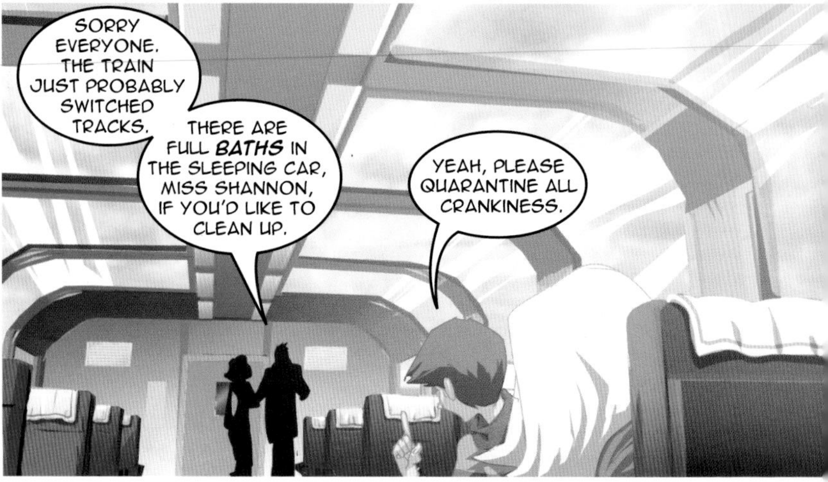
SORRY EVERYONE. THE TRAIN JUST PROBABLY SWITCHED TRACKS.
THERE ARE FULL **BATHS** IN THE SLEEPING CAR, MISS SHANNON, IF YOU'D LIKE TO CLEAN UP.
YEAH, PLEASE QUARANTINE ALL CRANKINESS.
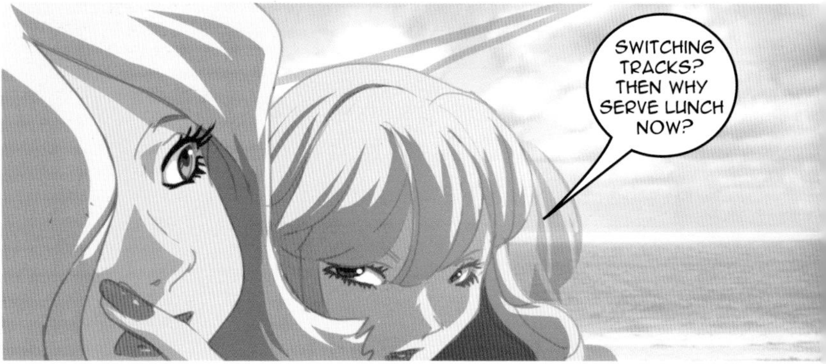
SWITCHING TRACKS? THEN WHY SERVE LUNCH NOW?
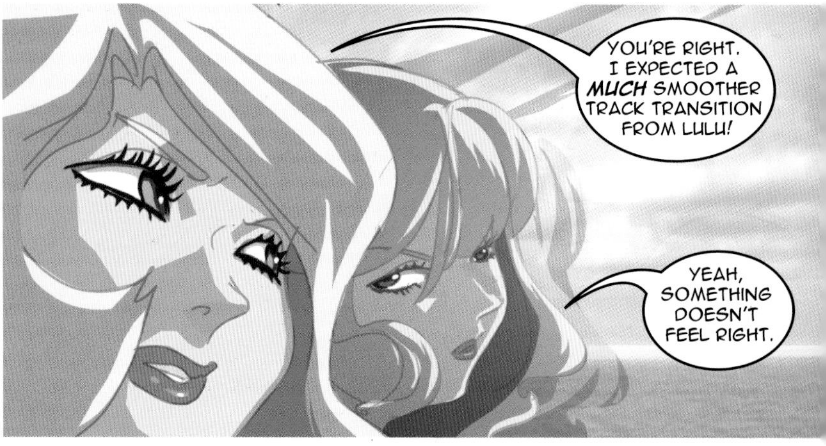
YOU'RE RIGHT. I EXPECTED A **MUCH** SMOOTHER TRACK TRANSITION FROM LULU!
YEAH, SOMETHING DOESN'T FEEL RIGHT.

WELL, EVEN WITH HEAD INJURIES WE ALL KNOW BETTER THAN TO NOT TRUST THOSE *FEELINGS* OF YOURS.

LET'S CHECK THE SYSTEM, SHALL WE?

IT'S EASY ENOUGH TO HACK INTO THE TRAIN'S LOVELY COMPUTER AND SCAN OUR PROGRESS.

LULU CAN TELL US *HERSELF* IF ANYTHING'S WRONG.

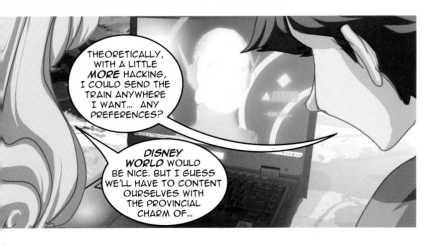

THEORETICALLY, WITH A LITTLE *MORE* HACKING, I COULD SEND THE TRAIN ANYWHERE I WANT... ANY PREFERENCES?

DISNEY WORLD WOULD BE NICE. BUT I GUESS WE'LL HAVE TO CONTENT OURSELVES WITH THE PROVINCIAL CHARM OF...

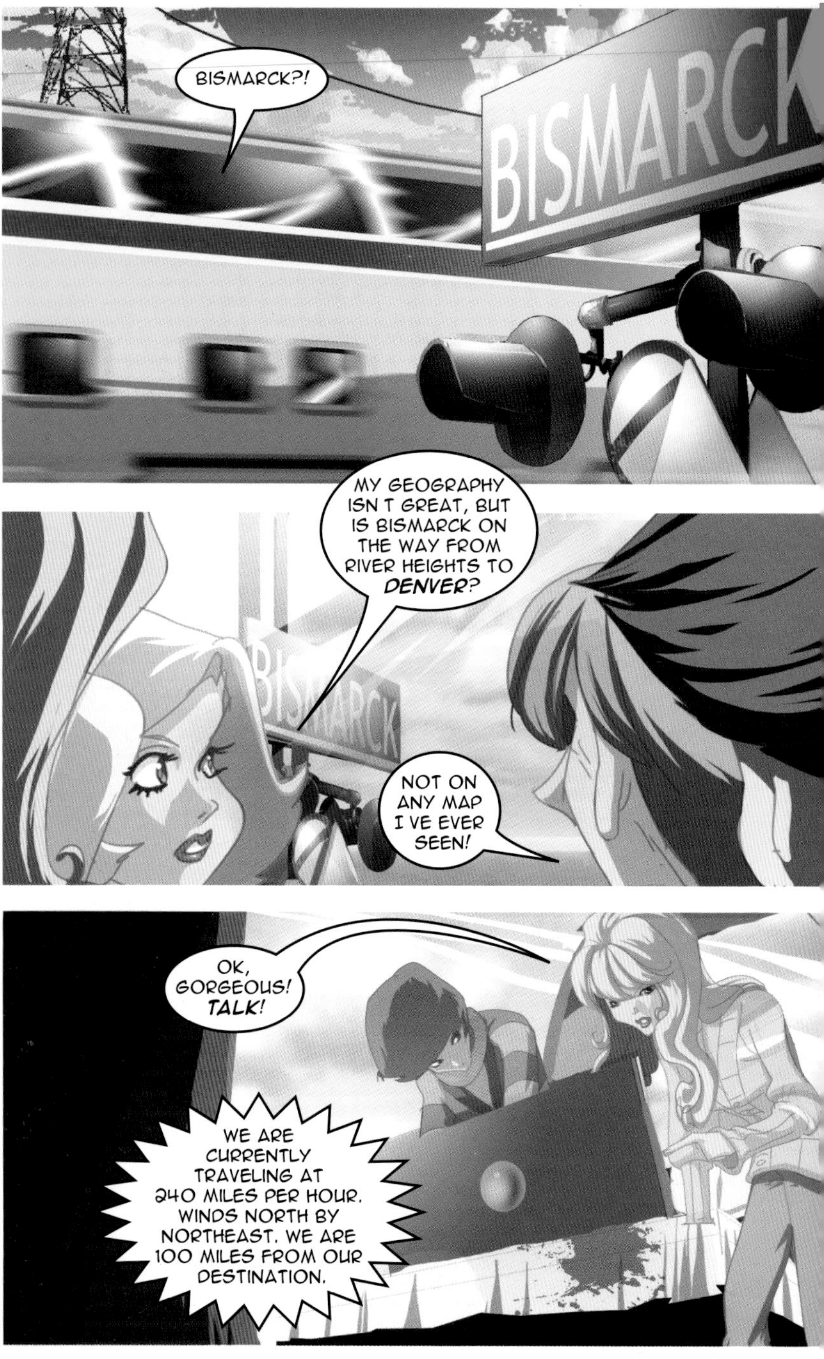
BISMARCK?!
BISMARCK
MY GEOGRAPHY ISN T GREAT, BUT IS BISMARCK ON THE WAY FROM RIVER HEIGHTS TO *DENVER*?
BISMARCK
NOT ON ANY MAP I VE EVER SEEN!
OK, GORGEOUS! *TALK*!
WE ARE CURRENTLY TRAVELING AT 240 MILES PER HOUR. WINDS NORTH BY NORTHEAST. WE ARE 100 MILES FROM OUR DESTINATION.

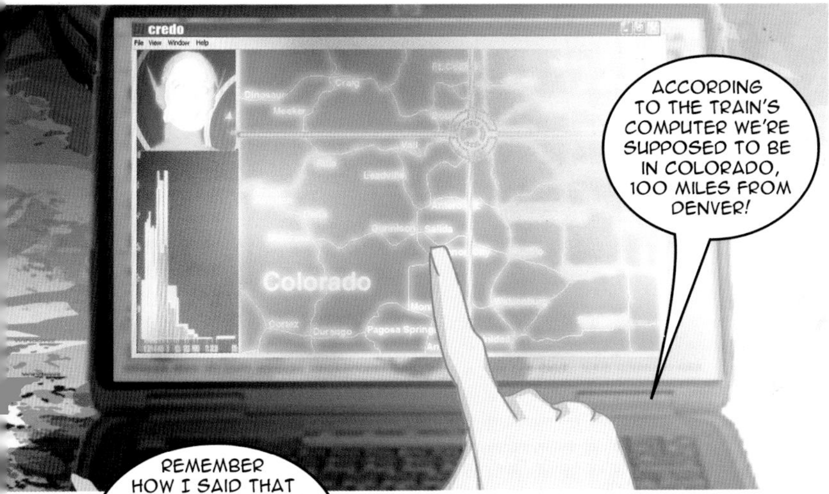
credo
File View Window Help
Colorado
Durango
Pagosa Springs
ACCORDING TO THE TRAIN'S COMPUTER WE'RE SUPPOSED TO BE IN COLORADO, 100 MILES FROM DENVER!

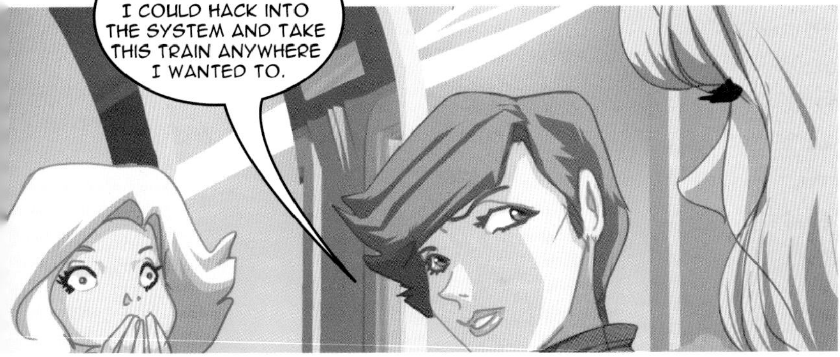
REMEMBER HOW I SAID THAT ***THEORETICALLY*** I COULD HACK INTO THE SYSTEM AND TAKE THIS TRAIN ANYWHERE I WANTED TO.

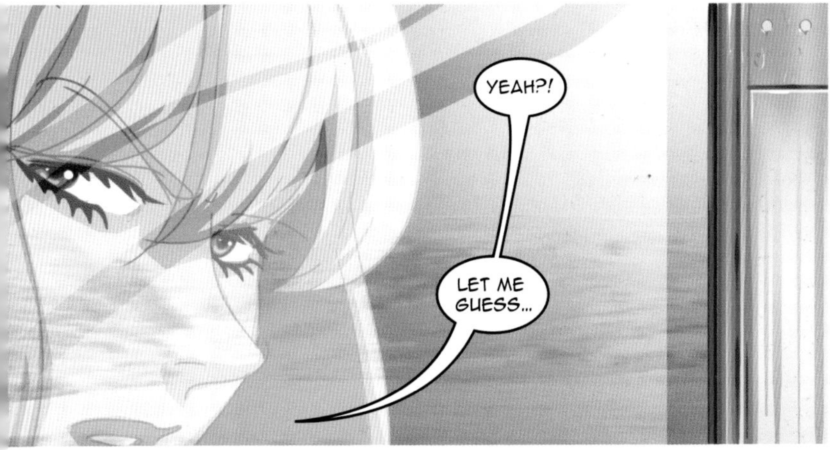
YEAH?!
LET ME GUESS...

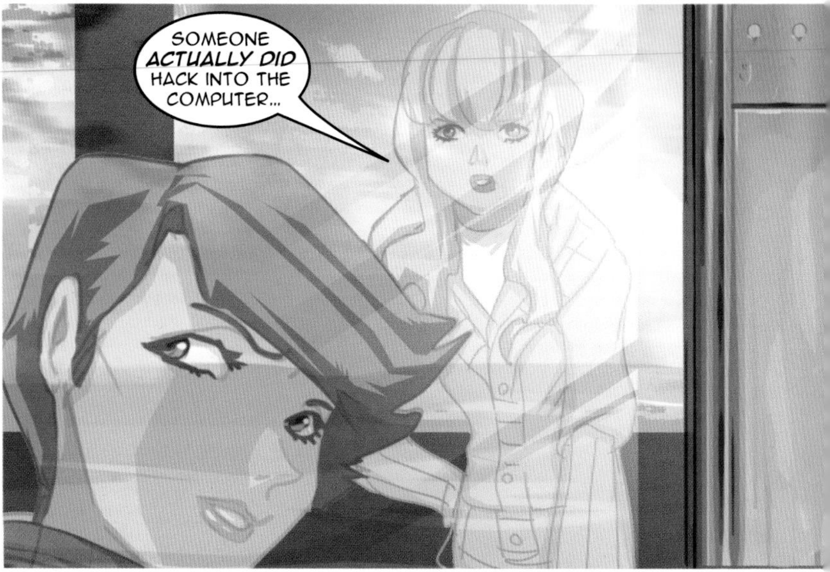
SOMEONE ACTUALLY DID HACK INTO THE COMPUTER...

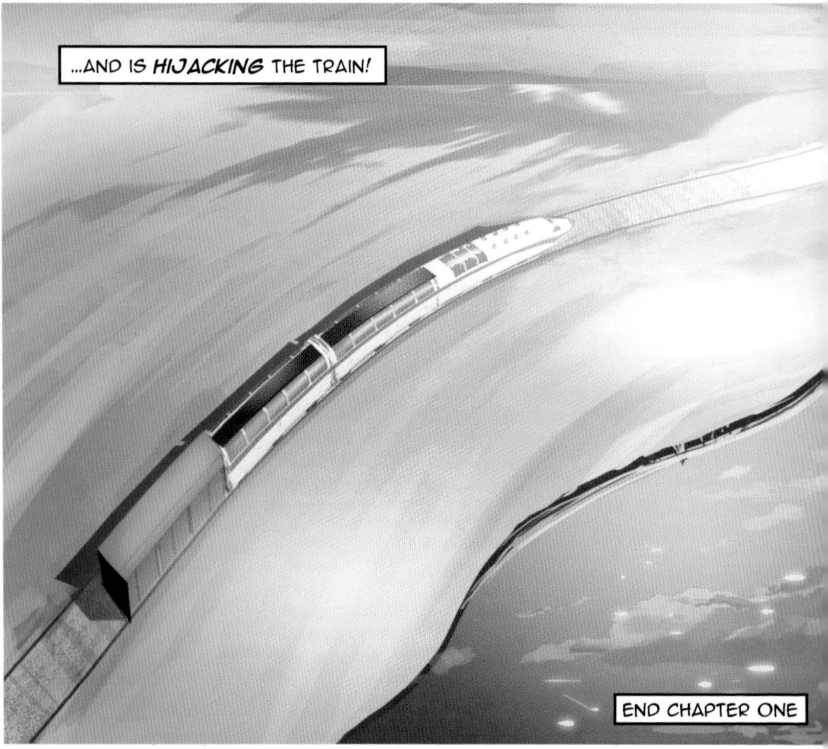
...AND IS HIJACKING THE TRAIN!
END CHAPTER ONE

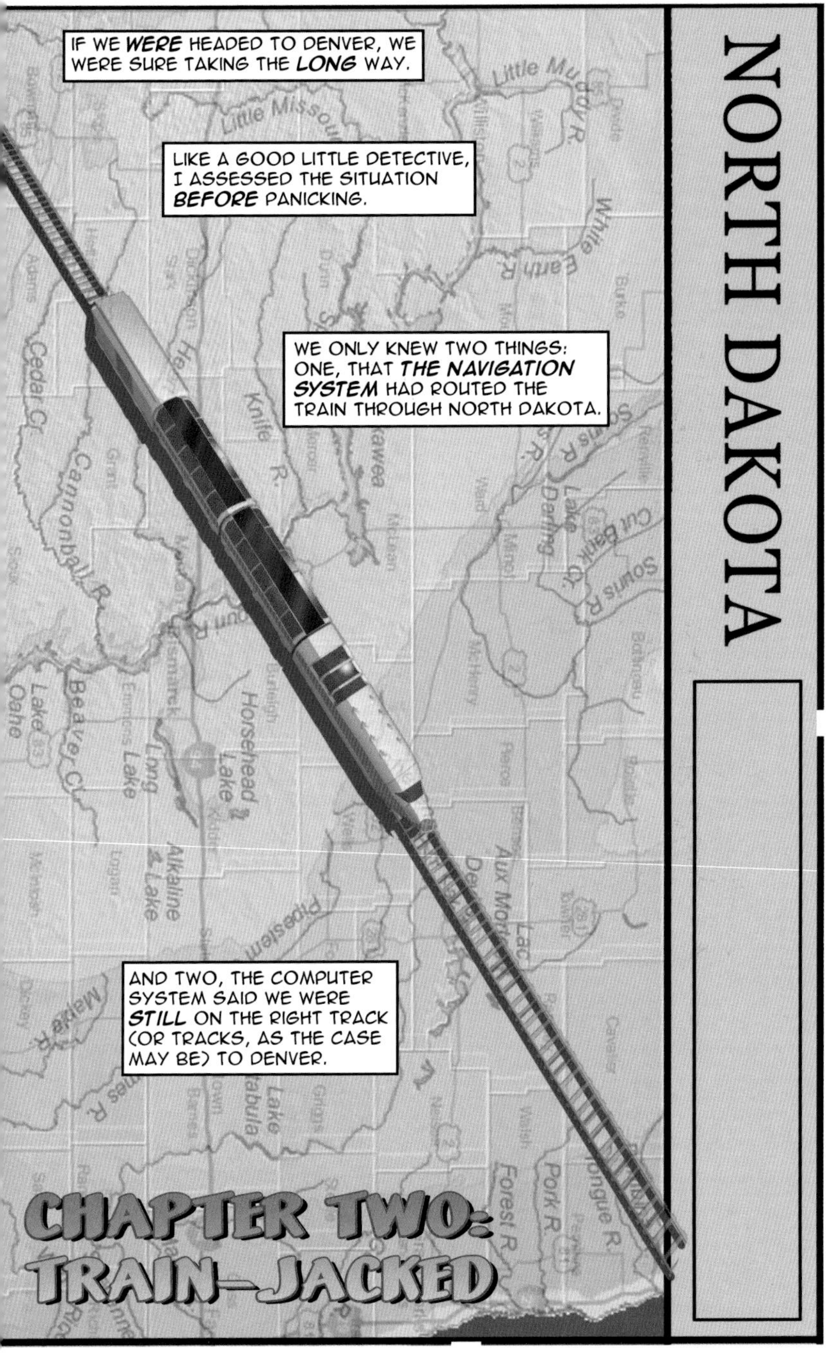

NORTH DAKOTA
IF WE *WERE* HEADED TO DENVER, WE WERE SURE TAKING THE *LONG* WAY.
LIKE A GOOD LITTLE DETECTIVE, I ASSESSED THE SITUATION *BEFORE* PANICKING.
WE ONLY KNEW TWO THINGS: ONE, THAT *THE NAVIGATION SYSTEM* HAD ROUTED THE TRAIN THROUGH NORTH DAKOTA.
AND TWO, THE COMPUTER SYSTEM SAID WE WERE *STILL* ON THE RIGHT TRACK (OR TRACKS, AS THE CASE MAY BE) TO DENVER.
CHAPTER TWO: TRAIN-JACKED

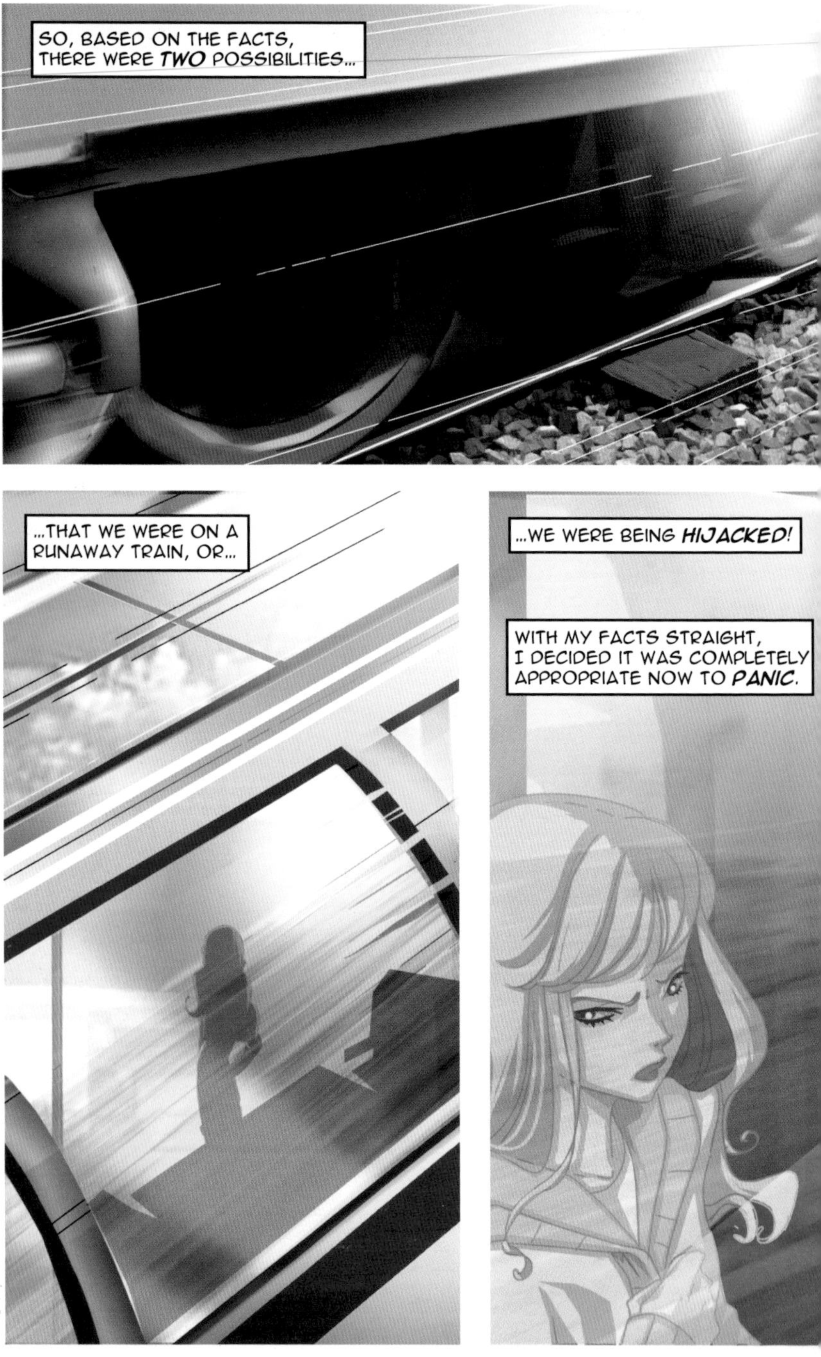
SO, BASED ON THE FACTS, THERE WERE TWO POSSIBILITIES...
...THAT WE WERE ON A RUNAWAY TRAIN, OR...
...WE WERE BEING HIJACKED!
WITH MY FACTS STRAIGHT, I DECIDED IT WAS COMPLETELY APPROPRIATE NOW TO PANIC.

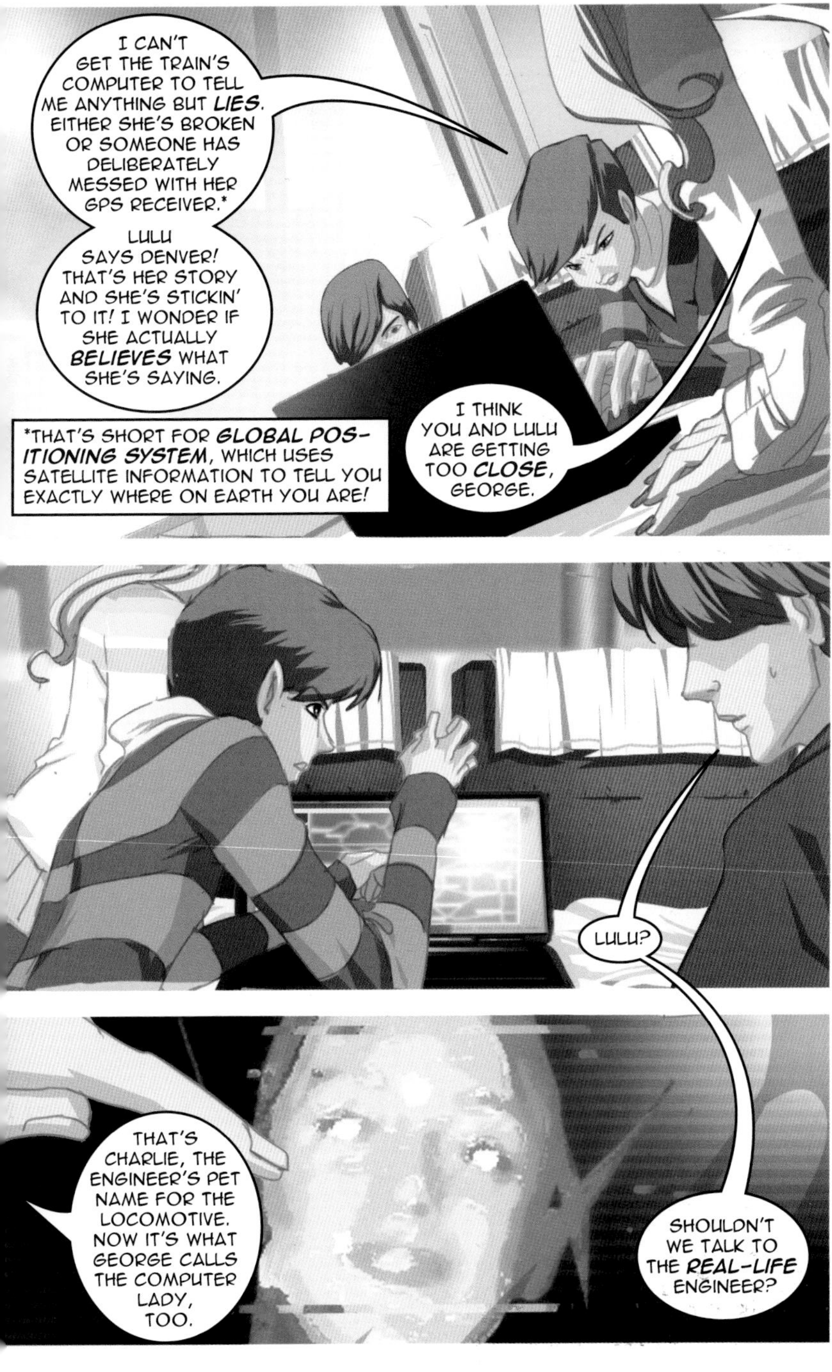
I CAN'T GET THE TRAIN'S COMPUTER TO TELL ME ANYTHING BUT LIES. EITHER SHE'S BROKEN OR SOMEONE HAS DELIBERATELY MESSED WITH HER GPS RECEIVER.*
LULU SAYS DENVER! THAT'S HER STORY AND SHE'S STICKIN' TO IT! I WONDER IF SHE ACTUALLY BELIEVES WHAT SHE'S SAYING.
*THAT'S SHORT FOR GLOBAL POSITIONING SYSTEM, WHICH USES SATELLITE INFORMATION TO TELL YOU EXACTLY WHERE ON EARTH YOU ARE!
I THINK YOU AND LULU ARE GETTING TOO CLOSE, GEORGE.
LULU?
THAT'S CHARLIE, THE ENGINEER'S PET NAME FOR THE LOCOMOTIVE. NOW IT'S WHAT GEORGE CALLS THE COMPUTER LADY, TOO.
SHOULDN'T WE TALK TO THE REAL-LIFE ENGINEER?

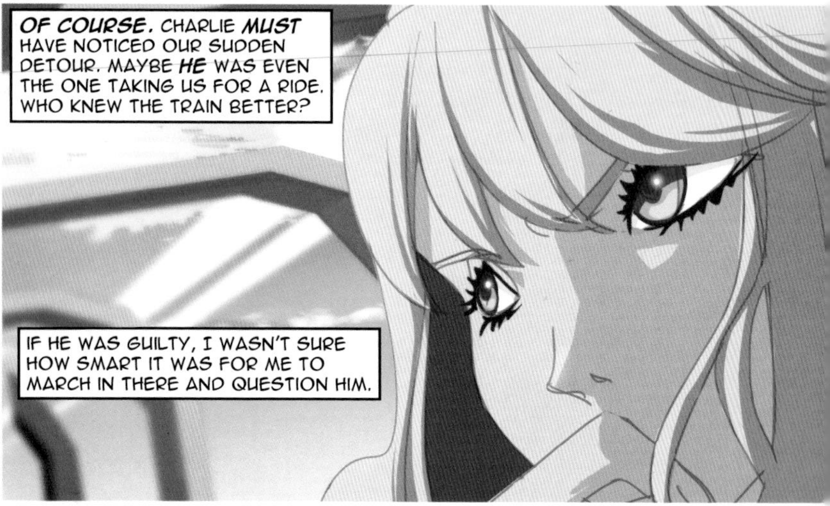
OF COURSE. CHARLIE MUST HAVE NOTICED OUR SUDDEN DETOUR. MAYBE HE WAS EVEN THE ONE TAKING US FOR A RIDE. WHO KNEW THE TRAIN BETTER?
IF HE WAS GUILTY, I WASN'T SURE HOW SMART IT WAS FOR ME TO MARCH IN THERE AND QUESTION HIM.

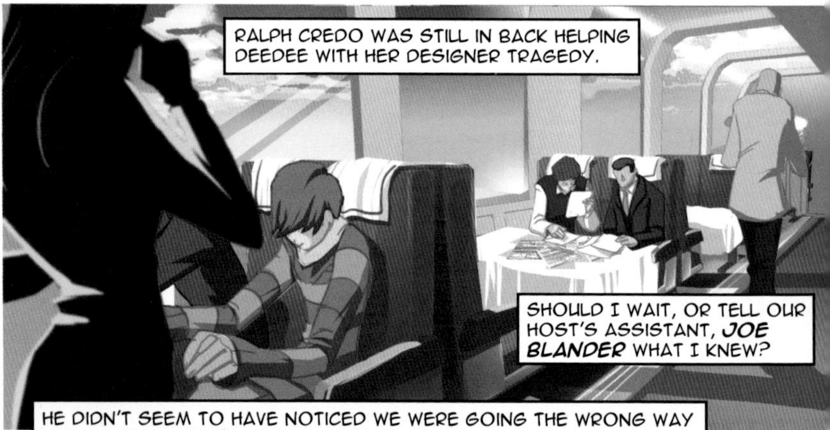
RALPH CREDO WAS STILL IN BACK HELPING DEEDEE WITH HER DESIGNER TRAGEDY.
SHOULD I WAIT, OR TELL OUR HOST'S ASSISTANT, JOE BLANDER WHAT I KNEW?

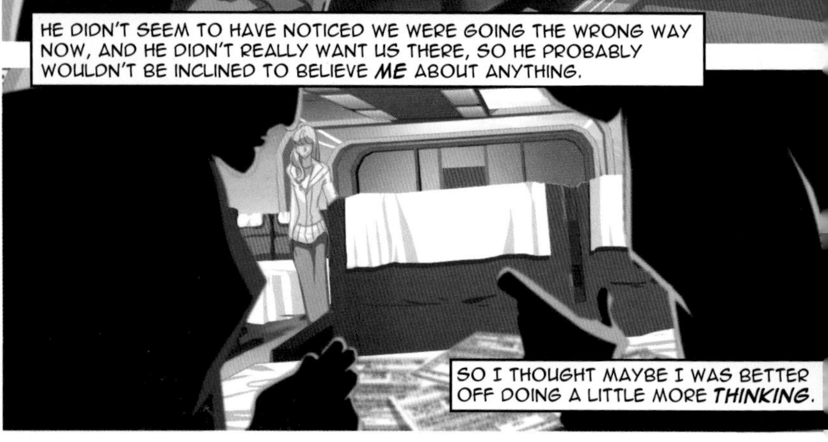
HE DIDN'T SEEM TO HAVE NOTICED WE WERE GOING THE WRONG WAY NOW, AND HE DIDN'T REALLY WANT US THERE, SO HE PROBABLY WOULDN'T BE INCLINED TO BELIEVE ME ABOUT ANYTHING.
SO I THOUGHT MAYBE I WAS BETTER OFF DOING A LITTLE MORE THINKING.

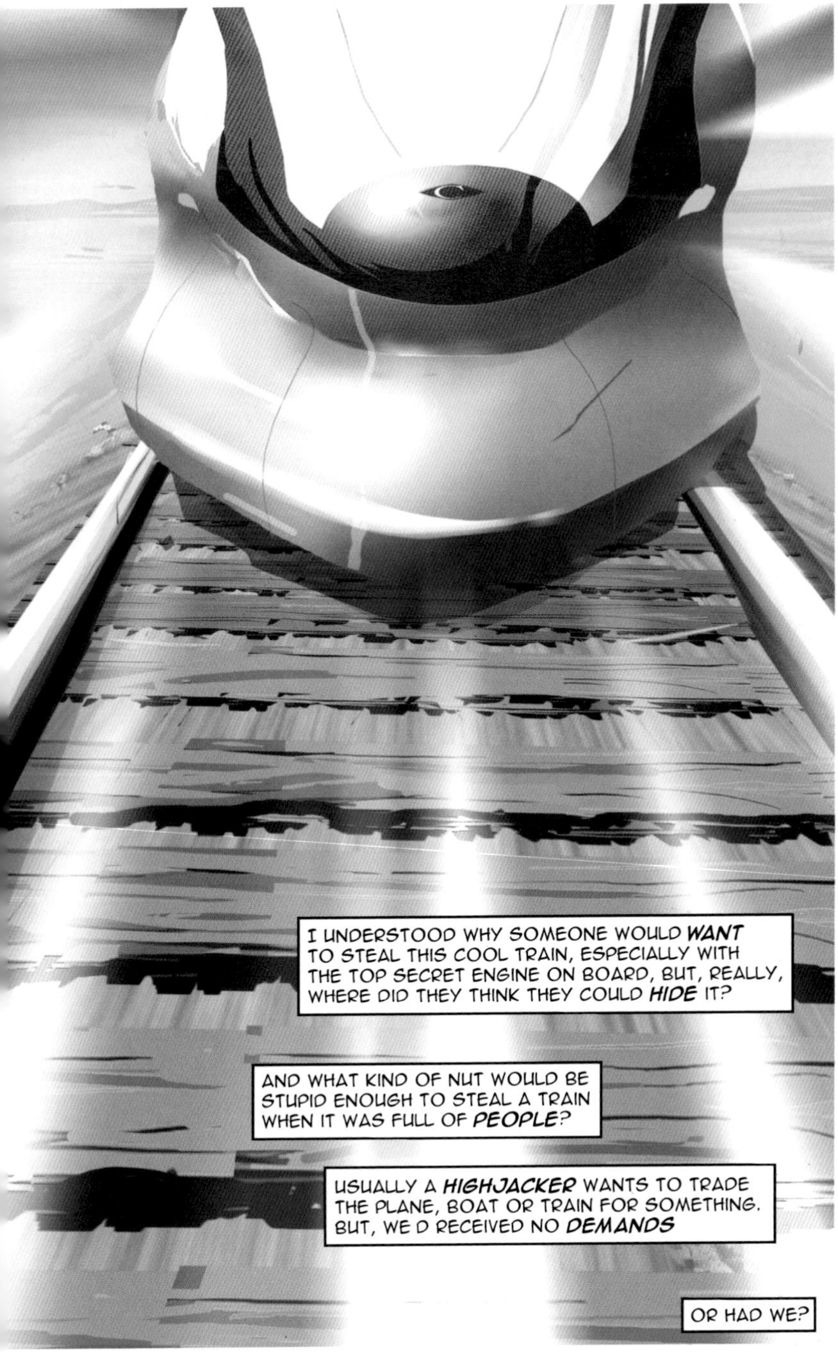
I UNDERSTOOD WHY SOMEONE WOULD WANT TO STEAL THIS COOL TRAIN, ESPECIALLY WITH THE TOP SECRET ENGINE ON BOARD, BUT, REALLY, WHERE DID THEY THINK THEY COULD HIDE IT?
AND WHAT KIND OF NUT WOULD BE STUPID ENOUGH TO STEAL A TRAIN WHEN IT WAS FULL OF PEOPLE?
USUALLY A HIGHJACKER WANTS TO TRADE THE PLANE, BOAT OR TRAIN FOR SOMETHING. BUT, WE D RECEIVED NO DEMANDS
OR HAD WE?

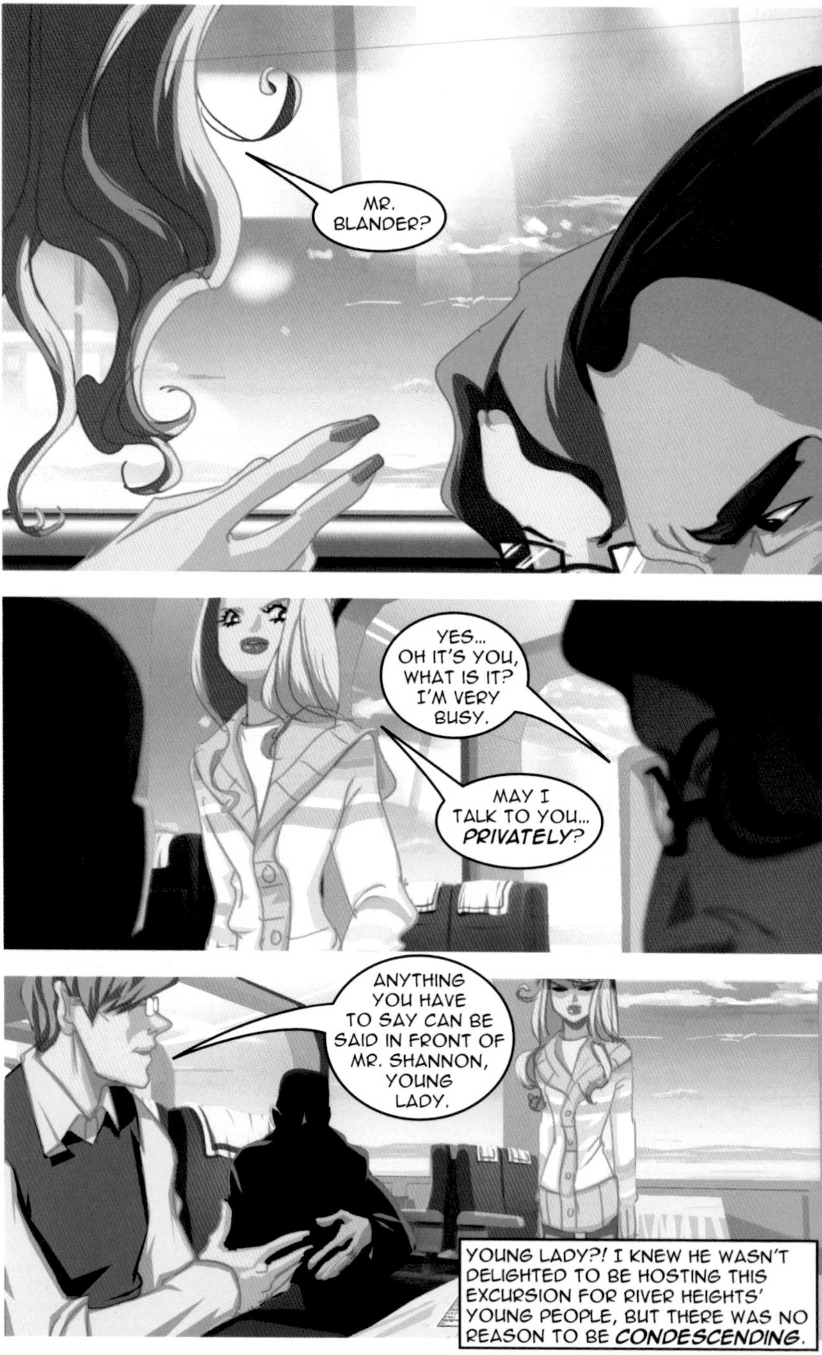

MR. BLANDER?
YES... OH IT'S YOU, WHAT IS IT? I'M VERY BUSY.
MAY I TALK TO YOU... *PRIVATELY*?
ANYTHING YOU HAVE TO SAY CAN BE SAID IN FRONT OF MR. SHANNON, YOUNG LADY.
YOUNG LADY?! I KNEW HE WASN'T DELIGHTED TO BE HOSTING THIS EXCURSION FOR RIVER HEIGHTS' YOUNG PEOPLE, BUT THERE WAS NO REASON TO BE *CONDESCENDING*.

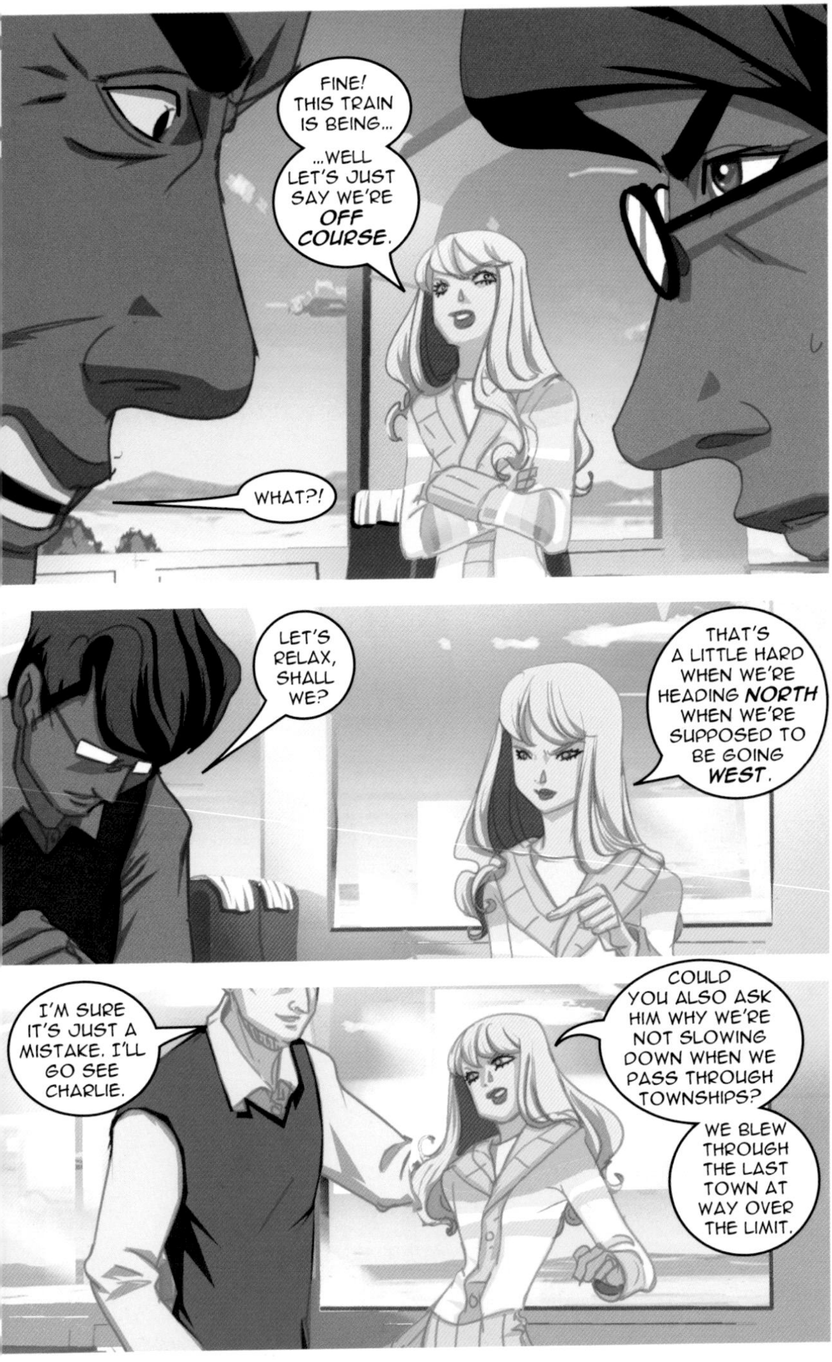
FINE! THIS TRAIN IS BEING...
...WELL LET'S JUST SAY WE'RE OFF COURSE.
WHAT?!
LET'S RELAX, SHALL WE?
THAT'S A LITTLE HARD WHEN WE'RE HEADING NORTH WHEN WE'RE SUPPOSED TO BE GOING WEST.
I'M SURE IT'S JUST A MISTAKE. I'LL GO SEE CHARLIE.
COULD YOU ALSO ASK HIM WHY WE'RE NOT SLOWING DOWN WHEN WE PASS THROUGH TOWNSHIPS?
WE BLEW THROUGH THE LAST TOWN AT WAY OVER THE LIMIT.

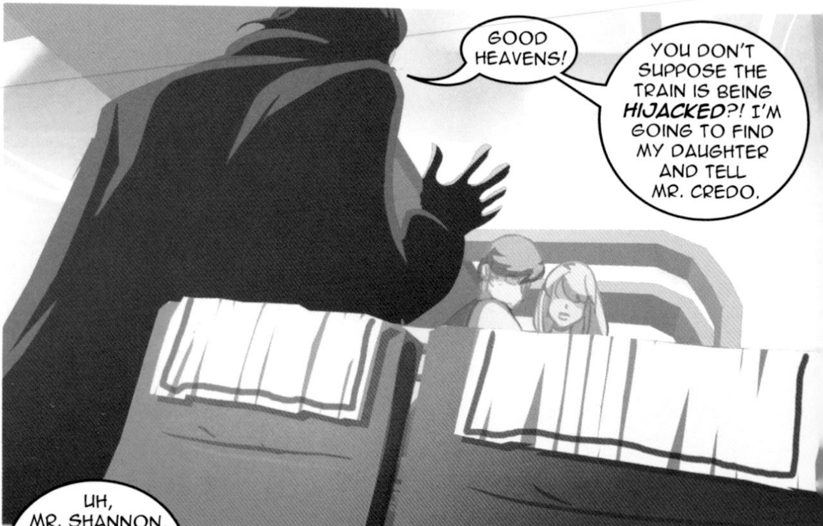
GOOD HEAVENS!
YOU DON'T SUPPOSE THE TRAIN IS BEING *HIJACKED*?! I'M GOING TO FIND MY DAUGHTER AND TELL MR. CREDO.
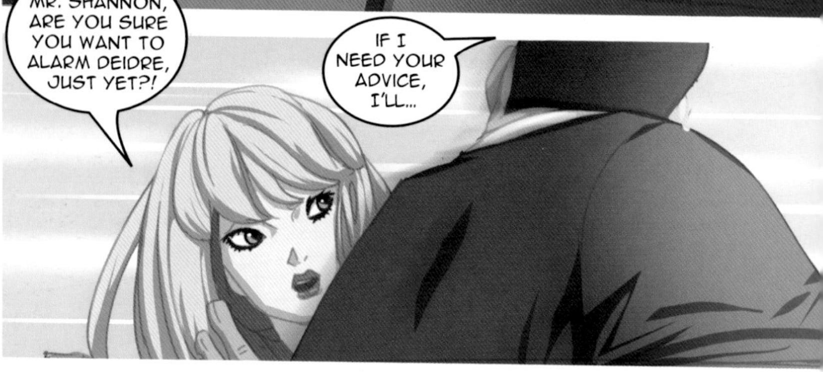
UH, MR. SHANNON, ARE YOU SURE YOU WANT TO ALARM DEIDRE, JUST YET?!
IF I NEED YOUR ADVICE, I'LL...
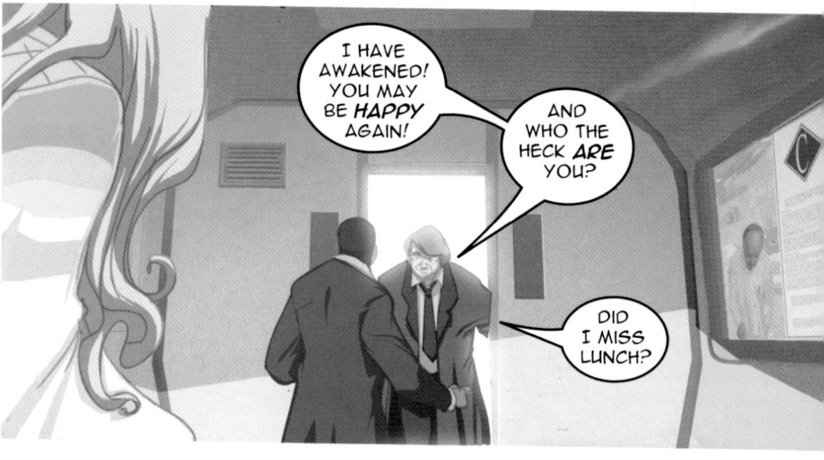
I HAVE AWAKENED! YOU MAY BE *HAPPY* AGAIN!
AND WHO THE HECK *ARE* YOU?
DID I MISS LUNCH?

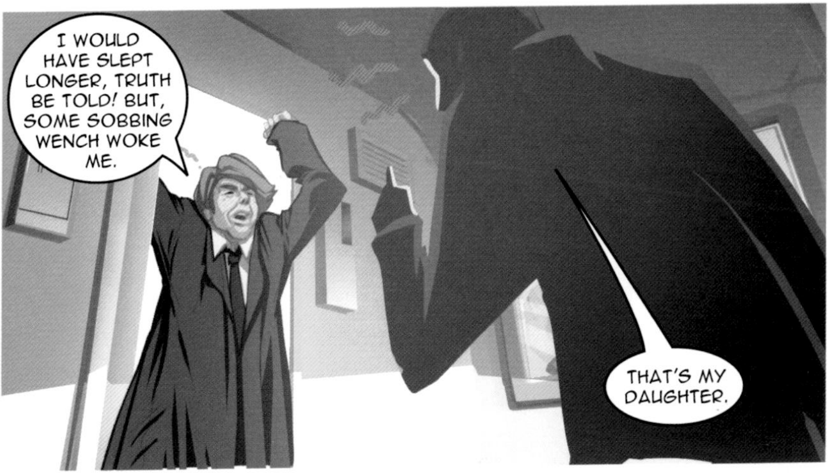
I WOULD HAVE SLEPT LONGER, TRUTH BE TOLD! BUT, SOME SOBBING WENCH WOKE ME.
THAT'S MY DAUGHTER.

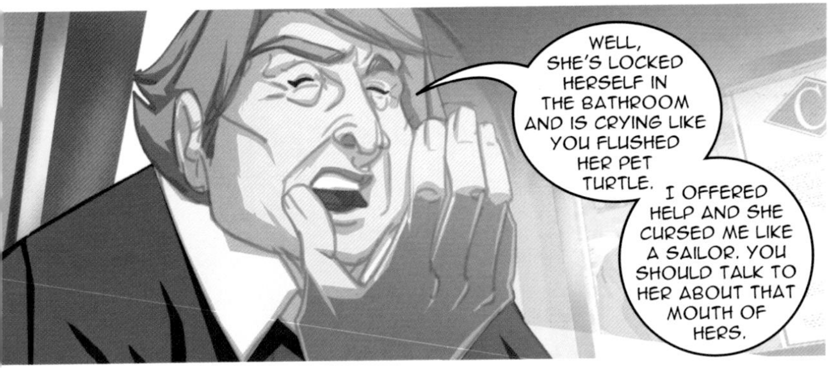
WELL, SHE'S LOCKED HERSELF IN THE BATHROOM AND IS CRYING LIKE YOU FLUSHED HER PET TURTLE.
I OFFERED HELP AND SHE CURSED ME LIKE A SAILOR. YOU SHOULD TALK TO HER ABOUT THAT MOUTH OF HERS.

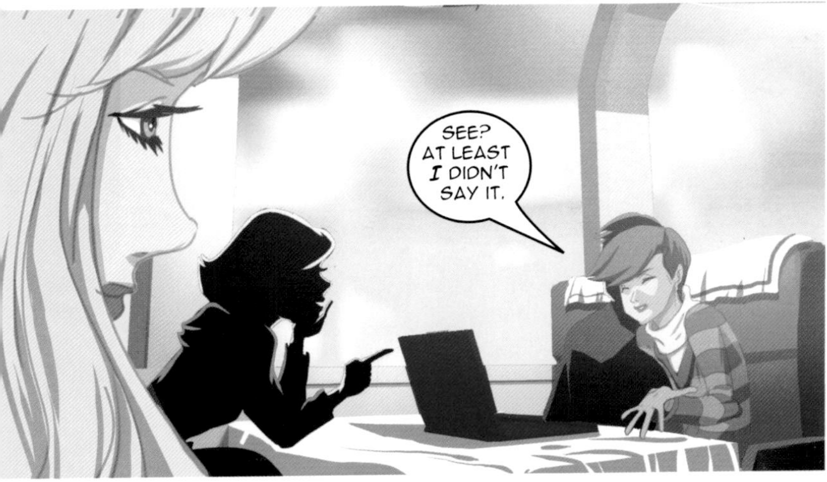
SEE? AT LEAST *I* DIDN'T SAY IT.

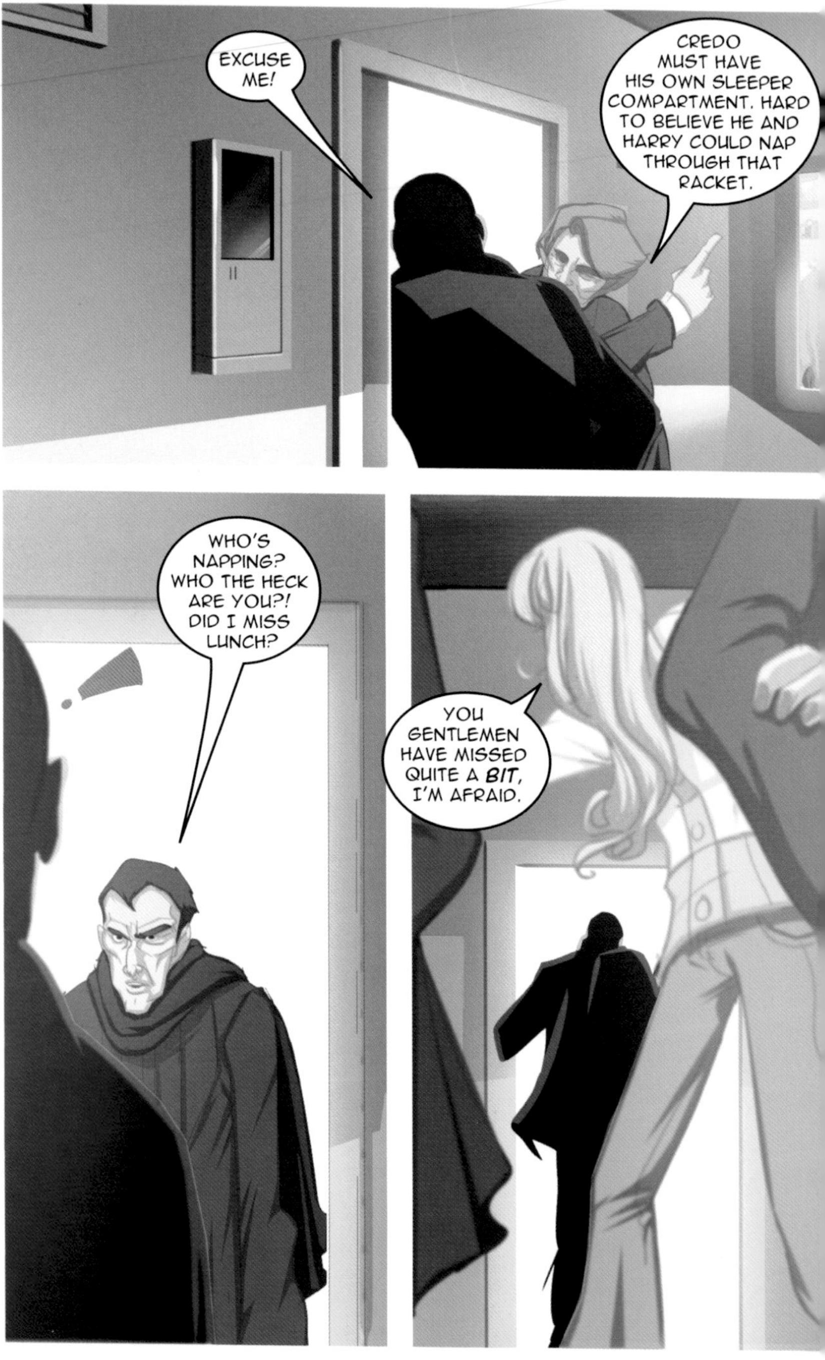
EXCUSE ME!
CREDO MUST HAVE HIS OWN SLEEPER COMPARTMENT. HARD TO BELIEVE HE AND HARRY COULD NAP THROUGH THAT RACKET.
WHO'S NAPPING? WHO THE HECK ARE YOU?! DID I MISS LUNCH?
YOU GENTLEMEN HAVE MISSED QUITE A *BIT*, I'M AFRAID.

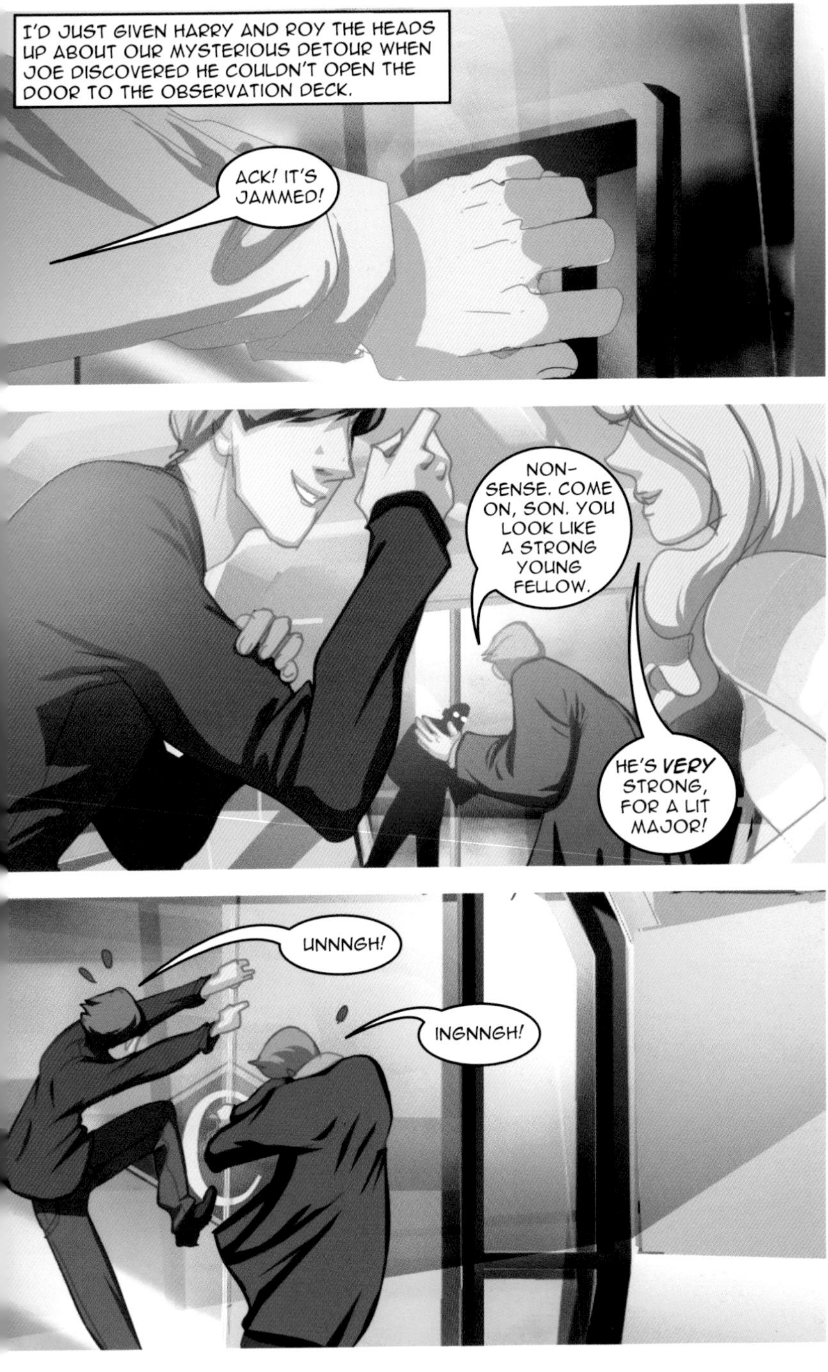
I'D JUST GIVEN HARRY AND ROY THE HEADS UP ABOUT OUR MYSTERIOUS DETOUR WHEN JOE DISCOVERED HE COULDN'T OPEN THE DOOR TO THE OBSERVATION DECK.
ACK! IT'S JAMMED!
NON-SENSE. COME ON, SON. YOU LOOK LIKE A STRONG YOUNG FELLOW.
HE'S *VERY* STRONG, FOR A LIT MAJOR!
UNNNGH!
INGNNGH!

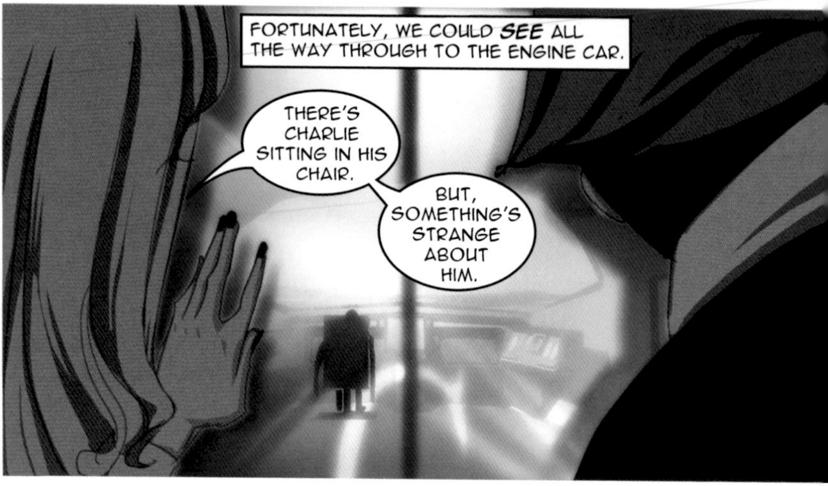
FORTUNATELY, WE COULD *SEE* ALL THE WAY THROUGH TO THE ENGINE CAR.
THERE'S CHARLIE SITTING IN HIS CHAIR.
BUT, SOMETHING'S STRANGE ABOUT HIM.

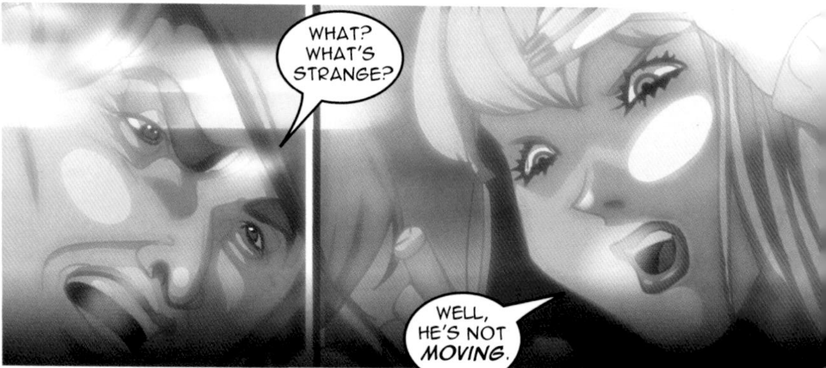
WHAT? WHAT'S STRANGE?
WELL, HE'S NOT *MOVING*.

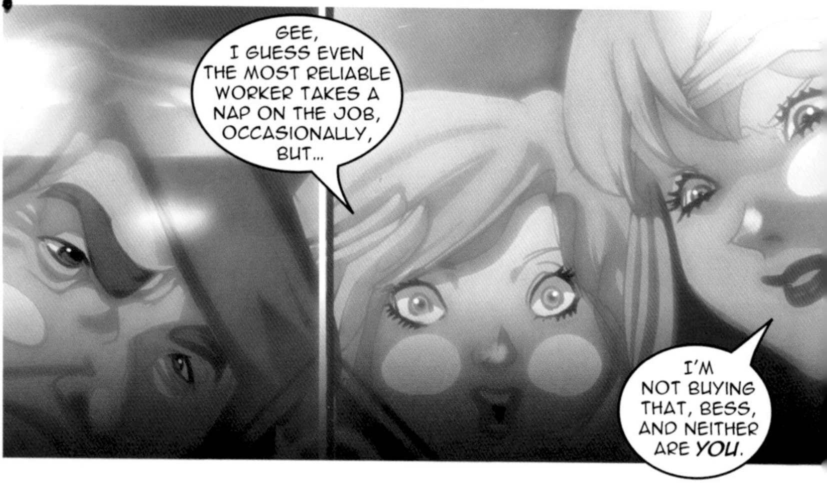
GEE, I GUESS EVEN THE MOST RELIABLE WORKER TAKES A NAP ON THE JOB, OCCASIONALLY, BUT...
I'M NOT BUYING THAT, BESS, AND NEITHER ARE *YOU*.

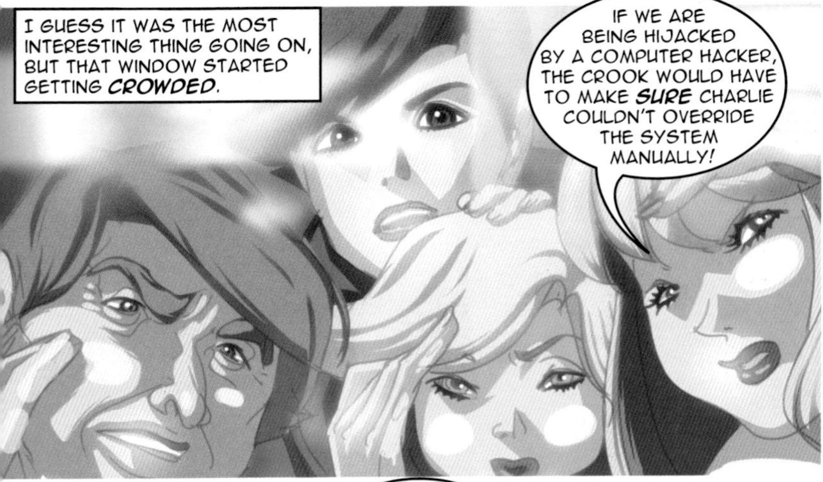
I GUESS IT WAS THE MOST INTERESTING THING GOING ON, BUT THAT WINDOW STARTED GETTING **CROWDED**.
IF WE ARE BEING HIJACKED BY A COMPUTER HACKER, THE CROOK WOULD HAVE TO MAKE **SURE** CHARLIE COULDN'T OVERRIDE THE SYSTEM MANUALLY!

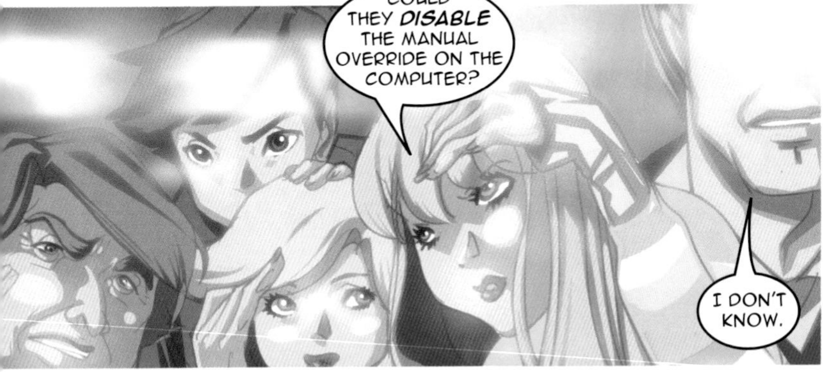
COULD THEY **DISABLE** THE MANUAL OVERRIDE ON THE COMPUTER?
I DON'T KNOW.

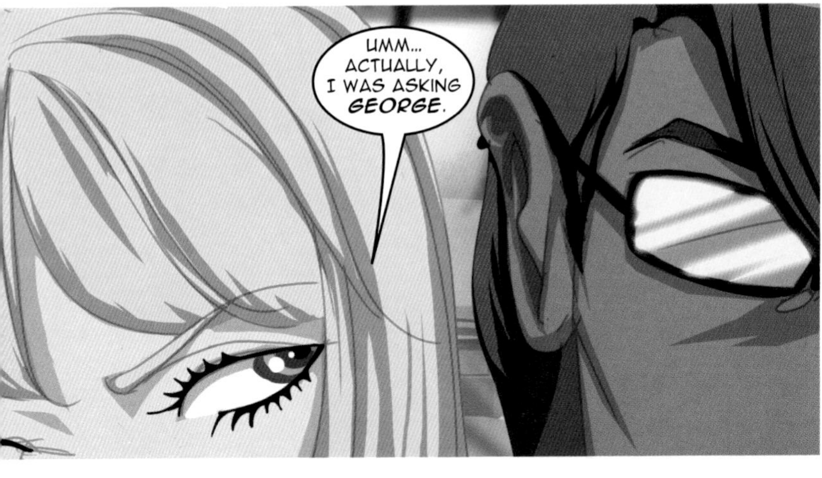
UMM... ACTUALLY, I WAS ASKING **GEORGE**.

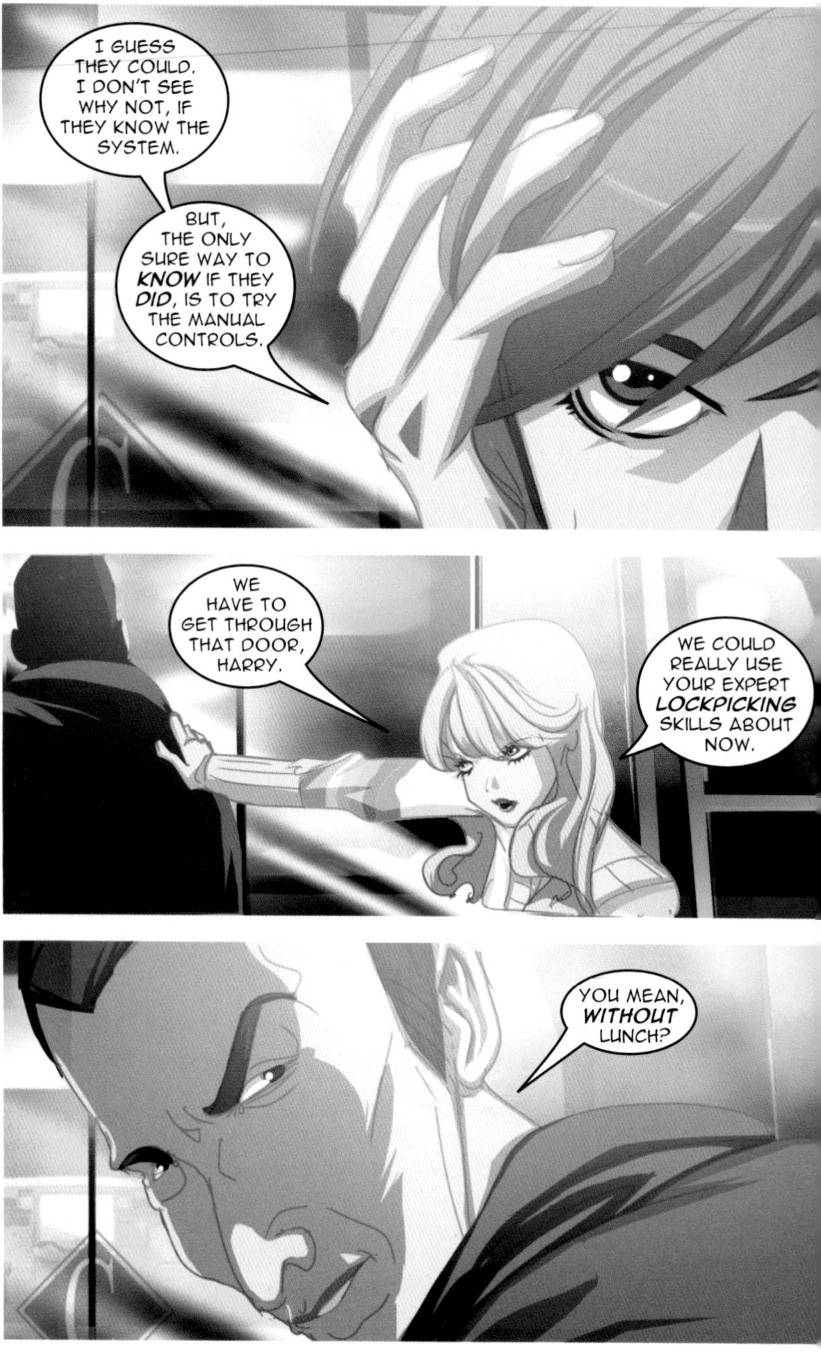
I GUESS THEY COULD. I DON'T SEE WHY NOT, IF THEY KNOW THE SYSTEM.
BUT, THE ONLY SURE WAY TO **KNOW** IF THEY **DID**, IS TO TRY THE MANUAL CONTROLS.
WE HAVE TO GET THROUGH THAT DOOR, HARRY.
WE COULD REALLY USE YOUR EXPERT **LOCKPICKING** SKILLS ABOUT NOW.
YOU MEAN, **WITHOUT** LUNCH?

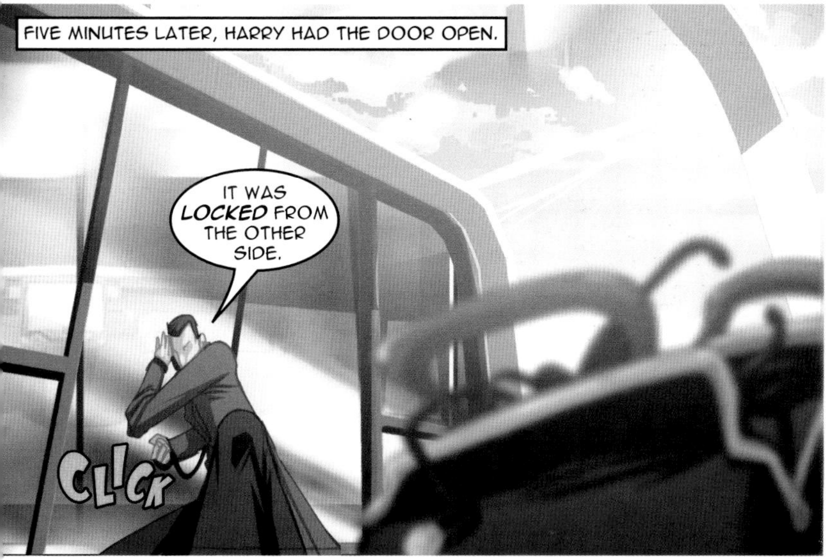
FIVE MINUTES LATER, HARRY HAD THE DOOR OPEN.
IT WAS LOCKED FROM THE OTHER SIDE.
CLICK
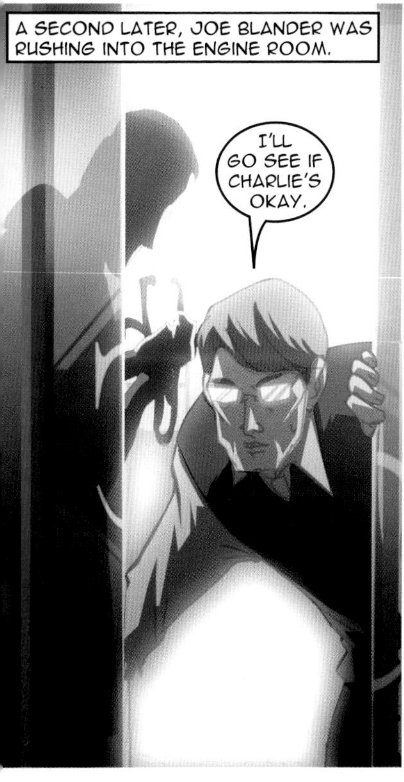
A SECOND LATER, JOE BLANDER WAS RUSHING INTO THE ENGINE ROOM.
I'LL GO SEE IF CHARLIE'S OKAY.
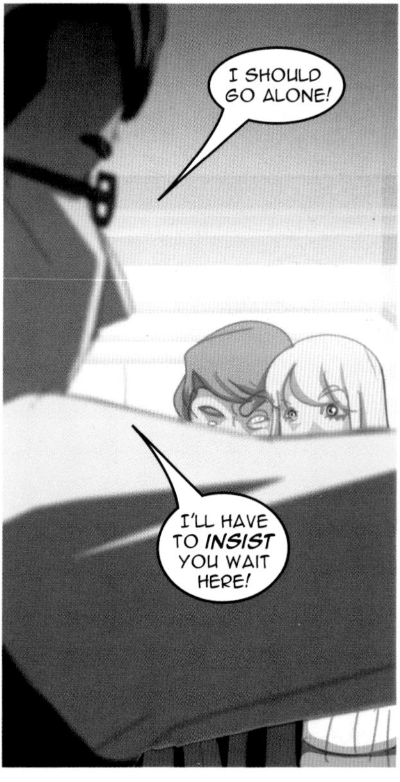
I SHOULD GO ALONE!
I'LL HAVE TO INSIST YOU WAIT HERE!

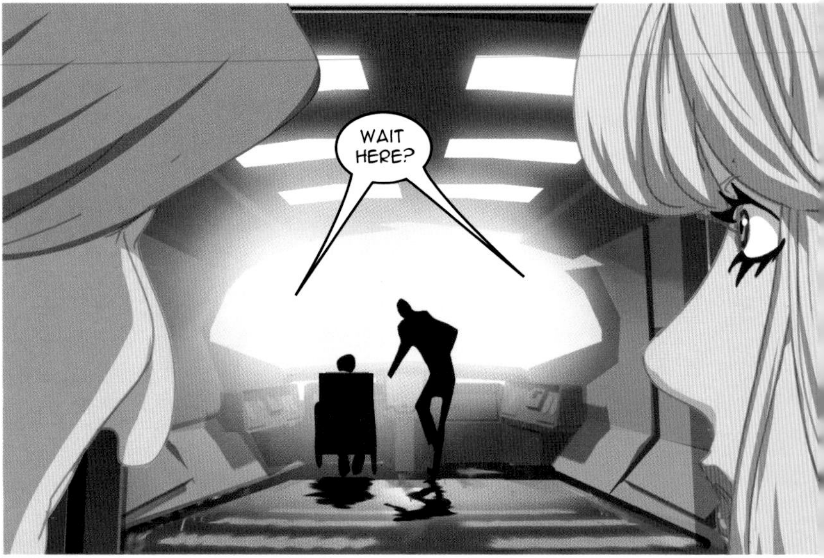
WAIT HERE?

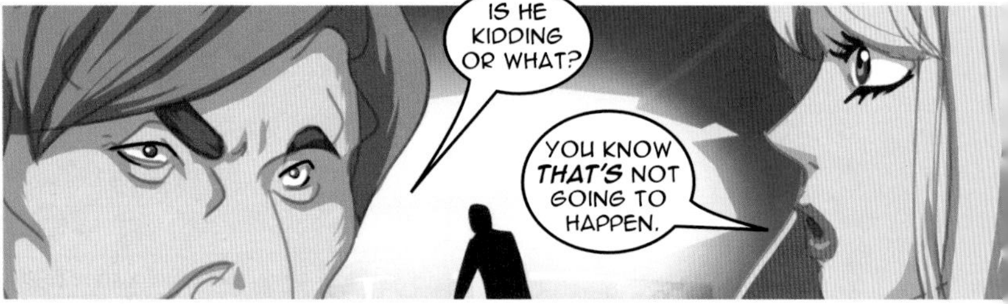
IS HE KIDDING OR WHAT?
YOU KNOW *THAT'S* NOT GOING TO HAPPEN.

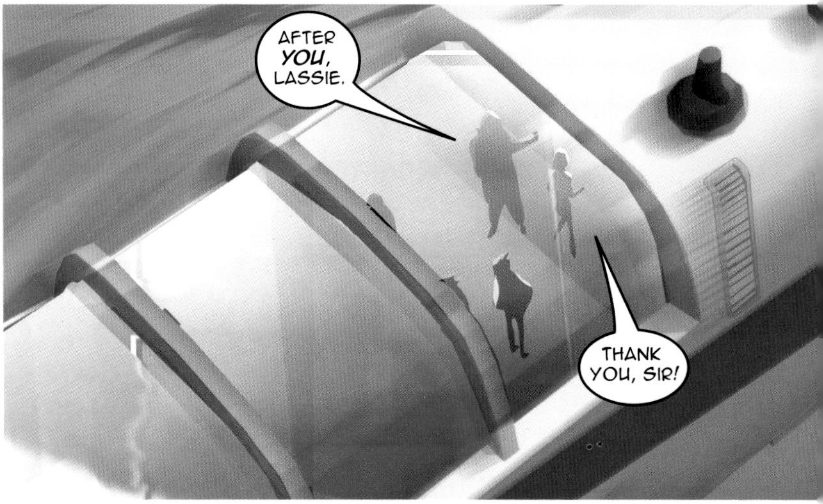
AFTER *YOU*, LASSIE.
THANK YOU, SIR!

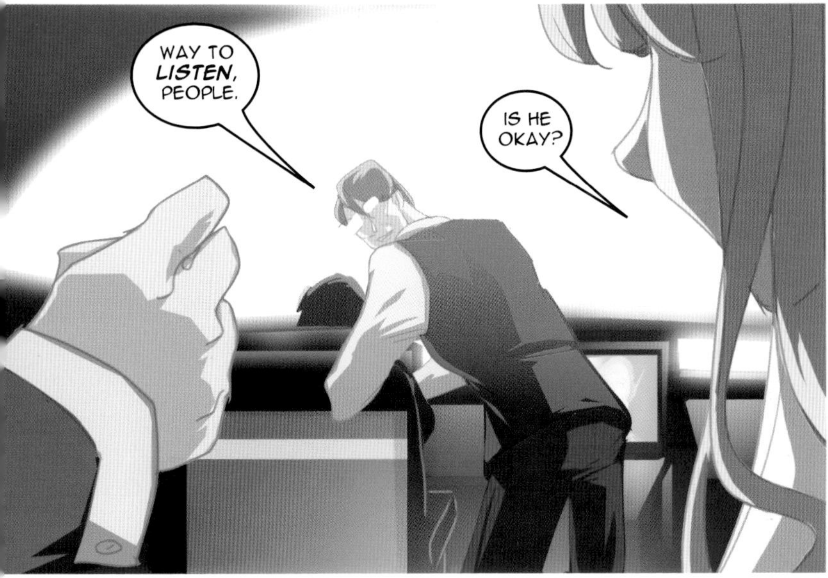
WAY TO LISTEN, PEOPLE.
IS HE OKAY?

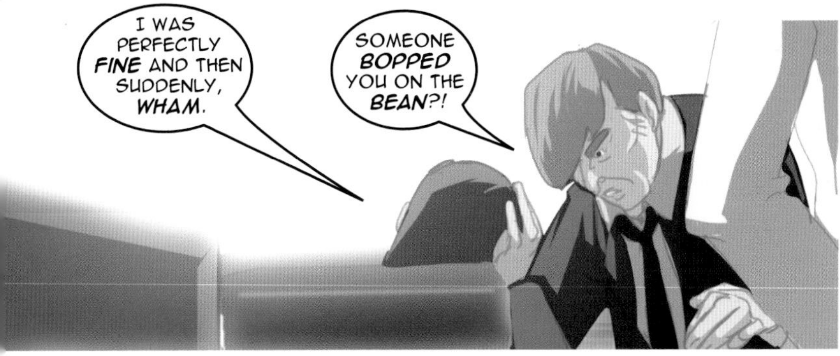
I WAS PERFECTLY FINE AND THEN SUDDENLY, WHAM.
SOMEONE BOPPED YOU ON THE BEAN?!

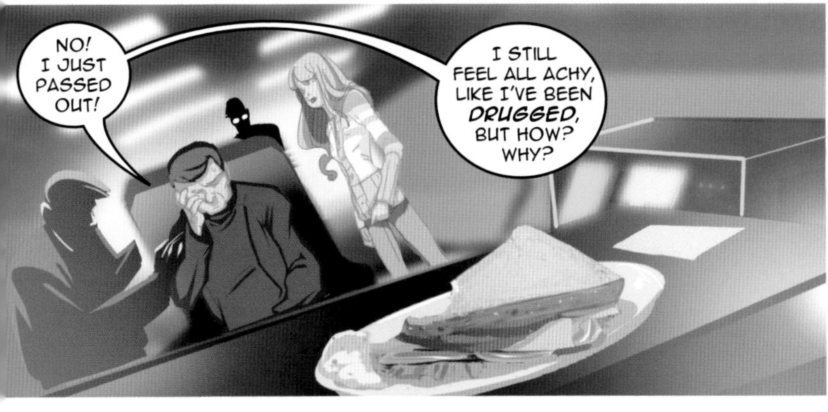
NO! I JUST PASSED OUT!
I STILL FEEL ALL ACHY, LIKE I'VE BEEN DRUGGED, BUT HOW? WHY?

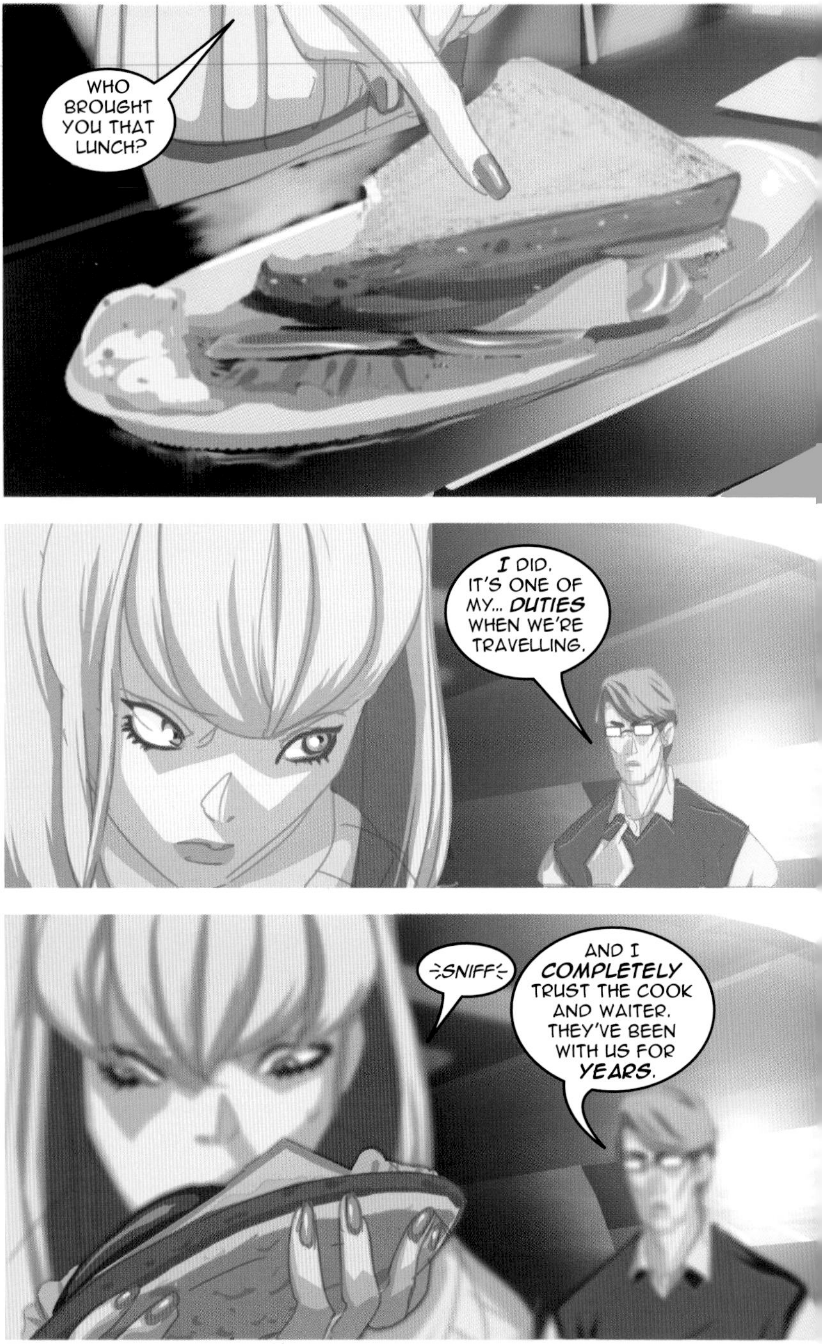
WHO BROUGHT YOU THAT LUNCH?
I DID. IT'S ONE OF MY... DUTIES WHEN WE'RE TRAVELLING.
SNIFF
AND I COMPLETELY TRUST THE COOK AND WAITER. THEY'VE BEEN WITH US FOR YEARS.

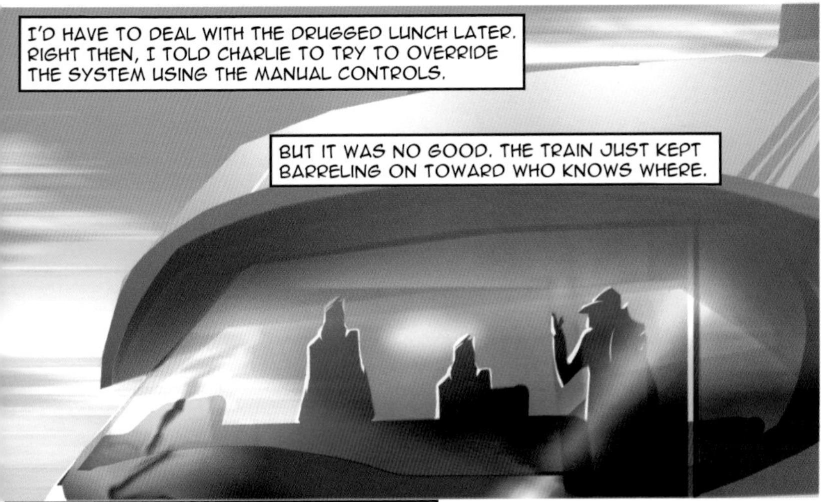
I'D HAVE TO DEAL WITH THE DRUGGED LUNCH LATER. RIGHT THEN, I TOLD CHARLIE TO TRY TO OVERRIDE THE SYSTEM USING THE MANUAL CONTROLS.
BUT IT WAS NO GOOD. THE TRAIN JUST KEPT BARRELING ON TOWARD WHO KNOWS WHERE.

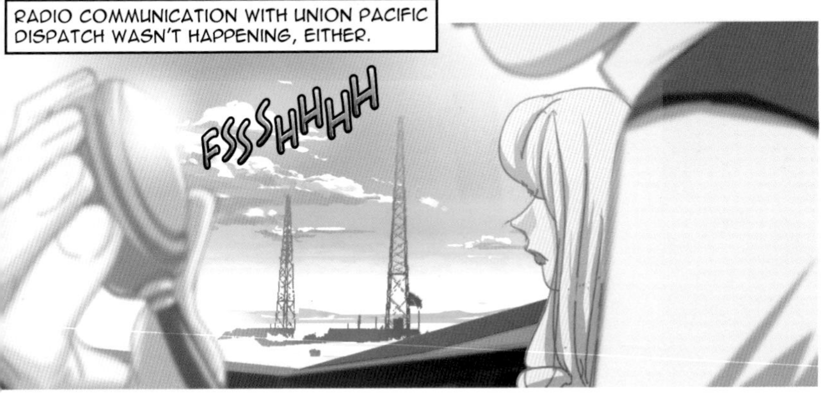
RADIO COMMUNICATION WITH UNION PACIFIC DISPATCH WASN'T HAPPENING, EITHER.
FSSSHHHHH

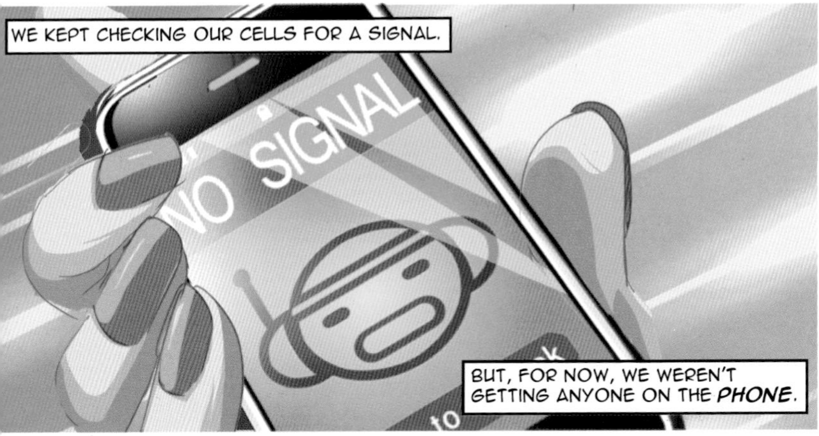
WE KEPT CHECKING OUR CELLS FOR A SIGNAL.
NO SIGNAL
BUT, FOR NOW, WE WEREN'T GETTING ANYONE ON THE *PHONE*.

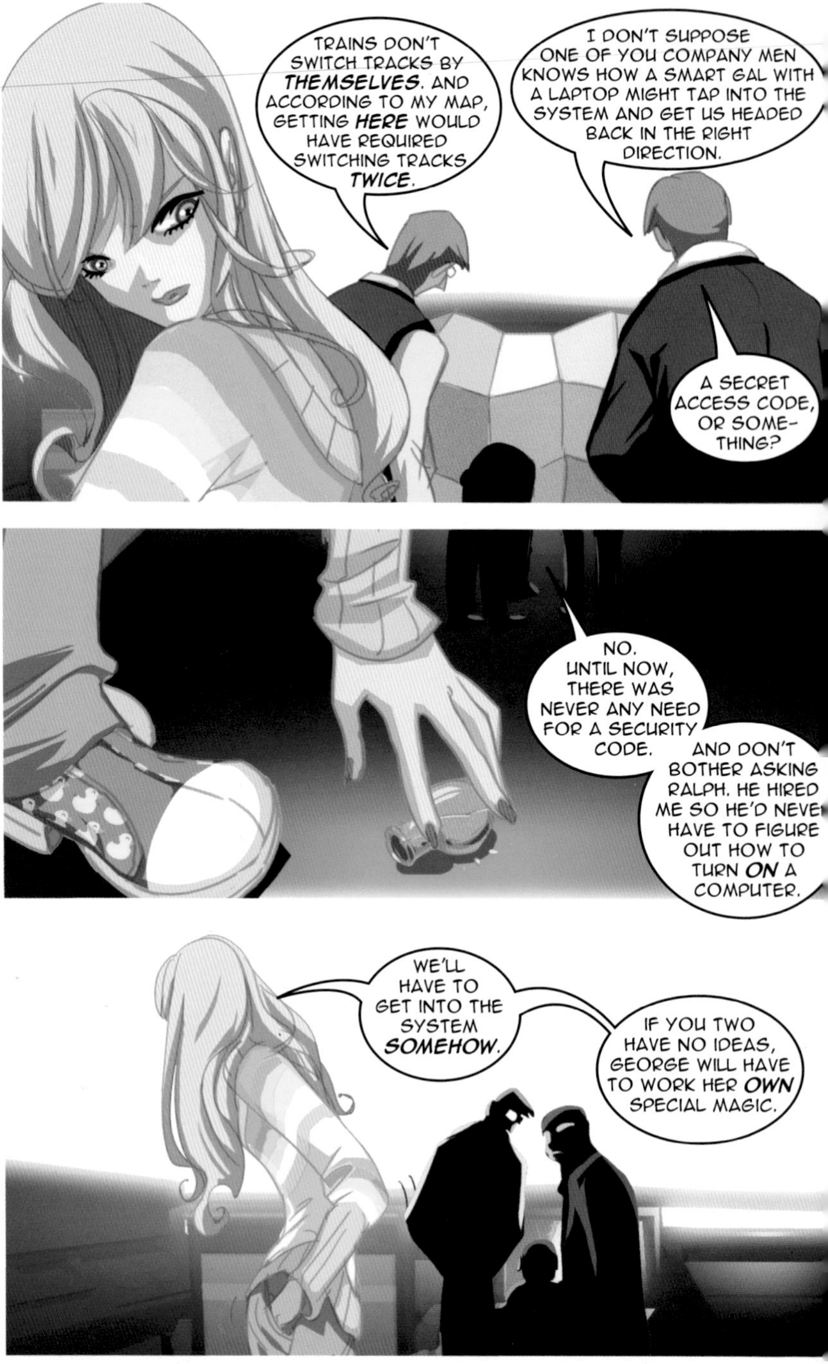
TRAINS DON'T SWITCH TRACKS BY THEMSELVES. AND ACCORDING TO MY MAP, GETTING HERE WOULD HAVE REQUIRED SWITCHING TRACKS TWICE.
I DON'T SUPPOSE ONE OF YOU COMPANY MEN KNOWS HOW A SMART GAL WITH A LAPTOP MIGHT TAP INTO THE SYSTEM AND GET US HEADED BACK IN THE RIGHT DIRECTION.
A SECRET ACCESS CODE, OR SOME-THING?
NO. UNTIL NOW, THERE WAS NEVER ANY NEED FOR A SECURITY CODE.
AND DON'T BOTHER ASKING RALPH. HE HIRED ME SO HE'D NEVE HAVE TO FIGURE OUT HOW TO TURN ON A COMPUTER.
WE'LL HAVE TO GET INTO THE SYSTEM SOMEHOW.
IF YOU TWO HAVE NO IDEAS, GEORGE WILL HAVE TO WORK HER OWN SPECIAL MAGIC.

CHARLIE ASSURED US HE WAS *FINE* AND HE'D KEEP TRYING TO CONTACT UNION PACIFIC DISPATCH AND OVERRIDE THE SYSTEM, MANUALLY.

I'D BETTER GO TELL MR. CREDO.

OUR BEST HOPE FOR REGAINING CONTROL OF THE TRAIN NOW WAS GEORGE. WHEN SHE WAS *FOCUSED,* GEORGE COULD HACK ANY COMPUTER SYSTEM.

WELL, I MANAGED TO GET A *FEW SECONDS* OF INTERNET ACCESS AS WE SPED THROUGH THAT LAST TOWN, BUT *LOST* IT BEFORE I COULD GET A SINGLE E-MAIL OFF. I'LL KEEP TRYING.

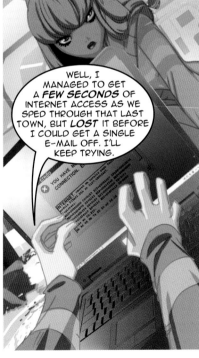

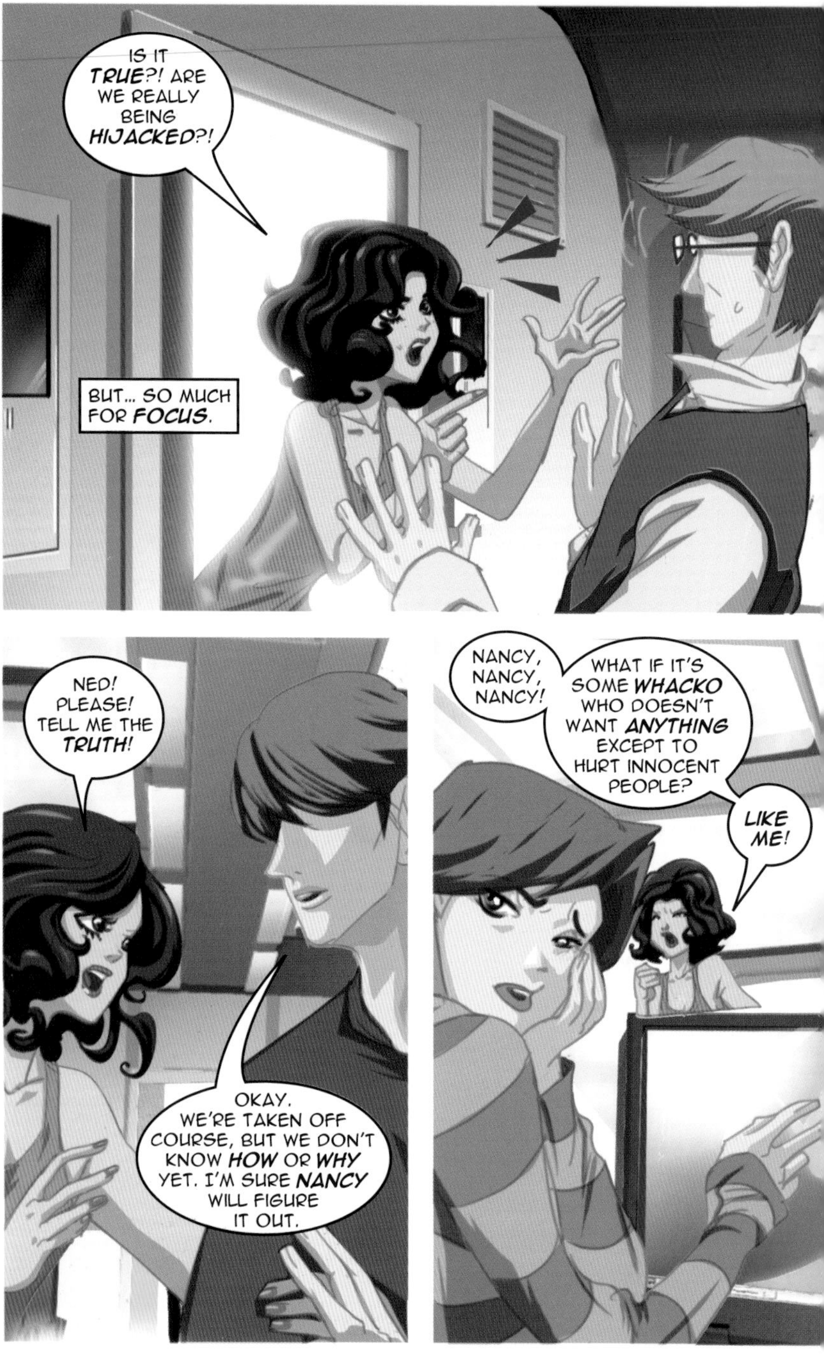
IS IT TRUE?! ARE WE REALLY BEING HIJACKED?!
BUT... SO MUCH FOR FOCUS.
NED! PLEASE! TELL ME THE TRUTH!
OKAY. WE'RE TAKEN OFF COURSE, BUT WE DON'T KNOW HOW OR WHY YET. I'M SURE NANCY WILL FIGURE IT OUT.
NANCY, NANCY, NANCY!
WHAT IF IT'S SOME WHACKO WHO DOESN'T WANT ANYTHING EXCEPT TO HURT INNOCENT PEOPLE?
LIKE ME!

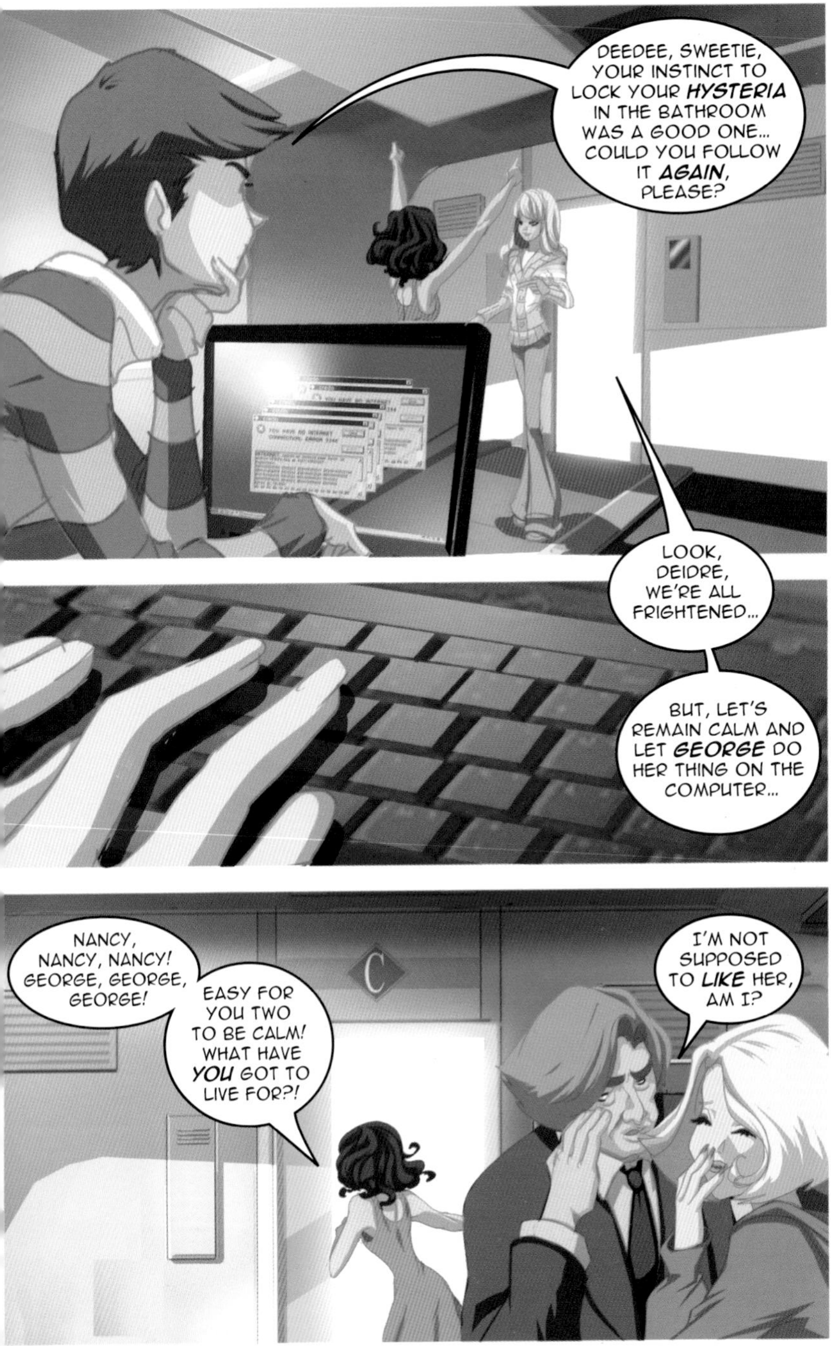
DEEDEE, SWEETIE, YOUR INSTINCT TO LOCK YOUR **HYSTERIA** IN THE BATHROOM WAS A GOOD ONE... COULD YOU FOLLOW IT **AGAIN**, PLEASE?
LOOK, DEIDRE, WE'RE ALL FRIGHTENED...
BUT, LET'S REMAIN CALM AND LET **GEORGE** DO HER THING ON THE COMPUTER...
NANCY, NANCY, NANCY! GEORGE, GEORGE, GEORGE!
EASY FOR YOU TWO TO BE CALM! WHAT HAVE **YOU** GOT TO LIVE FOR?!
I'M NOT SUPPOSED TO **LIKE** HER, AM I?

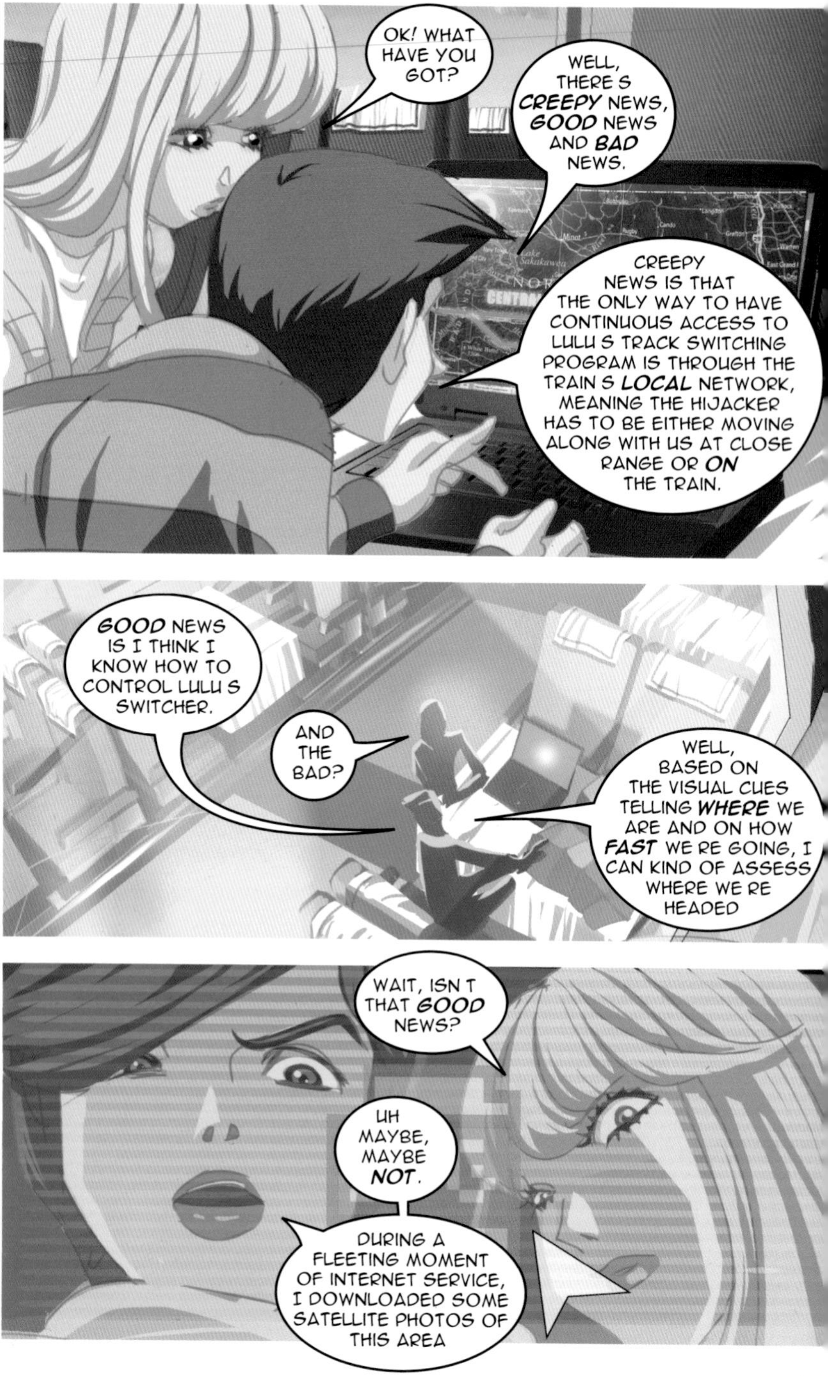
OK! WHAT HAVE YOU GOT?
WELL, THERE S *CREEPY* NEWS, *GOOD* NEWS AND *BAD* NEWS.
CREEPY NEWS IS THAT THE ONLY WAY TO HAVE CONTINUOUS ACCESS TO LULU S TRACK SWITCHING PROGRAM IS THROUGH THE TRAIN S *LOCAL* NETWORK, MEANING THE HIJACKER HAS TO BE EITHER MOVING ALONG WITH US AT CLOSE RANGE OR *ON* THE TRAIN.
GOOD NEWS IS I THINK I KNOW HOW TO CONTROL LULU S SWITCHER.
AND THE BAD?
WELL, BASED ON THE VISUAL CUES TELLING *WHERE* WE ARE AND ON HOW *FAST* WE RE GOING, I CAN KIND OF ASSESS WHERE WE RE HEADED
WAIT, ISN T THAT *GOOD* NEWS?
UH MAYBE, MAYBE *NOT*.
DURING A FLEETING MOMENT OF INTERNET SERVICE, I DOWNLOADED SOME SATELLITE PHOTOS OF THIS AREA

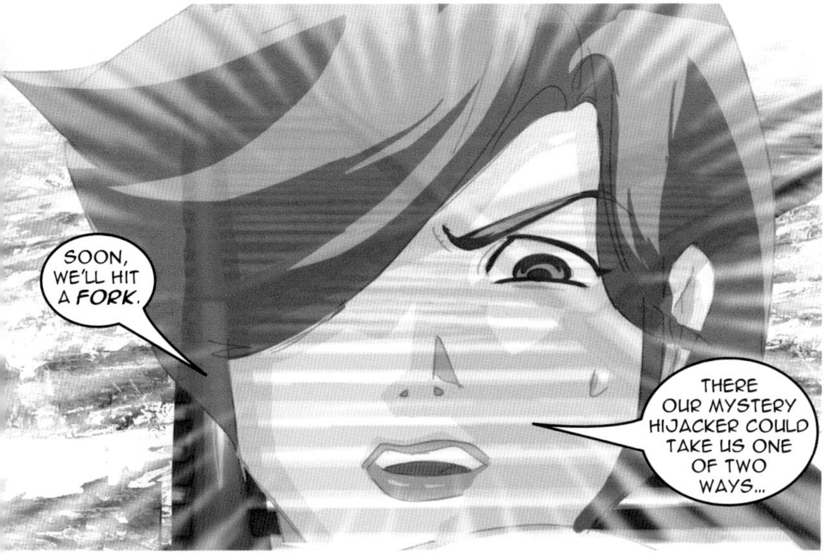
SOON, WE'LL HIT A **FORK**.
THERE OUR MYSTERY HIJACKER COULD TAKE US ONE OF TWO WAYS...

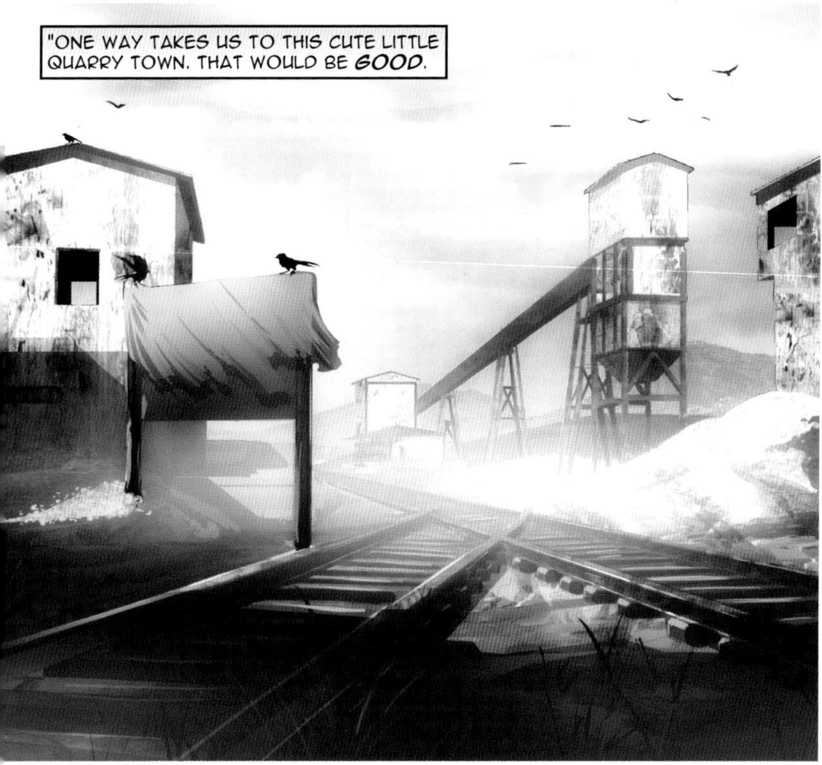
"ONE WAY TAKES US TO THIS CUTE LITTLE QUARRY TOWN. THAT WOULD BE **GOOD**.

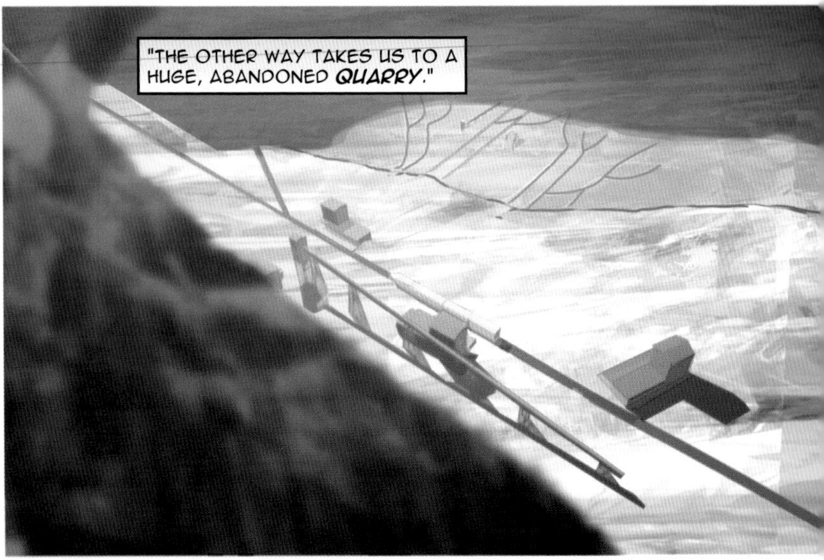
"THE OTHER WAY TAKES US TO A HUGE, ABANDONED **QUARRY**."

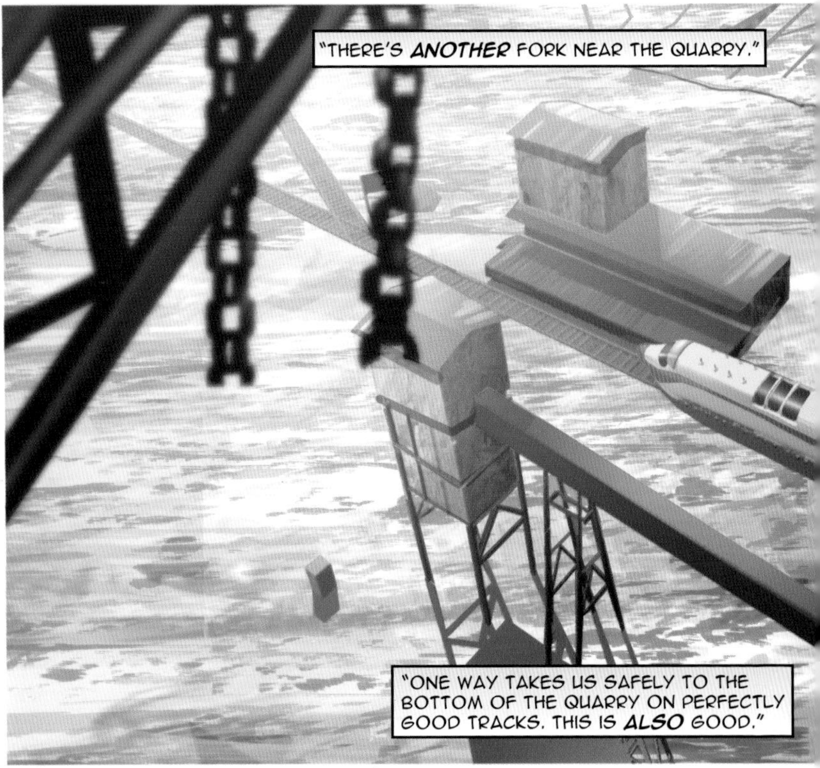
"THERE'S **ANOTHER** FORK NEAR THE QUARRY."
"ONE WAY TAKES US SAFELY TO THE BOTTOM OF THE QUARRY ON PERFECTLY GOOD TRACKS. THIS IS **ALSO** GOOD."

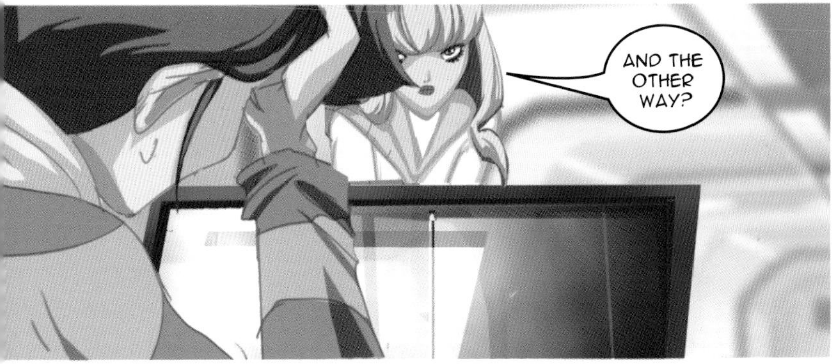
AND THE OTHER WAY?

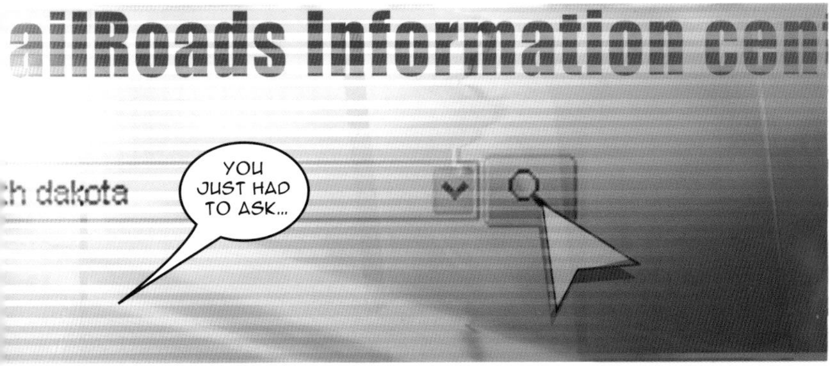
ailRoads Information cen
h dakota
YOU JUST HAD TO ASK...

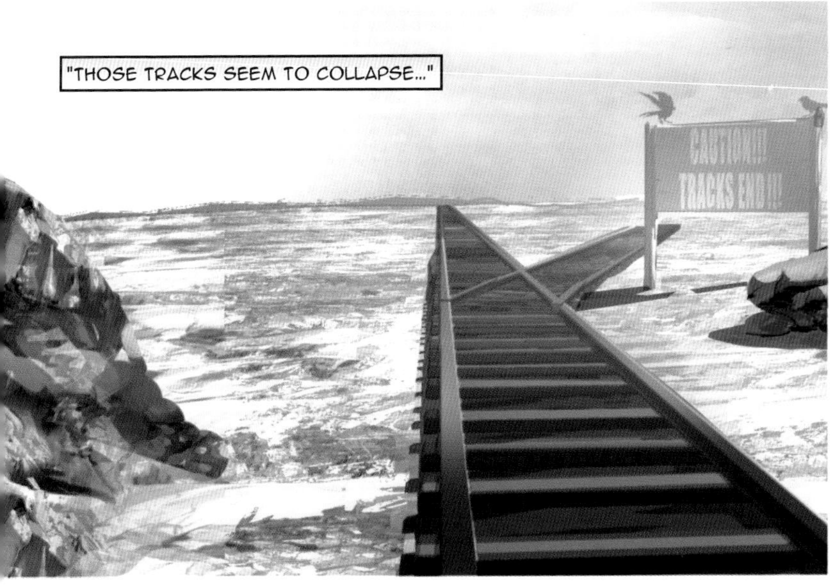
"THOSE TRACKS SEEM TO COLLAPSE..."
CAUTION!!!
TRACKS END!!!

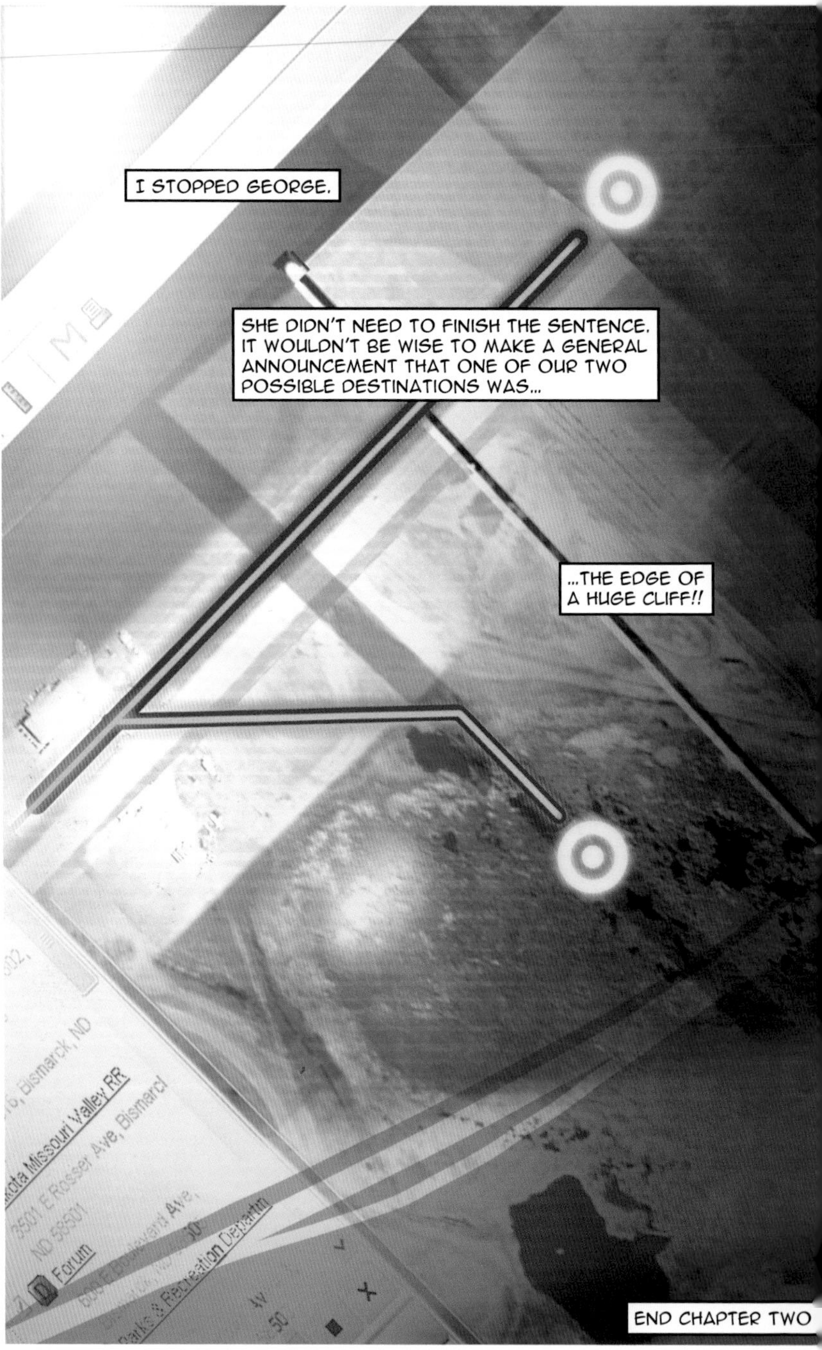
I STOPPED GEORGE.
SHE DIDN'T NEED TO FINISH THE SENTENCE. IT WOULDN'T BE WISE TO MAKE A GENERAL ANNOUNCEMENT THAT ONE OF OUR TWO POSSIBLE DESTINATIONS WAS...
...THE EDGE OF A HUGE CLIFF!!
END CHAPTER TWO

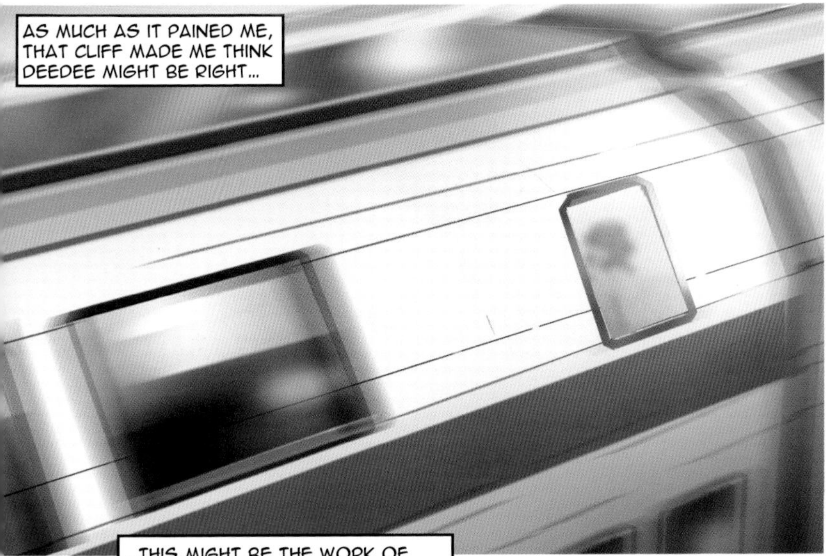
AS MUCH AS IT PAINED ME, THAT CLIFF MADE ME THINK DEEDEE MIGHT BE RIGHT...

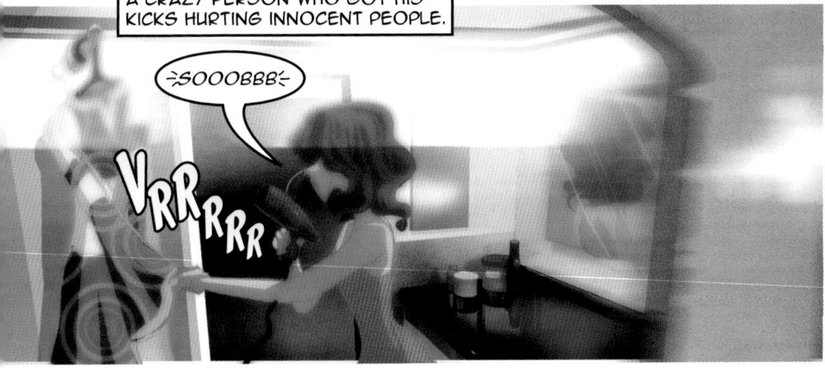
...THIS MIGHT BE THE WORK OF A CRAZY PERSON WHO GOT HIS KICKS HURTING INNOCENT PEOPLE.
SOOOBBB
VRRRRR

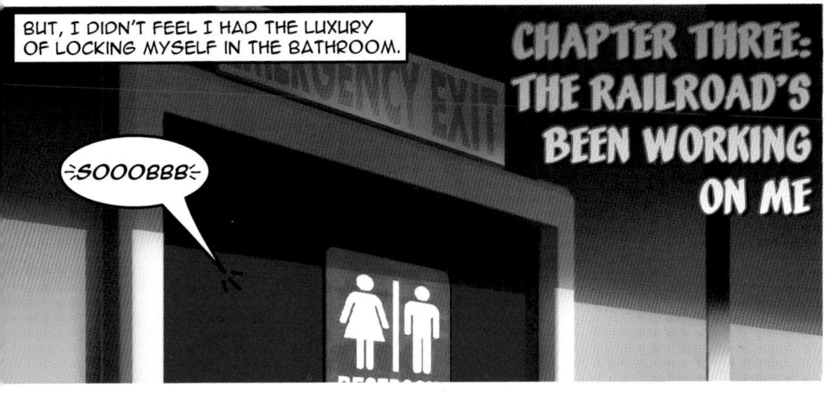
BUT, I DIDN'T FEEL I HAD THE LUXURY OF LOCKING MYSELF IN THE BATHROOM.
CHAPTER THREE: THE RAILROAD'S BEEN WORKING ON ME
SOOOBBB

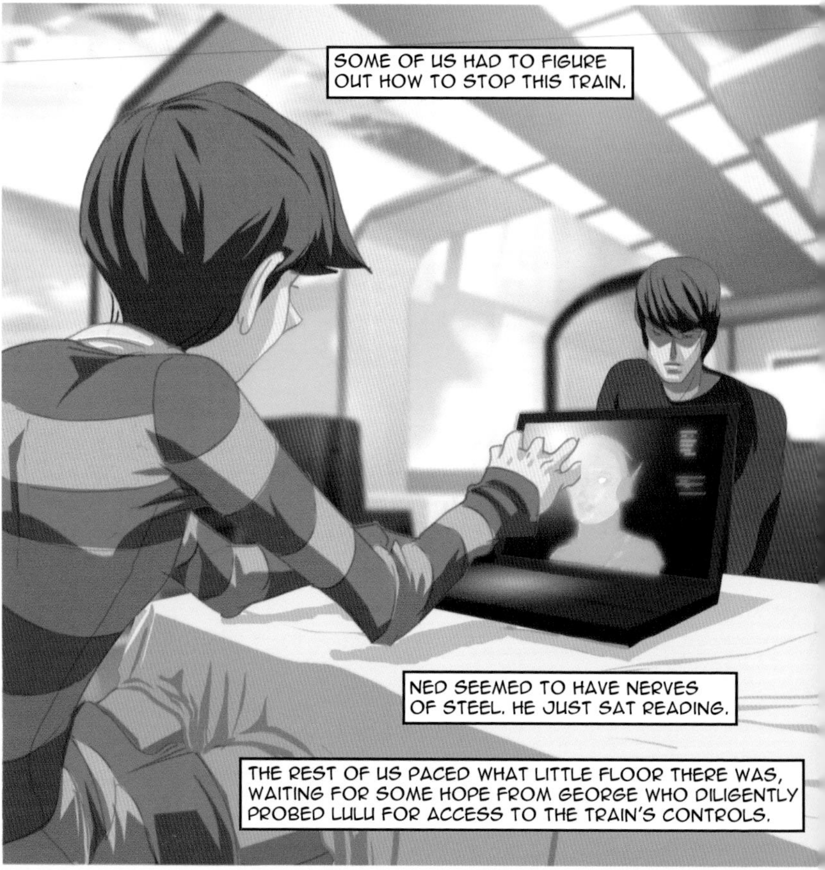
SOME OF US HAD TO FIGURE OUT HOW TO STOP THIS TRAIN.
NED SEEMED TO HAVE NERVES OF STEEL. HE JUST SAT READING.
THE REST OF US PACED WHAT LITTLE FLOOR THERE WAS, WAITING FOR SOME HOPE FROM GEORGE WHO DILIGENTLY PROBED LULU FOR ACCESS TO THE TRAIN'S CONTROLS.

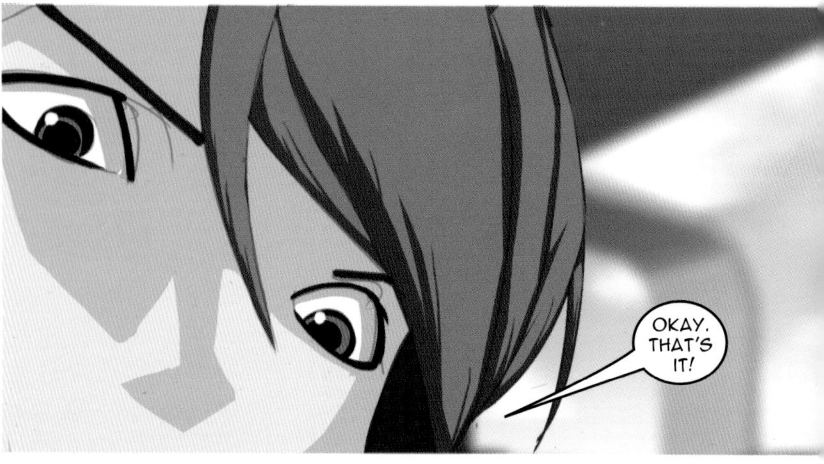
OKAY. THAT'S IT!

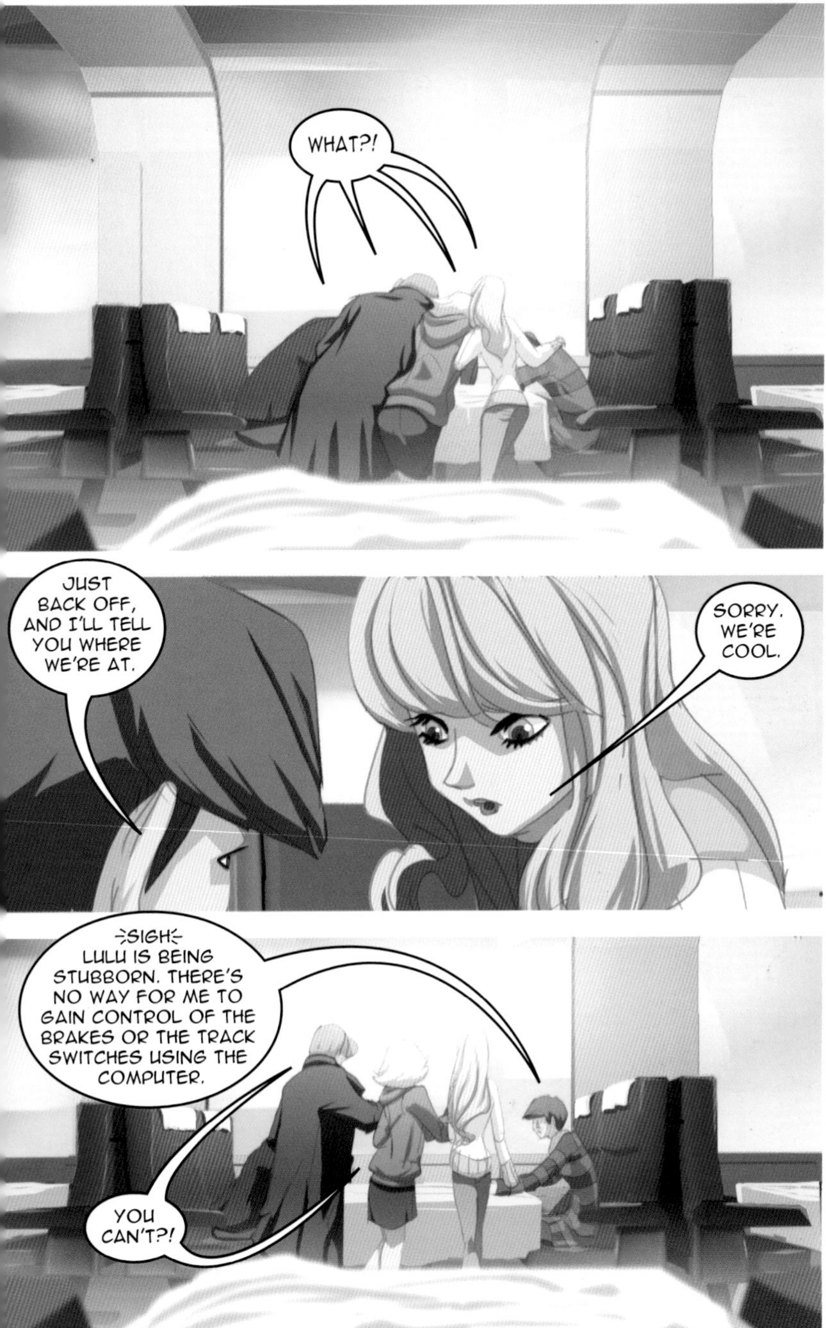
WHAT?!
JUST BACK OFF, AND I'LL TELL YOU WHERE WE'RE AT.
SORRY. WE'RE COOL.
SIGH
LULU IS BEING STUBBORN. THERE'S NO WAY FOR ME TO GAIN CONTROL OF THE BRAKES OR THE TRACK SWITCHES USING THE COMPUTER.
YOU CAN'T?!

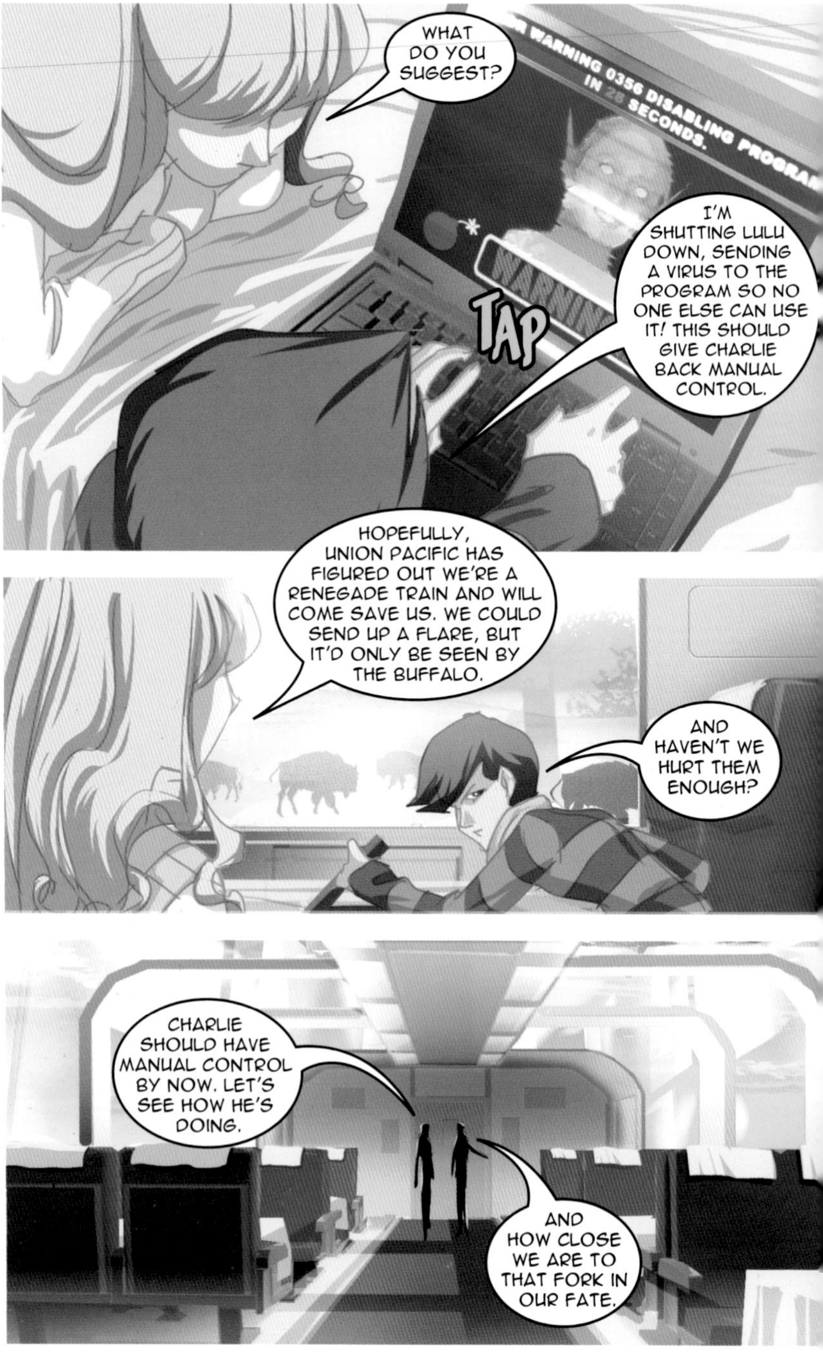
WHAT DO YOU SUGGEST?
TAP
I'M SHUTTING LULU DOWN, SENDING A VIRUS TO THE PROGRAM SO NO ONE ELSE CAN USE IT! THIS SHOULD GIVE CHARLIE BACK MANUAL CONTROL.
HOPEFULLY, UNION PACIFIC HAS FIGURED OUT WE'RE A RENEGADE TRAIN AND WILL COME SAVE US. WE COULD SEND UP A FLARE, BUT IT'D ONLY BE SEEN BY THE BUFFALO.
AND HAVEN'T WE HURT THEM ENOUGH?
CHARLIE SHOULD HAVE MANUAL CONTROL BY NOW. LET'S SEE HOW HE'S DOING.
AND HOW CLOSE WE ARE TO THAT FORK IN OUR FATE.

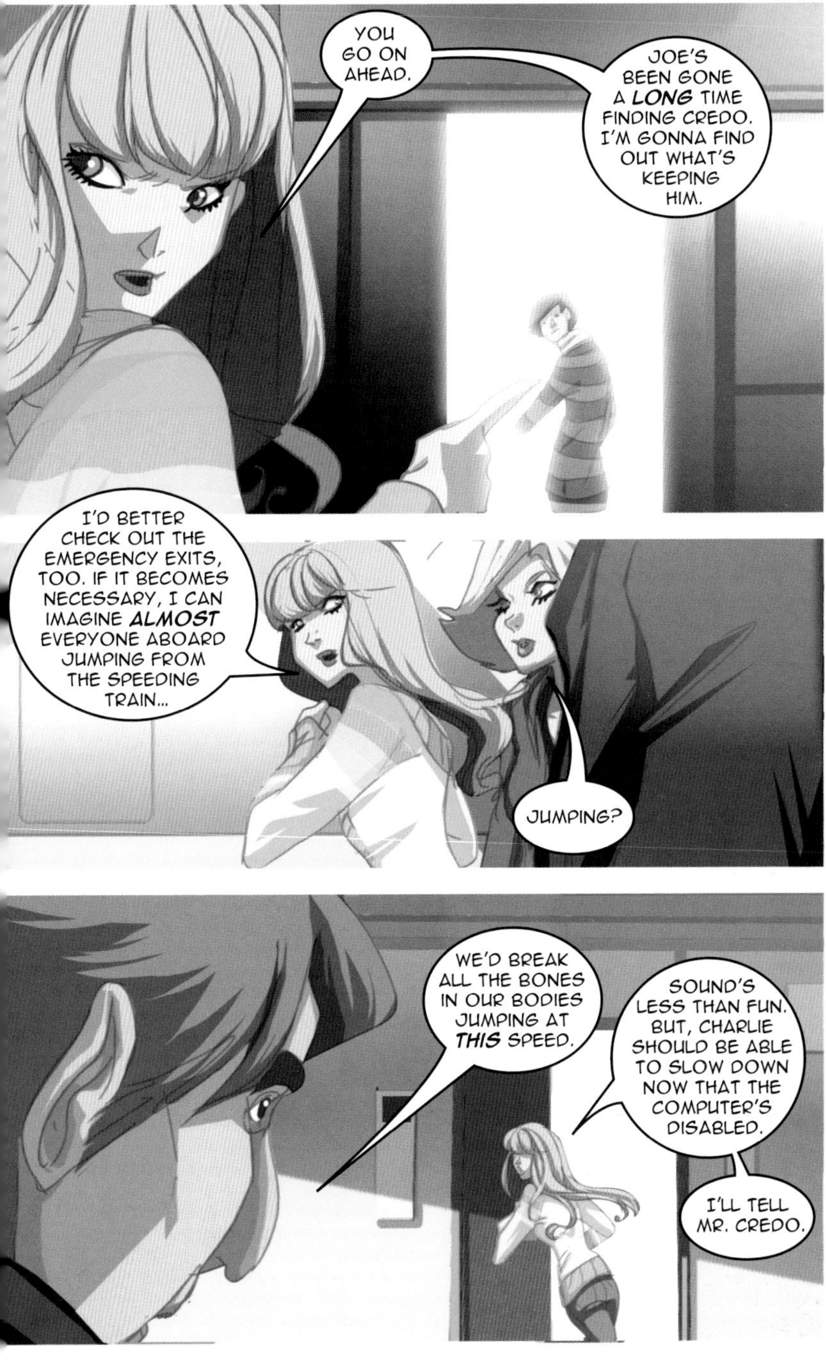
YOU GO ON AHEAD.
JOE'S BEEN GONE A **LONG** TIME FINDING CREDO. I'M GONNA FIND OUT WHAT'S KEEPING HIM.
I'D BETTER CHECK OUT THE EMERGENCY EXITS, TOO. IF IT BECOMES NECESSARY, I CAN IMAGINE ***ALMOST*** EVERYONE ABOARD JUMPING FROM THE SPEEDING TRAIN...
JUMPING?
WE'D BREAK ALL THE BONES IN OUR BODIES JUMPING AT ***THIS*** SPEED.
SOUND'S LESS THAN FUN. BUT, CHARLIE SHOULD BE ABLE TO SLOW DOWN NOW THAT THE COMPUTER'S DISABLED.
I'LL TELL MR. CREDO.

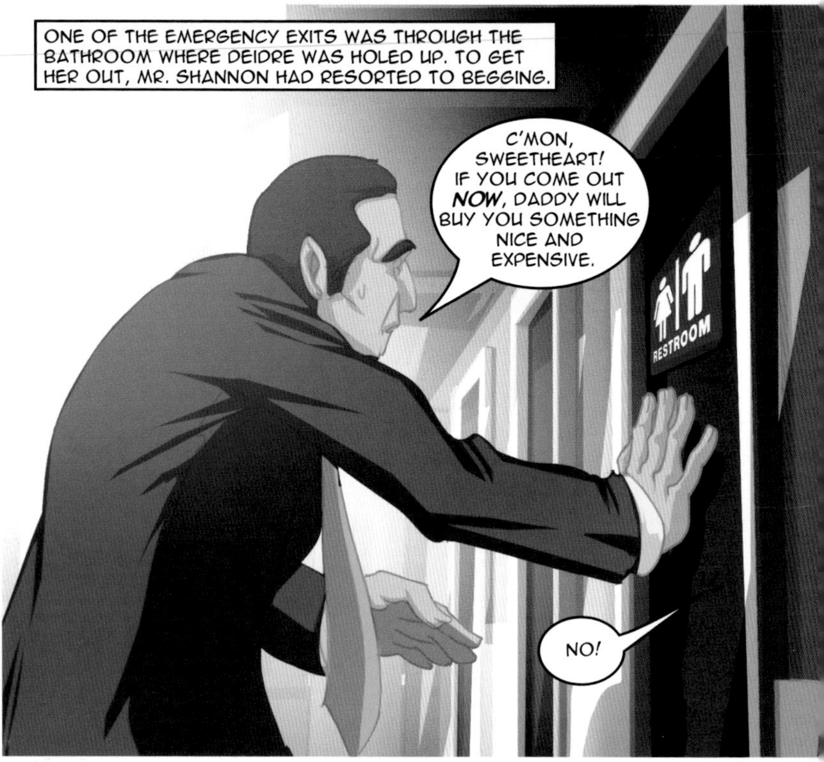
ONE OF THE EMERGENCY EXITS WAS THROUGH THE BATHROOM WHERE DEIDRE WAS HOLED UP. TO GET HER OUT, MR. SHANNON HAD RESORTED TO BEGGING.
C'MON, SWEETHEART! IF YOU COME OUT **NOW**, DADDY WILL BUY YOU SOMETHING NICE AND EXPENSIVE.
RESTROOM
NO!

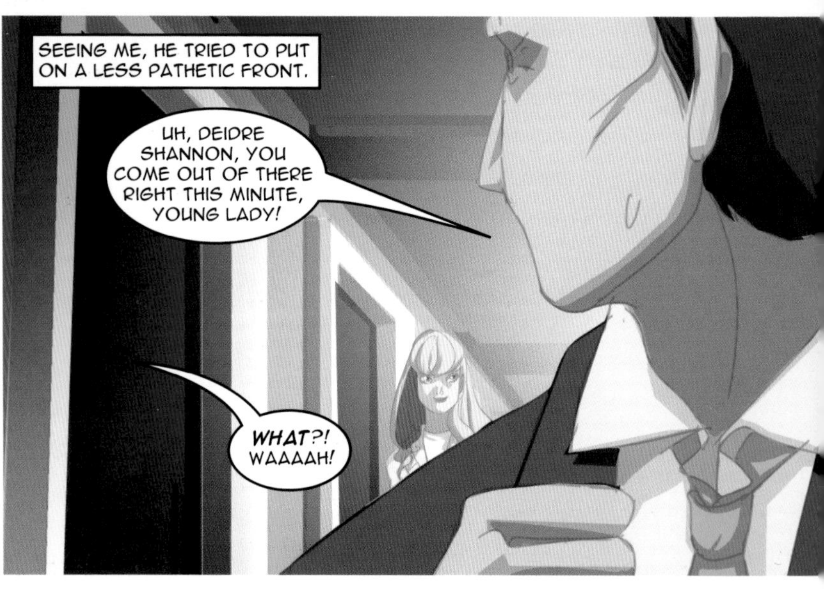
SEEING ME, HE TRIED TO PUT ON A LESS PATHETIC FRONT.
UH, DEIDRE SHANNON, YOU COME OUT OF THERE RIGHT THIS MINUTE, YOUNG LADY!
WHAT?! WAAAAH!

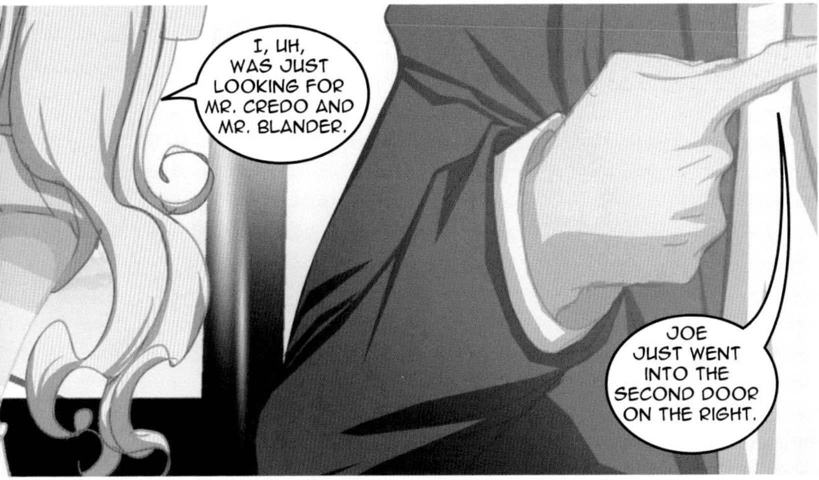
I, UH, WAS JUST LOOKING FOR MR. CREDO AND MR. BLANDER.
JOE JUST WENT INTO THE SECOND DOOR ON THE RIGHT.

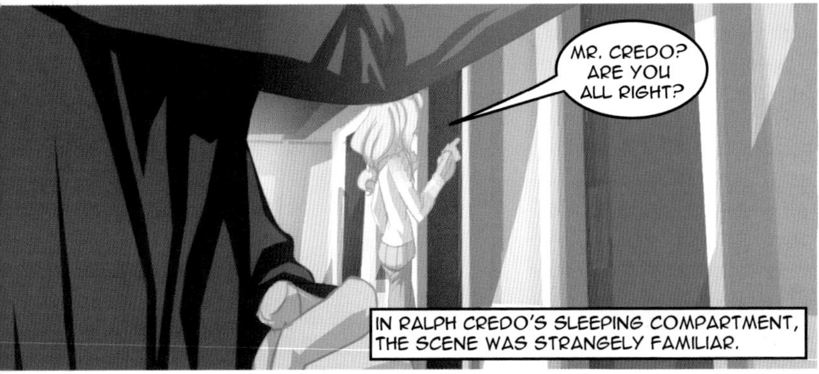
MR. CREDO? ARE YOU ALL RIGHT?
IN RALPH CREDO'S SLEEPING COMPARTMENT, THE SCENE WAS STRANGELY FAMILIAR.

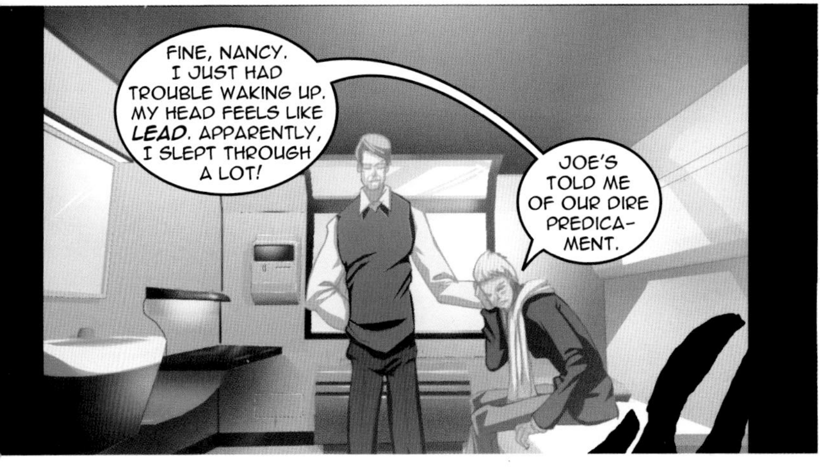
FINE, NANCY. I JUST HAD TROUBLE WAKING UP. MY HEAD FEELS LIKE ***LEAD***. APPARENTLY, I SLEPT THROUGH A LOT!
JOE'S TOLD ME OF OUR DIRE PREDICA- MENT.

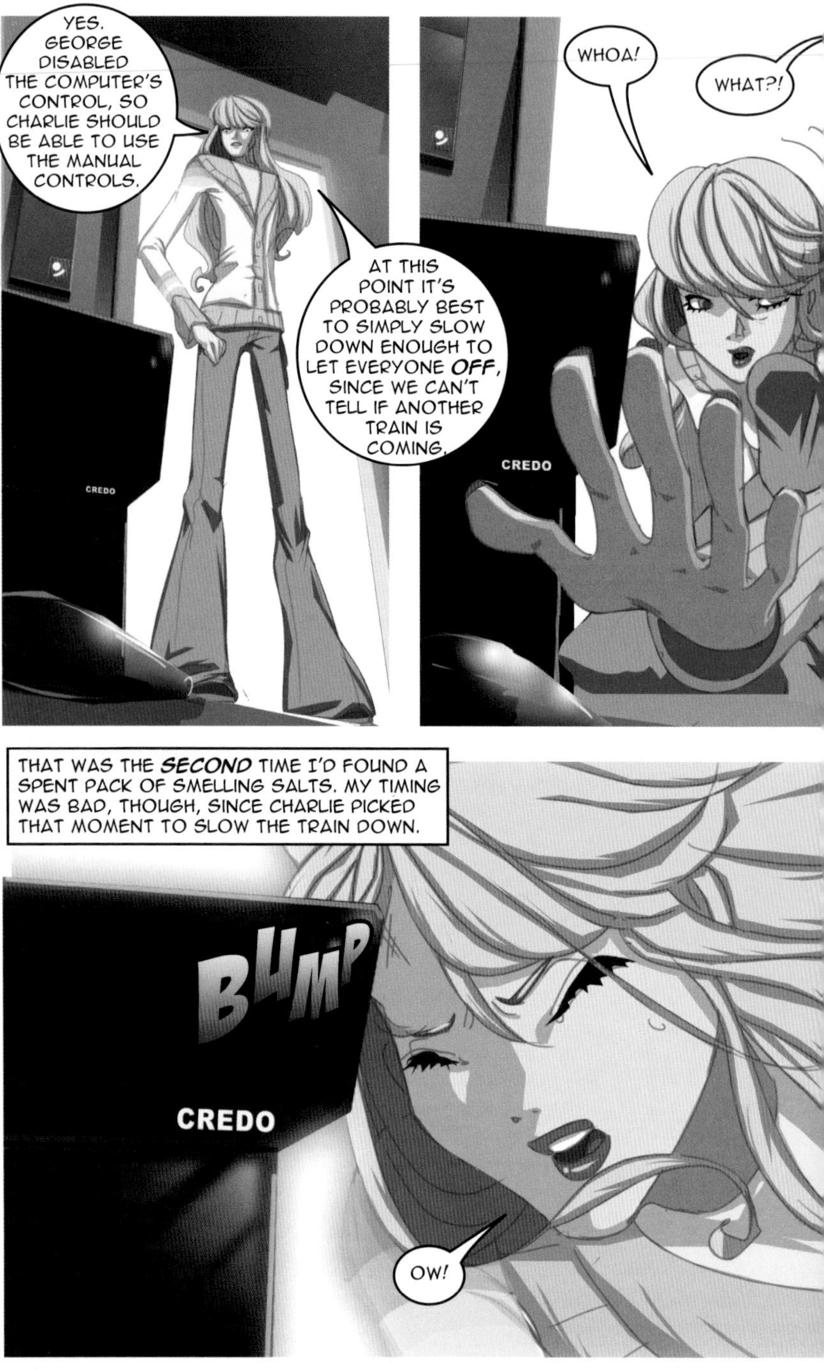
YES. GEORGE DISABLED THE COMPUTER'S CONTROL, SO CHARLIE SHOULD BE ABLE TO USE THE MANUAL CONTROLS.
AT THIS POINT IT'S PROBABLY BEST TO SIMPLY SLOW DOWN ENOUGH TO LET EVERYONE *OFF*, SINCE WE CAN'T TELL IF ANOTHER TRAIN IS COMING.
CREDO
WHOA!
WHAT?!
CREDO
THAT WAS THE *SECOND* TIME I'D FOUND A SPENT PACK OF SMELLING SALTS. MY TIMING WAS BAD, THOUGH, SINCE CHARLIE PICKED THAT MOMENT TO SLOW THE TRAIN DOWN.
BUMP
CREDO
OW!

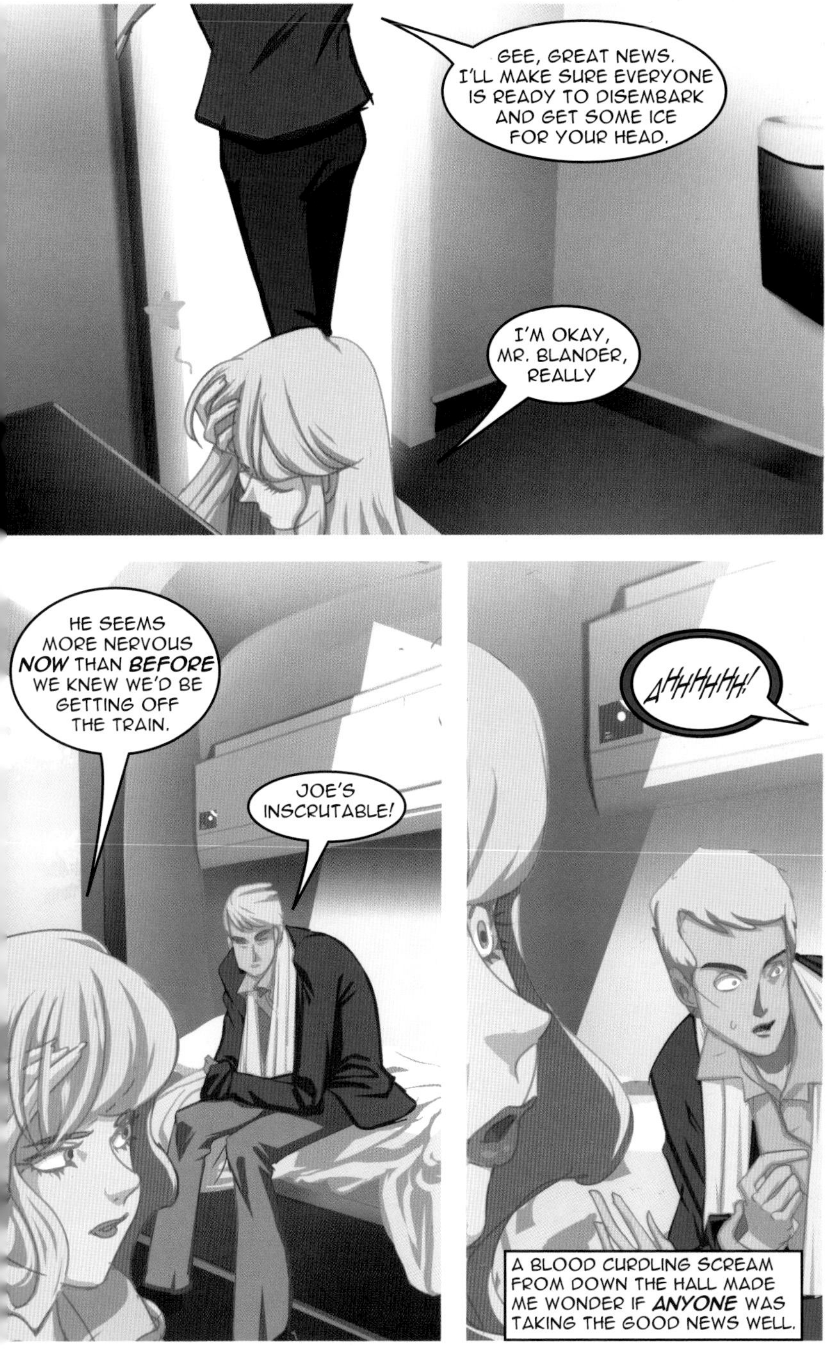
GEE, GREAT NEWS. I'LL MAKE SURE EVERYONE IS READY TO DISEMBARK AND GET SOME ICE FOR YOUR HEAD.
I'M OKAY, MR. BLANDER, REALLY
HE SEEMS MORE NERVOUS **NOW** THAN **BEFORE** WE KNEW WE'D BE GETTING OFF THE TRAIN.
JOE'S INSCRUTABLE!
AHHHHHH!
A BLOOD CURDLING SCREAM FROM DOWN THE HALL MADE ME WONDER IF ***ANYONE*** WAS TAKING THE GOOD NEWS WELL.

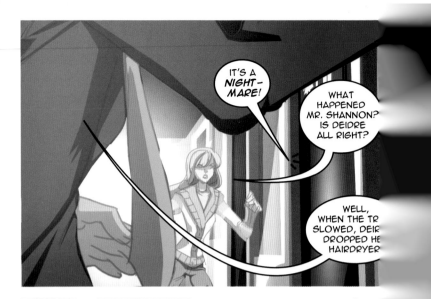

IT'S A **NIGHT-MARE!**

WHAT HAPPENED MR. SHANNON? IS DEIDRE ALL RIGHT?

WELL, WHEN THE TR... SLOWED, DEIR... DROPPED HE... HAIRDRYER...

I DROPPED THE HAIRDRYER IN THE **TOILET!**

NOW HOW WILL I DRY MY DRESS?!

WELL... WOULD IT MAKE YOU FEEL BETTER TO KNOW WE'RE PROBABLY GOING TO **LIVE** THROUGH THIS HIJACKING?

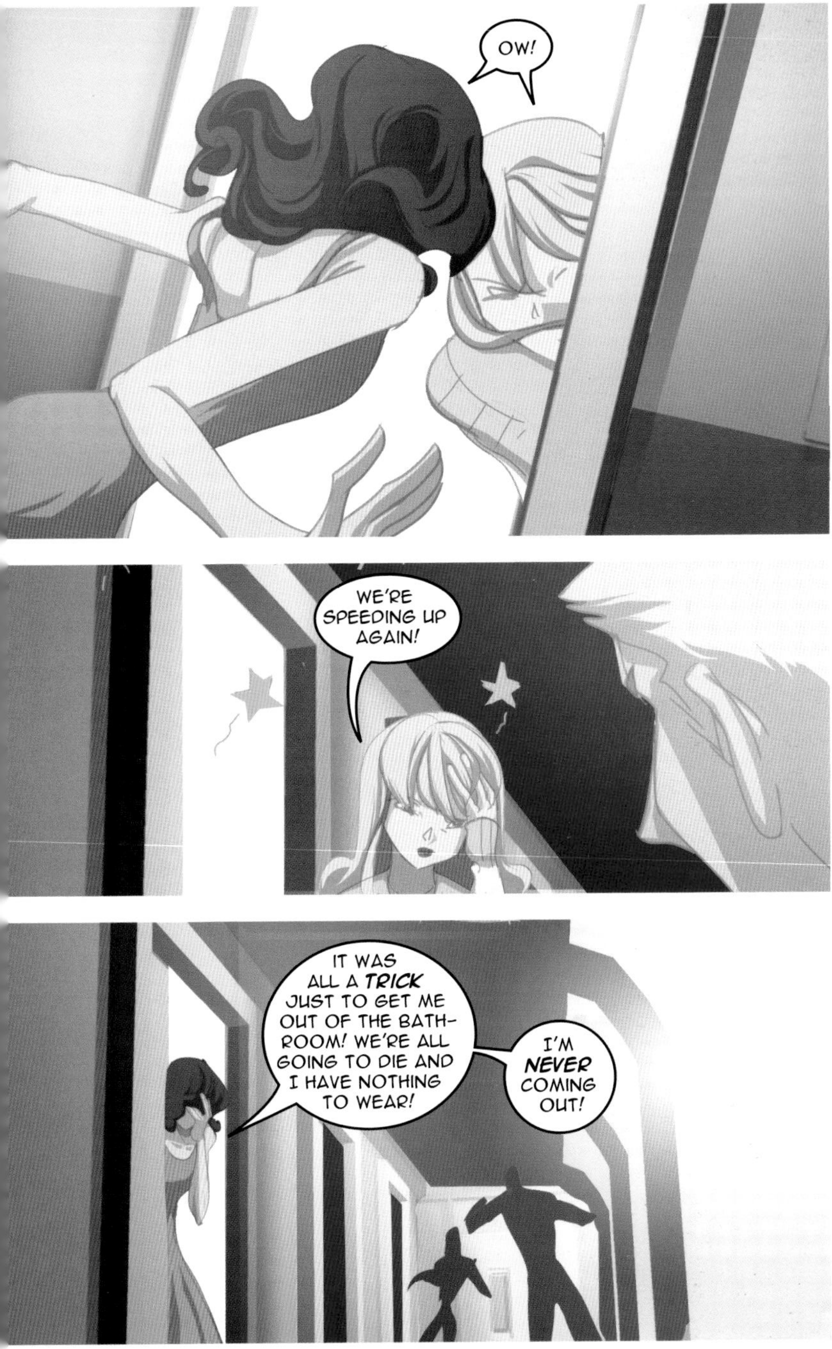
OW!
WE'RE SPEEDING UP AGAIN!
IT WAS ALL A **TRICK** JUST TO GET ME OUT OF THE BATH-ROOM! WE'RE ALL GOING TO DIE AND I HAVE NOTHING TO WEAR!
I'M **NEVER** COMING OUT!

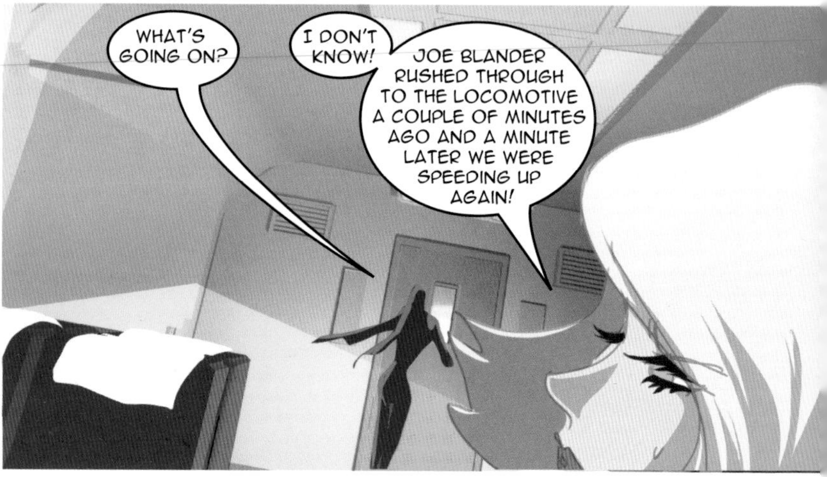
WHAT'S GOING ON?
I DON'T KNOW!
JOE BLANDER RUSHED THROUGH TO THE LOCOMOTIVE A COUPLE OF MINUTES AGO AND A MINUTE LATER WE WERE SPEEDING UP AGAIN!

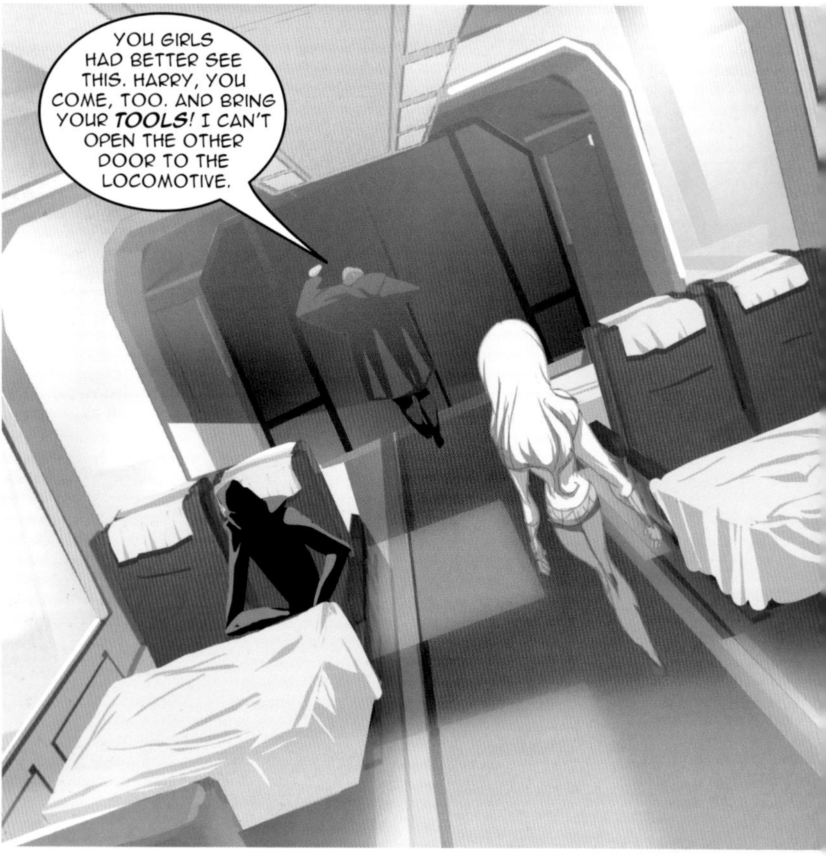
YOU GIRLS HAD BETTER SEE THIS. HARRY, YOU COME, TOO. AND BRING YOUR ***TOOLS!*** I CAN'T OPEN THE OTHER DOOR TO THE LOCOMOTIVE.

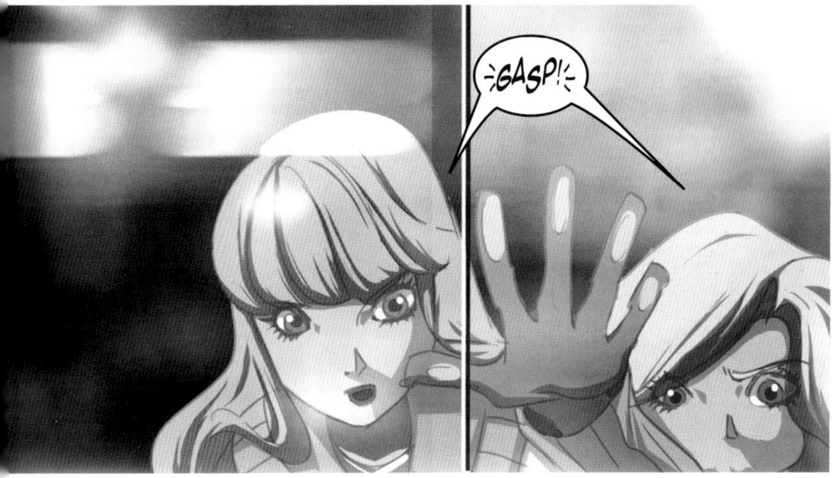
GASP!

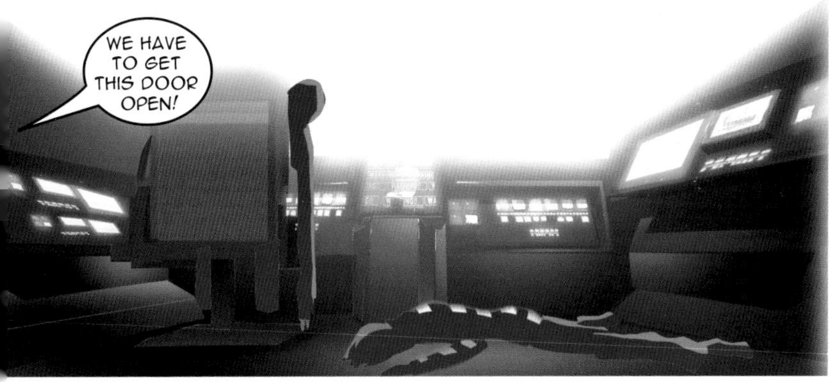
WE HAVE TO GET THIS DOOR OPEN!

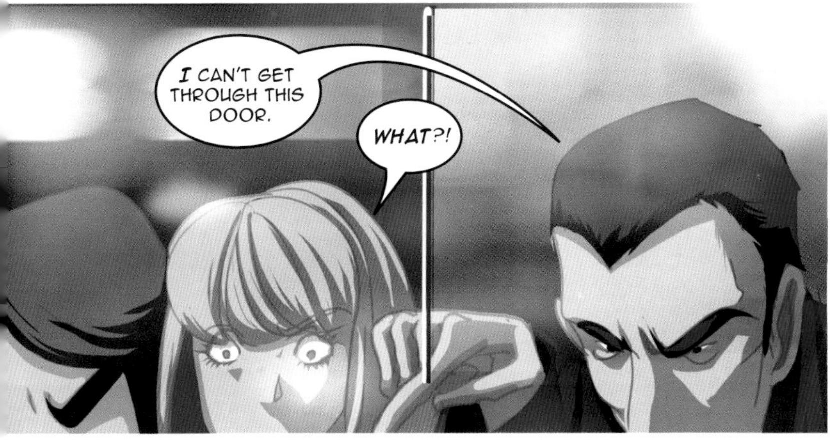
I CAN'T GET THROUGH THIS DOOR.
WHAT?!

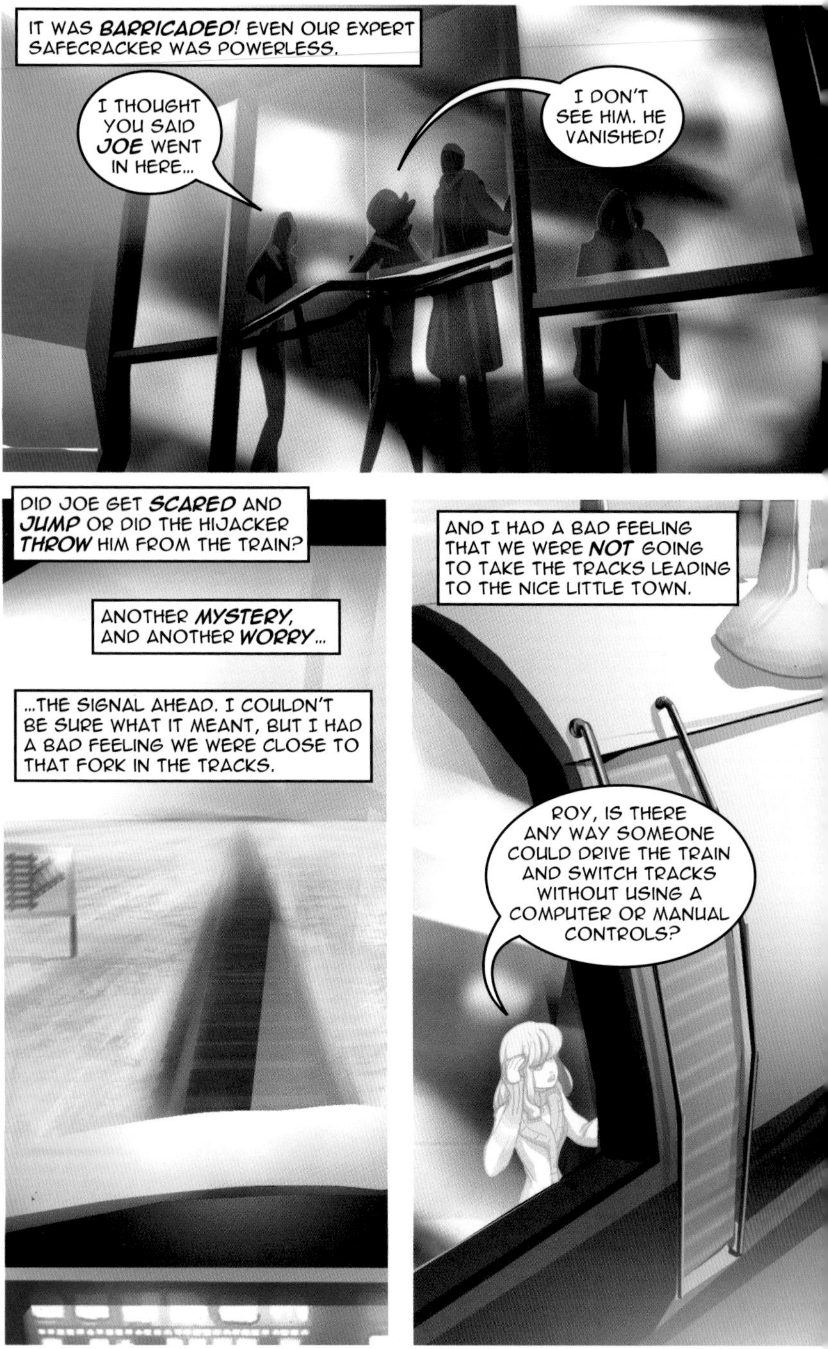
IT WAS BARRICADED! EVEN OUR EXPERT SAFECRACKER WAS POWERLESS.
I THOUGHT YOU SAID JOE WENT IN HERE...
I DON'T SEE HIM. HE VANISHED!
DID JOE GET SCARED AND JUMP OR DID THE HIJACKER THROW HIM FROM THE TRAIN?
ANOTHER MYSTERY, AND ANOTHER WORRY...
...THE SIGNAL AHEAD. I COULDN'T BE SURE WHAT IT MEANT, BUT I HAD A BAD FEELING WE WERE CLOSE TO THAT FORK IN THE TRACKS.
AND I HAD A BAD FEELING THAT WE WERE NOT GOING TO TAKE THE TRACKS LEADING TO THE NICE LITTLE TOWN.
ROY, IS THERE ANY WAY SOMEONE COULD DRIVE THE TRAIN AND SWITCH TRACKS WITHOUT USING A COMPUTER OR MANUAL CONTROLS?

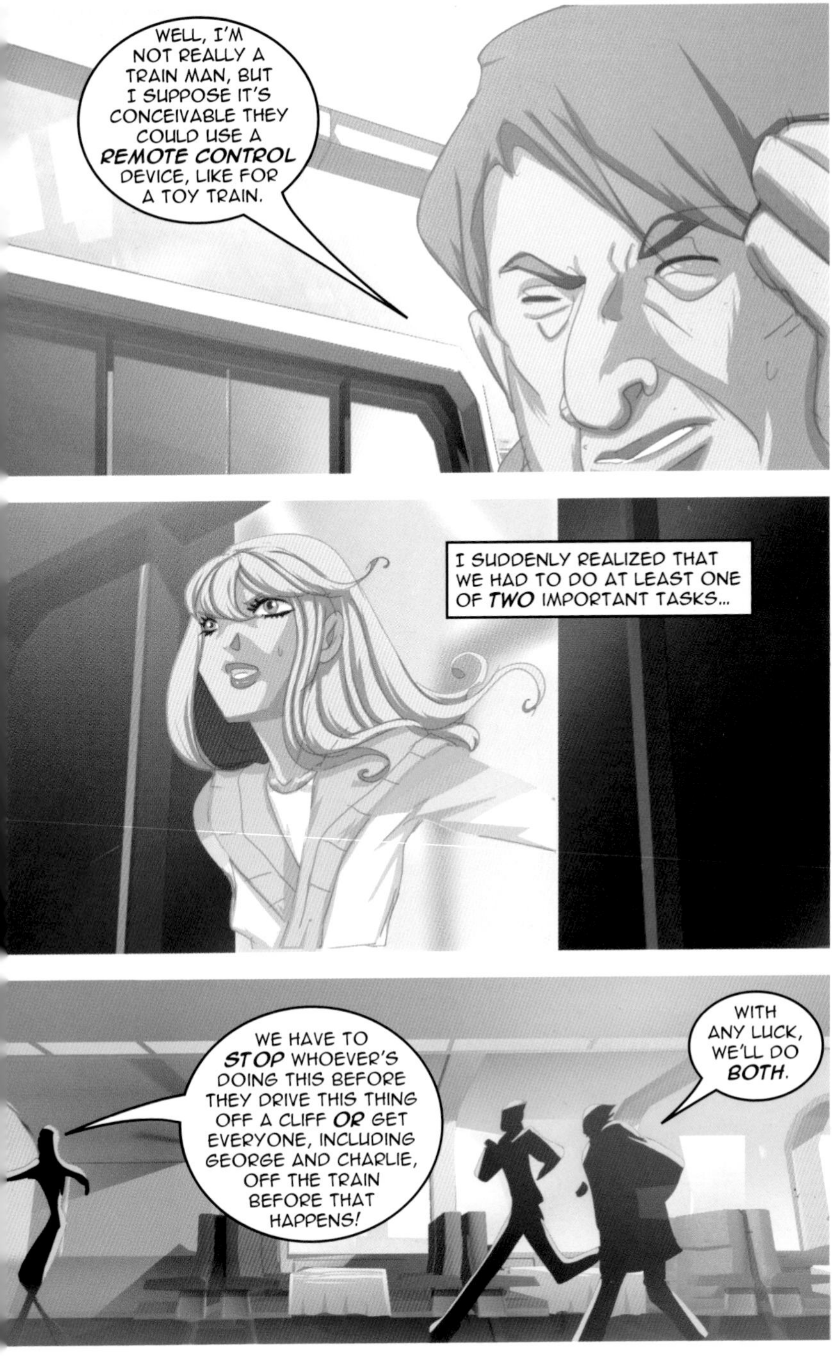
WELL, I'M NOT REALLY A TRAIN MAN, BUT I SUPPOSE IT'S CONCEIVABLE THEY COULD USE A *REMOTE CONTROL* DEVICE, LIKE FOR A TOY TRAIN.
I SUDDENLY REALIZED THAT WE HAD TO DO AT LEAST ONE OF *TWO* IMPORTANT TASKS...
WE HAVE TO *STOP* WHOEVER'S DOING THIS BEFORE THEY DRIVE THIS THING OFF A CLIFF *OR* GET EVERYONE, INCLUDING GEORGE AND CHARLIE, OFF THE TRAIN BEFORE THAT HAPPENS!
WITH ANY LUCK, WE'LL DO *BOTH*.

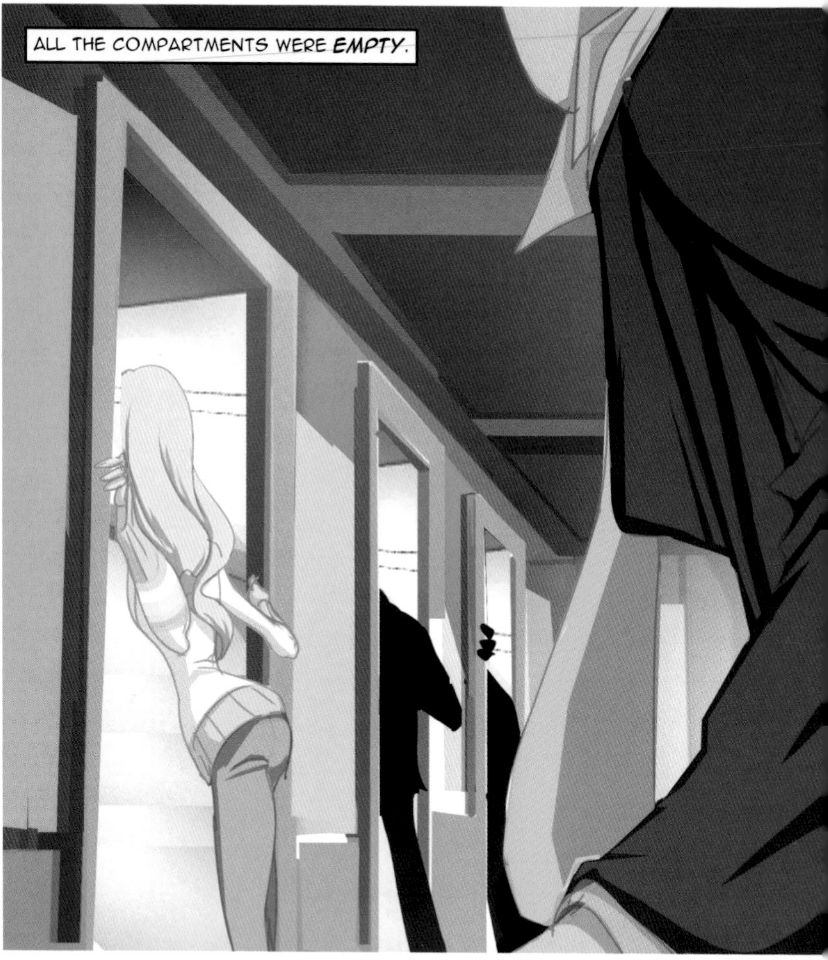
ALL THE COMPARTMENTS WERE EMPTY.
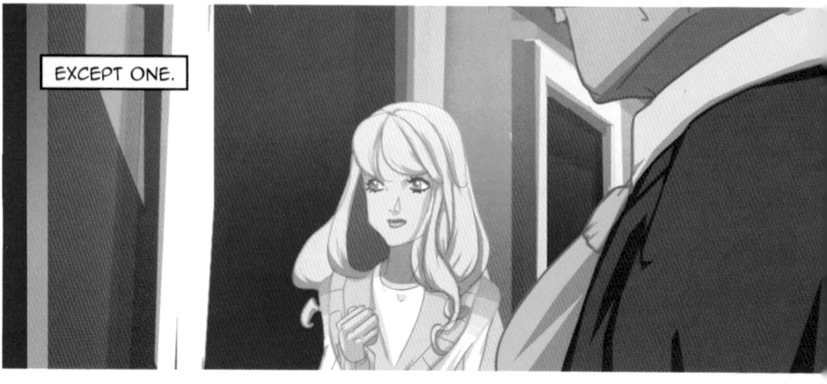
EXCEPT ONE.

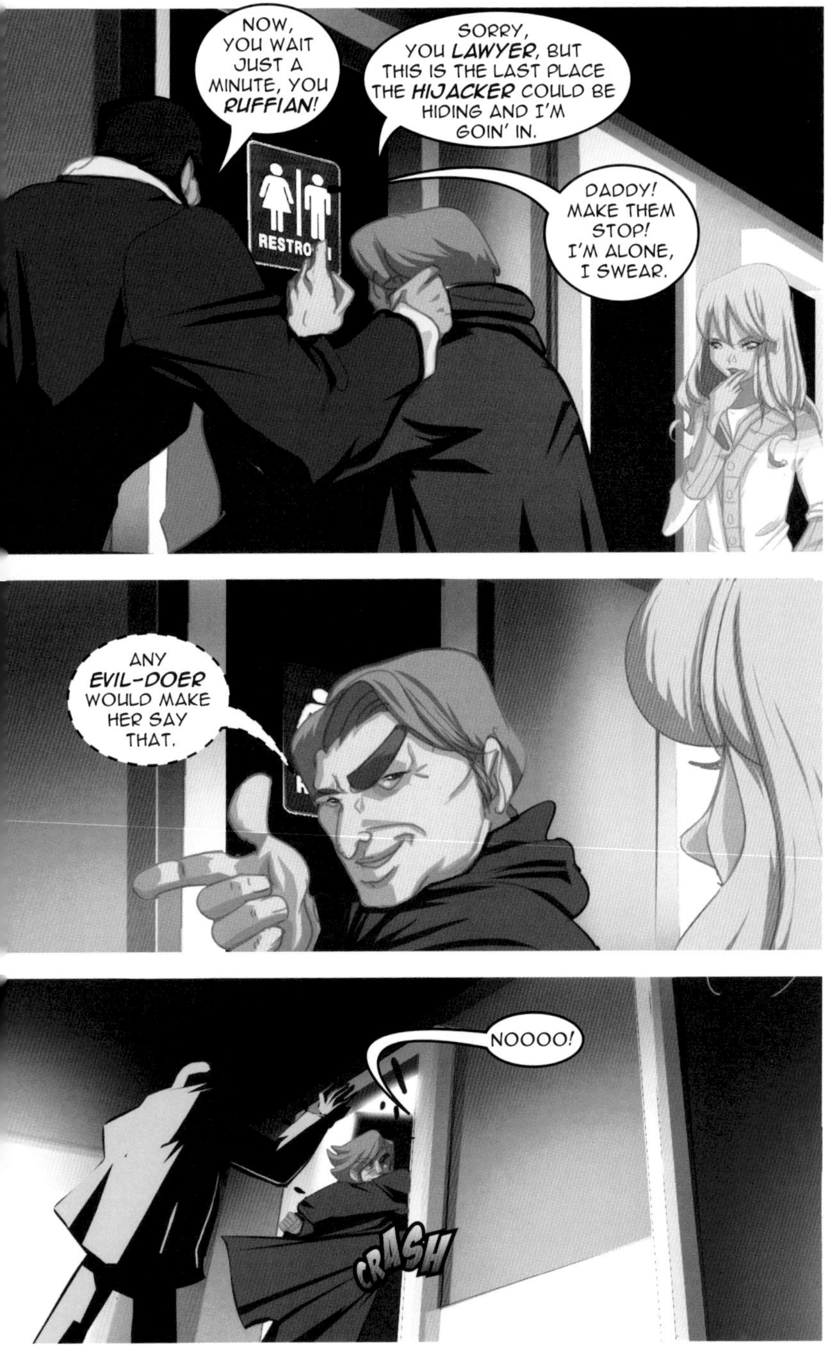
NOW, YOU WAIT JUST A MINUTE, YOU RUFFIAN!
SORRY, YOU LAWYER, BUT THIS IS THE LAST PLACE THE HIJACKER COULD BE HIDING AND I'M GOIN' IN.
RESTRO
DADDY! MAKE THEM STOP! I'M ALONE, I SWEAR.
ANY EVIL-DOER WOULD MAKE HER SAY THAT.
NOOOO!
CRASH

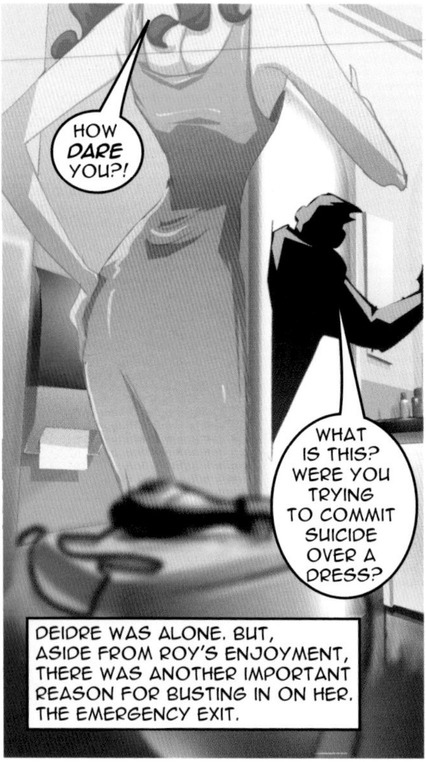
HOW *DARE* YOU?!
WHAT IS THIS? WERE YOU TRYING TO COMMIT SUICIDE OVER A DRESS?
DEIDRE WAS ALONE. BUT, ASIDE FROM ROY'S ENJOYMENT, THERE WAS ANOTHER IMPORTANT REASON FOR BUSTING IN ON HER. THE EMERGENCY EXIT.

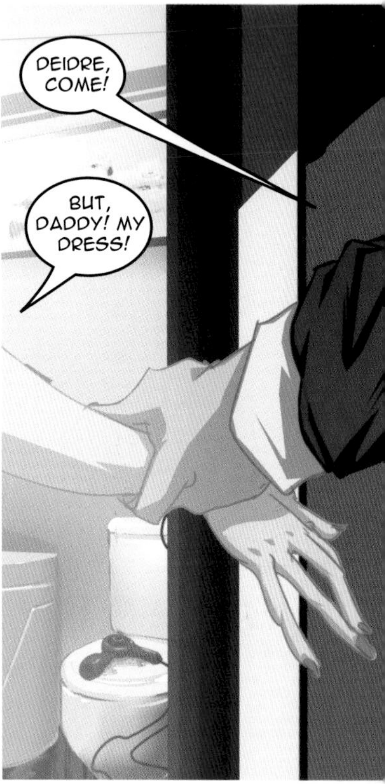
DEIDRE, COME!
BUT, DADDY! MY DRESS!

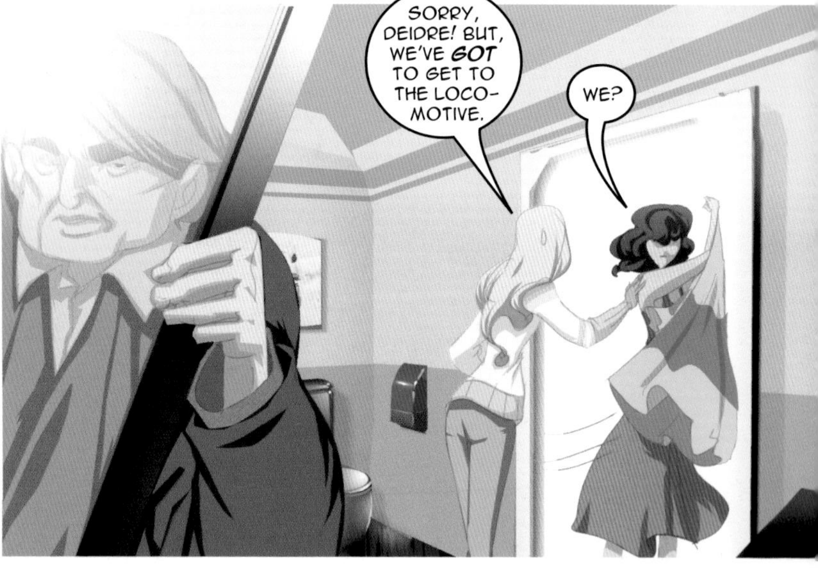
SORRY, DEIDRE! BUT, WE'VE *GOT* TO GET TO THE LOCO-MOTIVE.
WE?

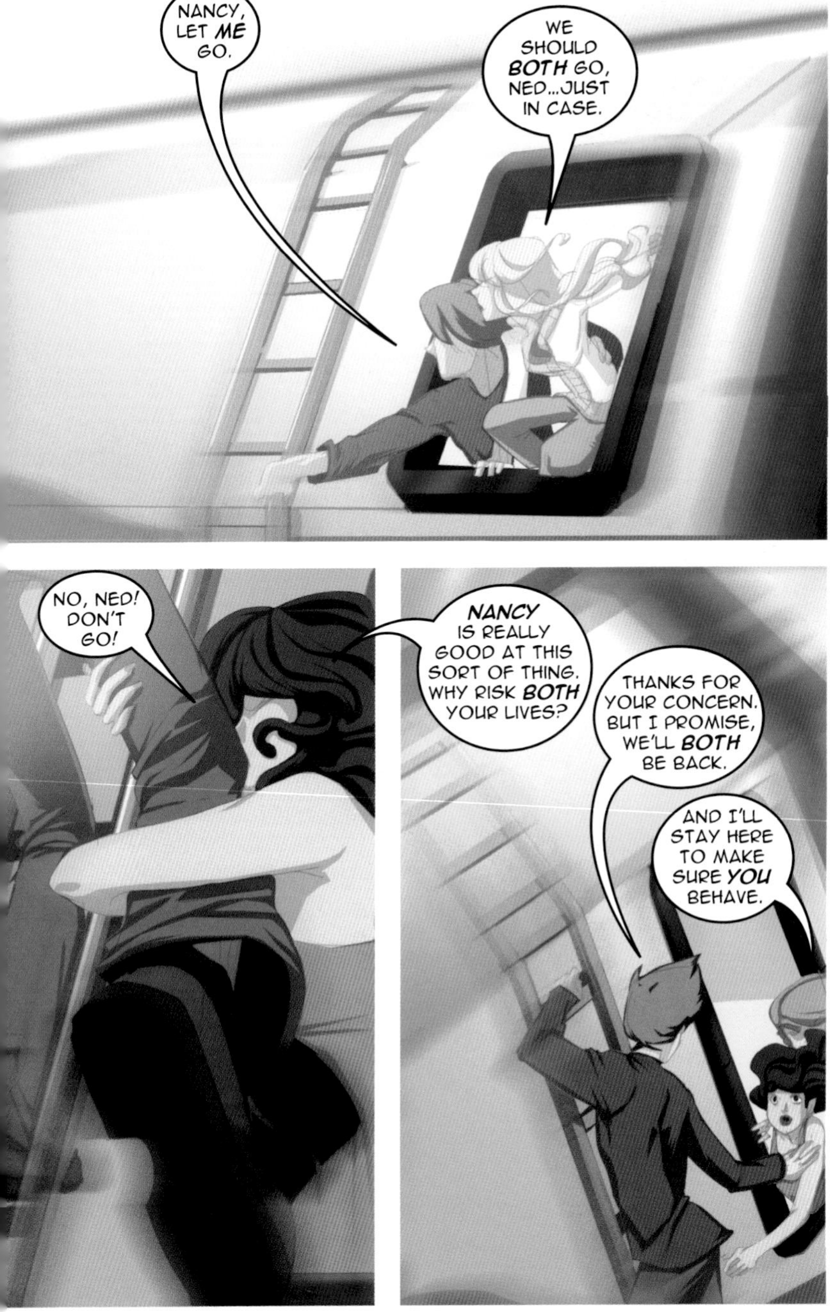
NANCY, LET *ME* GO.
WE SHOULD ***BOTH*** GO, NED...JUST IN CASE.
NO, NED! DON'T GO!
NANCY IS REALLY GOOD AT THIS SORT OF THING. WHY RISK ***BOTH*** YOUR LIVES?
THANKS FOR YOUR CONCERN. BUT I PROMISE, WE'LL ***BOTH*** BE BACK.
AND I'LL STAY HERE TO MAKE SURE ***YOU*** BEHAVE.

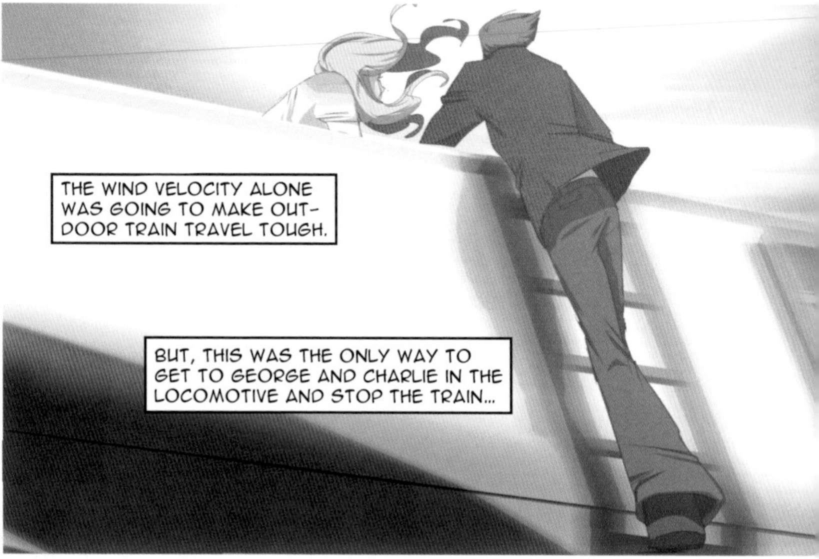
THE WIND VELOCITY ALONE WAS GOING TO MAKE OUT-DOOR TRAIN TRAVEL TOUGH.
BUT, THIS WAS THE ONLY WAY TO GET TO GEORGE AND CHARLIE IN THE LOCOMOTIVE AND STOP THE TRAIN...

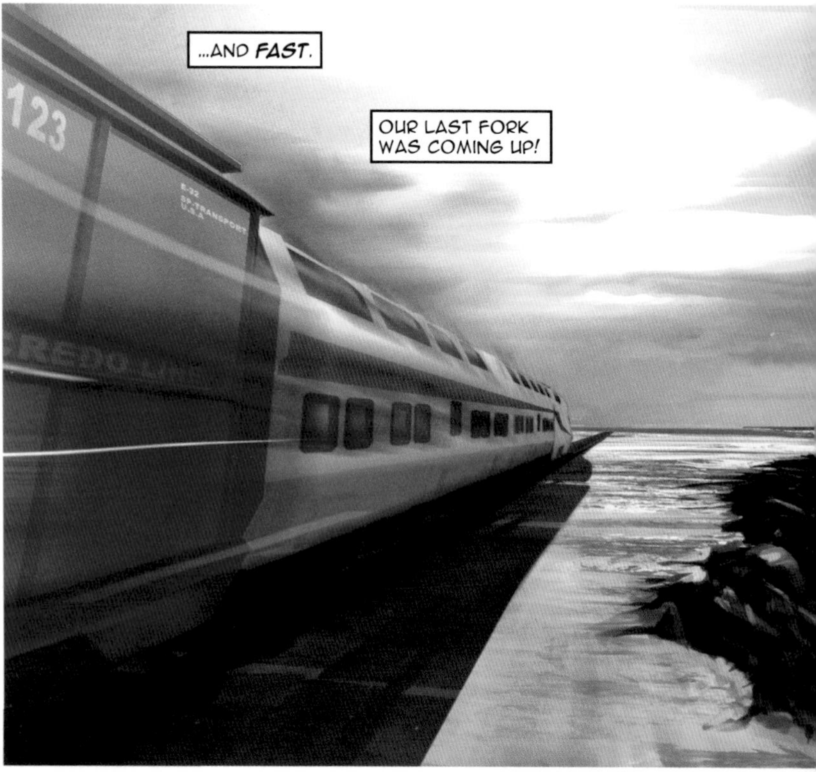
...AND FAST.
123
OUR LAST FORK WAS COMING UP!

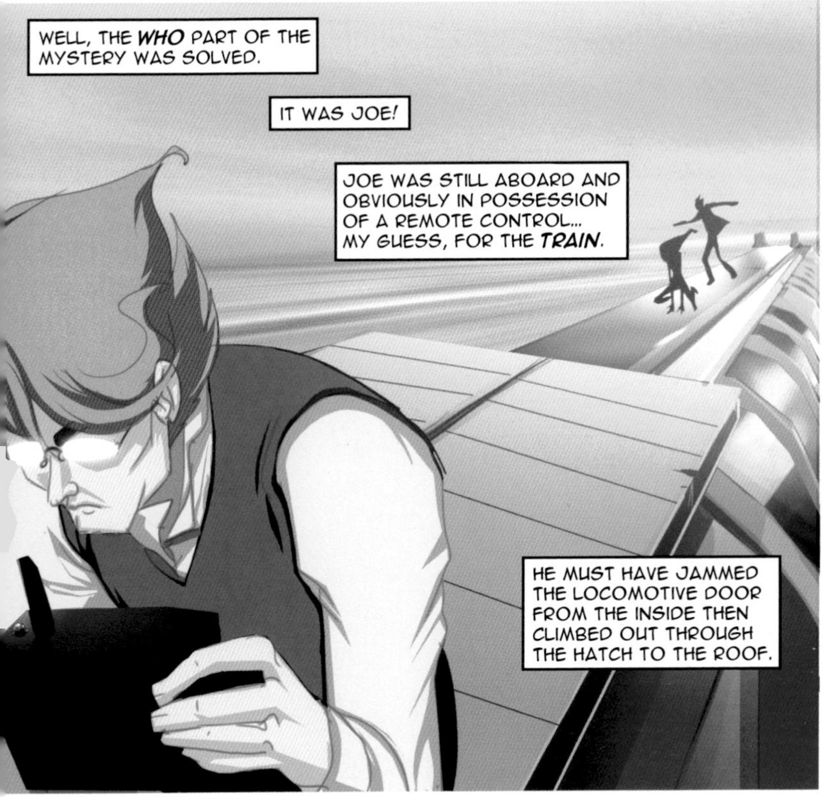
WELL, THE ***WHO*** PART OF THE MYSTERY WAS SOLVED.
IT WAS JOE!
JOE WAS STILL ABOARD AND OBVIOUSLY IN POSSESSION OF A REMOTE CONTROL... MY GUESS, FOR THE ***TRAIN***.
HE MUST HAVE JAMMED THE LOCOMOTIVE DOOR FROM THE INSIDE THEN CLIMBED OUT THROUGH THE HATCH TO THE ROOF.

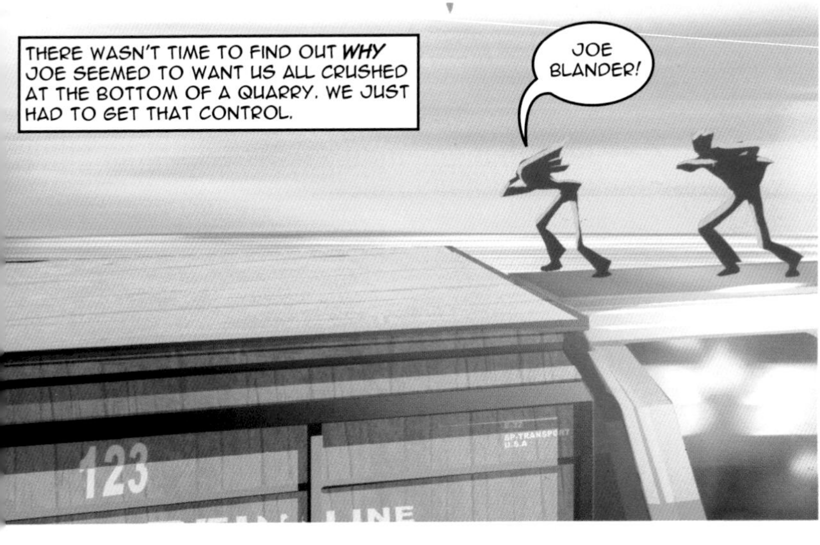
THERE WASN'T TIME TO FIND OUT ***WHY*** JOE SEEMED TO WANT US ALL CRUSHED AT THE BOTTOM OF A QUARRY. WE JUST HAD TO GET THAT CONTROL.
JOE BLANDER!
123

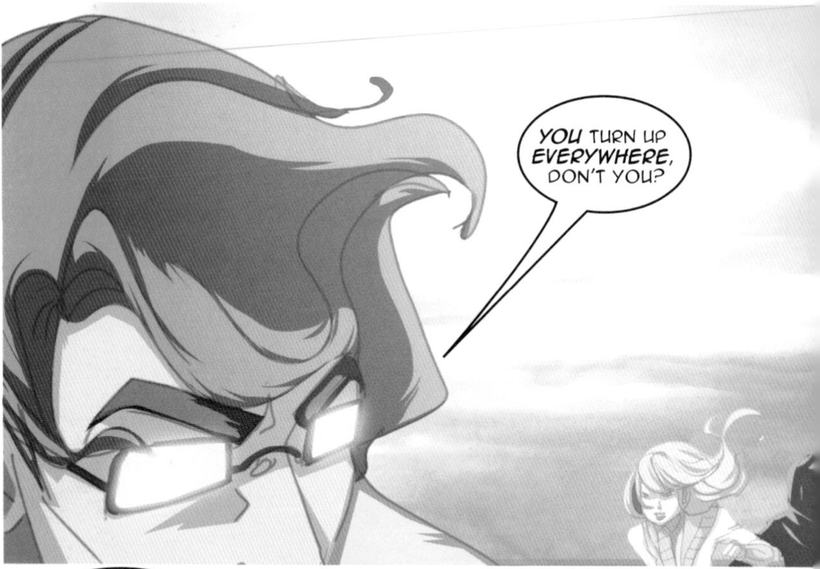
YOU TURN UP *EVERYWHERE,* DON'T YOU?
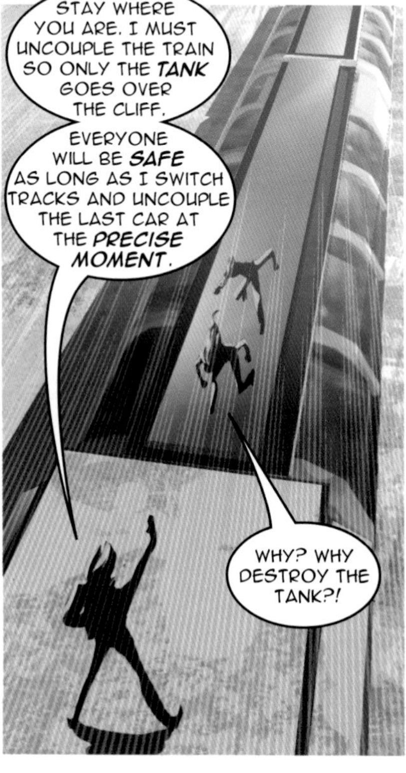
STAY WHERE YOU ARE. I MUST UNCOUPLE THE TRAIN SO ONLY THE *TANK* GOES OVER THE CLIFF.
EVERYONE WILL BE *SAFE* AS LONG AS I SWITCH TRACKS AND UNCOUPLE THE LAST CAR AT THE *PRECISE MOMENT*.
WHY? WHY DESTROY THE TANK?!
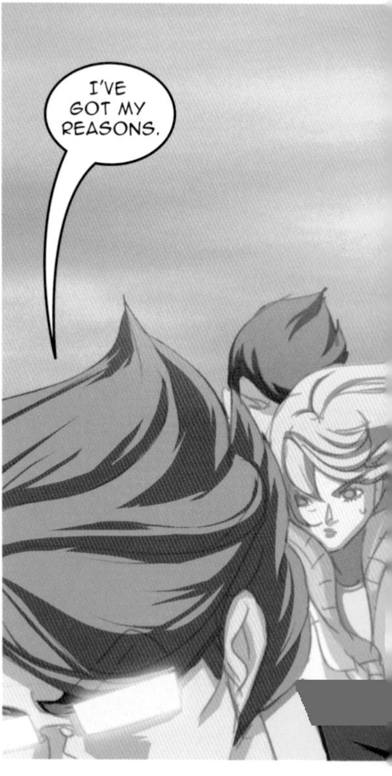
I'VE GOT MY REASONS.

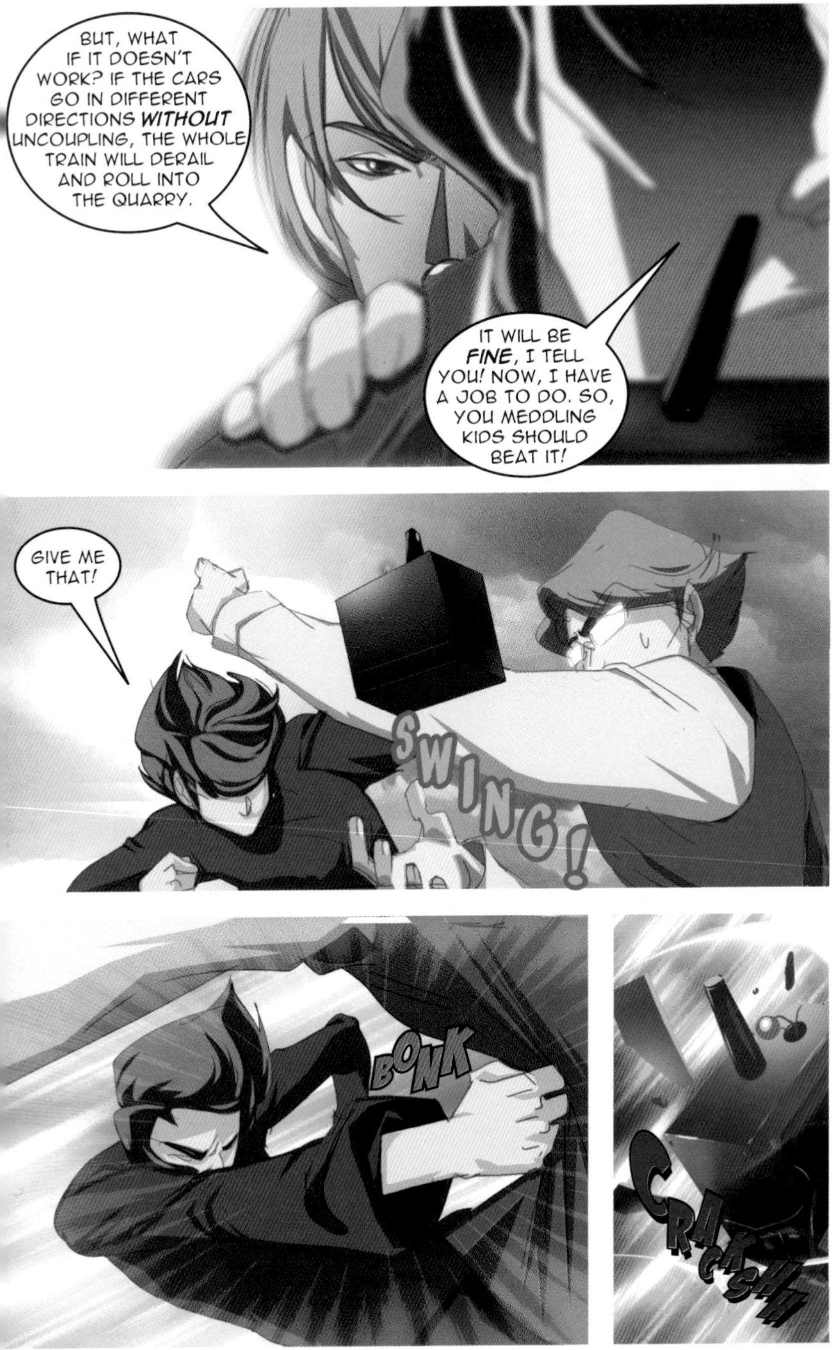
BUT, WHAT IF IT DOESN'T WORK? IF THE CARS GO IN DIFFERENT DIRECTIONS **WITHOUT** UNCOUPLING, THE WHOLE TRAIN WILL DERAIL AND ROLL INTO THE QUARRY.
IT WILL BE **FINE**, I TELL YOU! NOW, I HAVE A JOB TO DO. SO, YOU MEDDLING KIDS SHOULD BEAT IT!
GIVE ME THAT!
SWING!
BONK
CRACKSHH!!

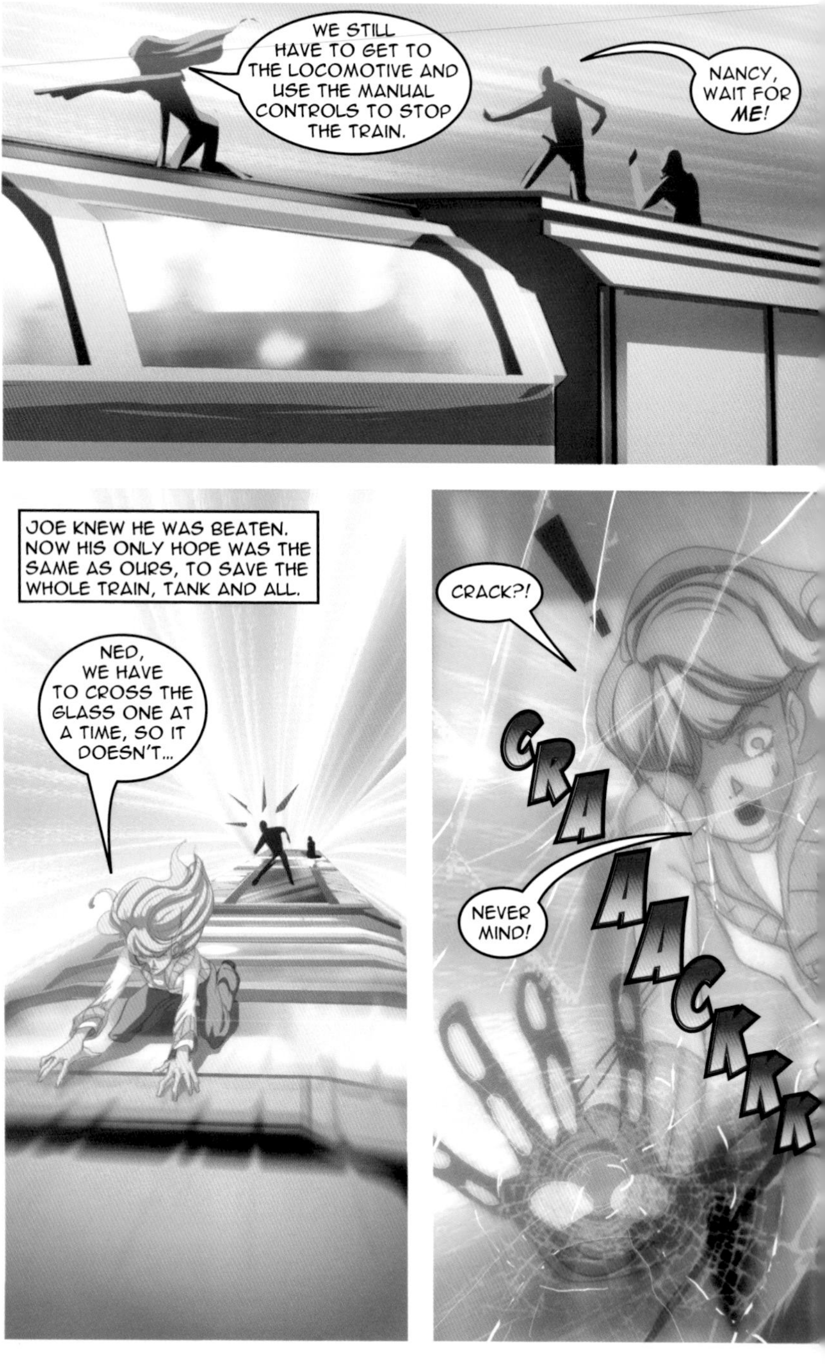
WE STILL HAVE TO GET TO THE LOCOMOTIVE AND USE THE MANUAL CONTROLS TO STOP THE TRAIN.
NANCY, WAIT FOR *ME!*
JOE KNEW HE WAS BEATEN. NOW HIS ONLY HOPE WAS THE SAME AS OURS, TO SAVE THE WHOLE TRAIN, TANK AND ALL.
NED, WE HAVE TO CROSS THE GLASS ONE AT A TIME, SO IT DOESN'T...
CRACK?!
CRAAACKKK
NEVER MIND!

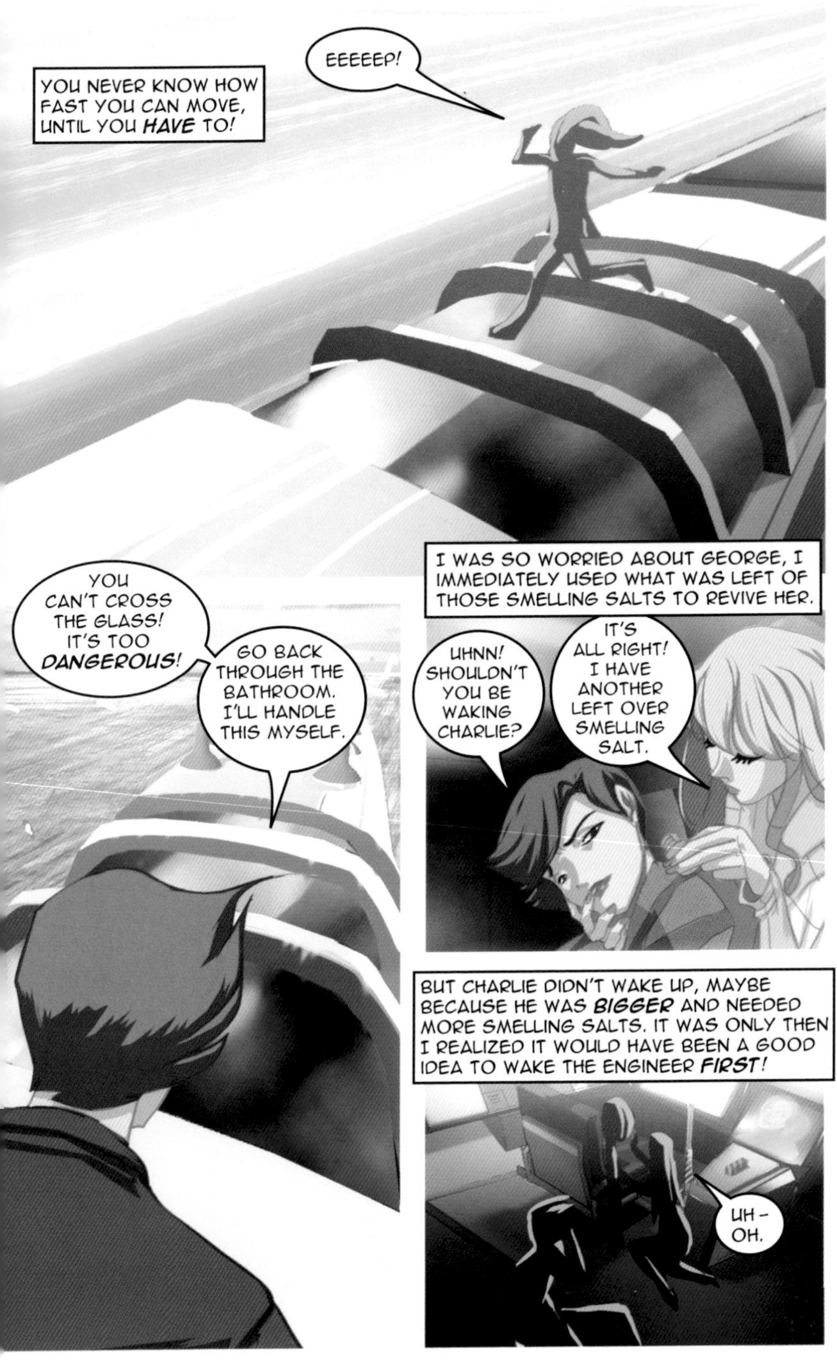
YOU NEVER KNOW HOW FAST YOU CAN MOVE, UNTIL YOU *HAVE* TO!
EEEEEP!
YOU CAN'T CROSS THE GLASS! IT'S TOO *DANGEROUS*!
GO BACK THROUGH THE BATHROOM. I'LL HANDLE THIS MYSELF.
I WAS SO WORRIED ABOUT GEORGE, I IMMEDIATELY USED WHAT WAS LEFT OF THOSE SMELLING SALTS TO REVIVE HER.
UHNN! SHOULDN'T YOU BE WAKING CHARLIE?
IT'S ALL RIGHT! I HAVE ANOTHER LEFT OVER SMELLING SALT.
BUT CHARLIE DIDN'T WAKE UP, MAYBE BECAUSE HE WAS *BIGGER* AND NEEDED MORE SMELLING SALTS. IT WAS ONLY THEN I REALIZED IT WOULD HAVE BEEN A GOOD IDEA TO WAKE THE ENGINEER *FIRST*!
UH-OH.

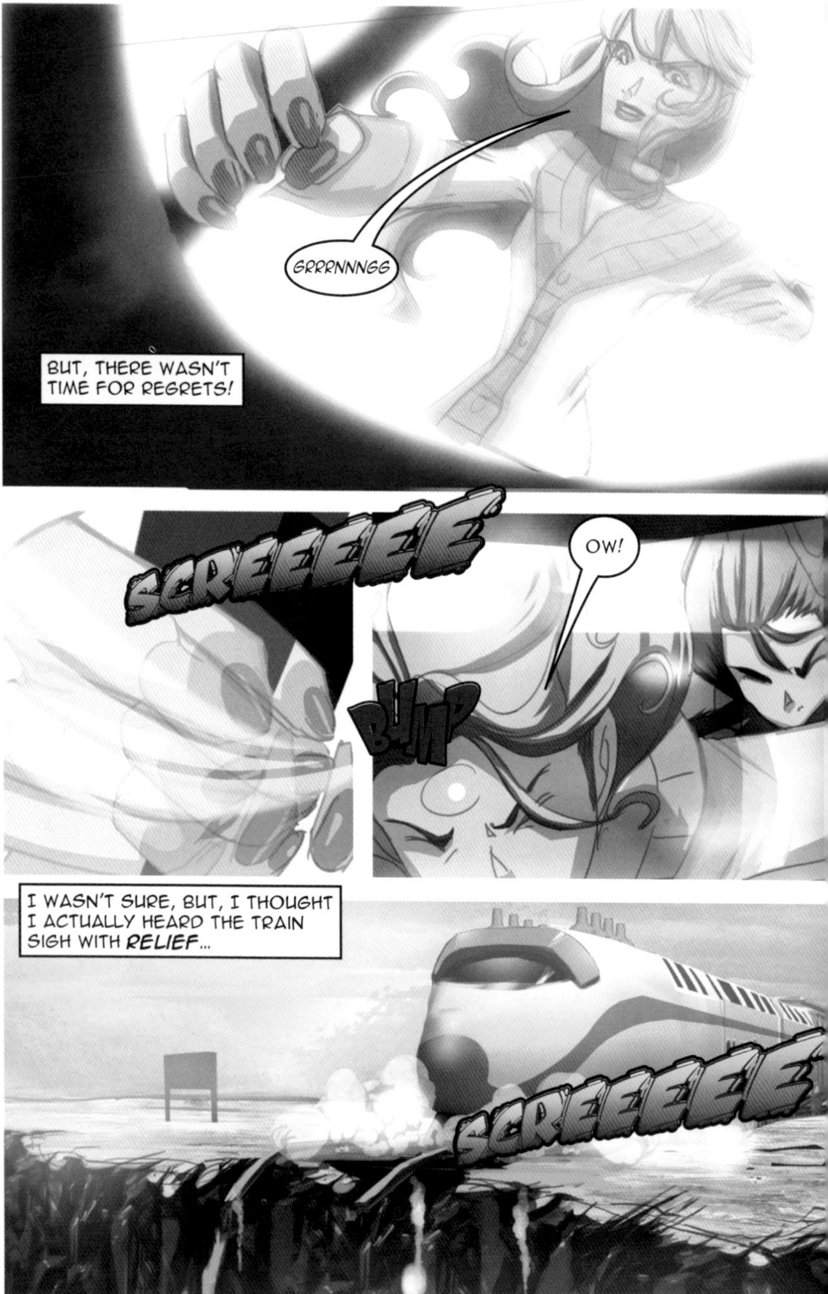
GRRRNNNGG
BUT, THERE WASN'T TIME FOR REGRETS!
SCREEEEEE
OW!
BUMP
I WASN'T SURE, BUT, I THOUGHT I ACTUALLY HEARD THE TRAIN SIGH WITH RELIEF...
SCREEEEEE
...MAYBE IT WAS ME.

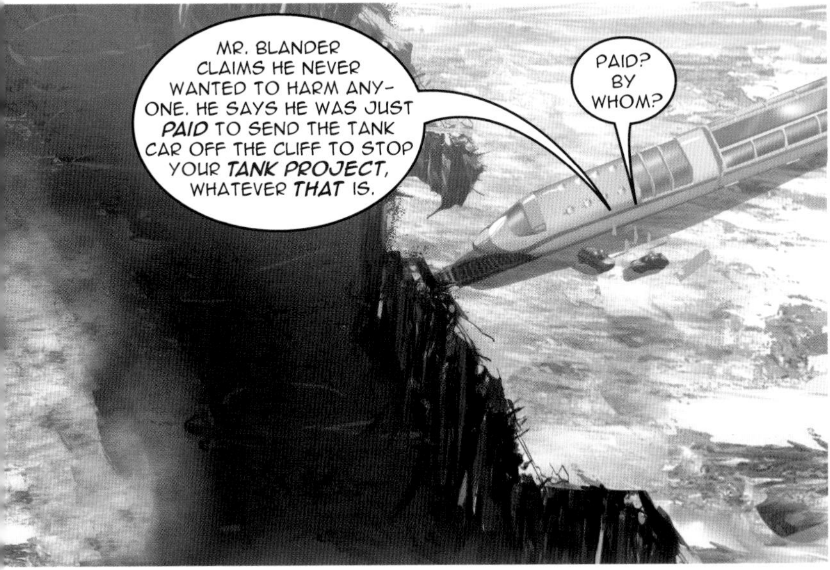
MR. BLANDER CLAIMS HE NEVER WANTED TO HARM ANY-ONE. HE SAYS HE WAS JUST *PAID* TO SEND THE TANK CAR OFF THE CLIFF TO STOP YOUR *TANK PROJECT*, WHATEVER *THAT* IS.
PAID? BY WHOM?

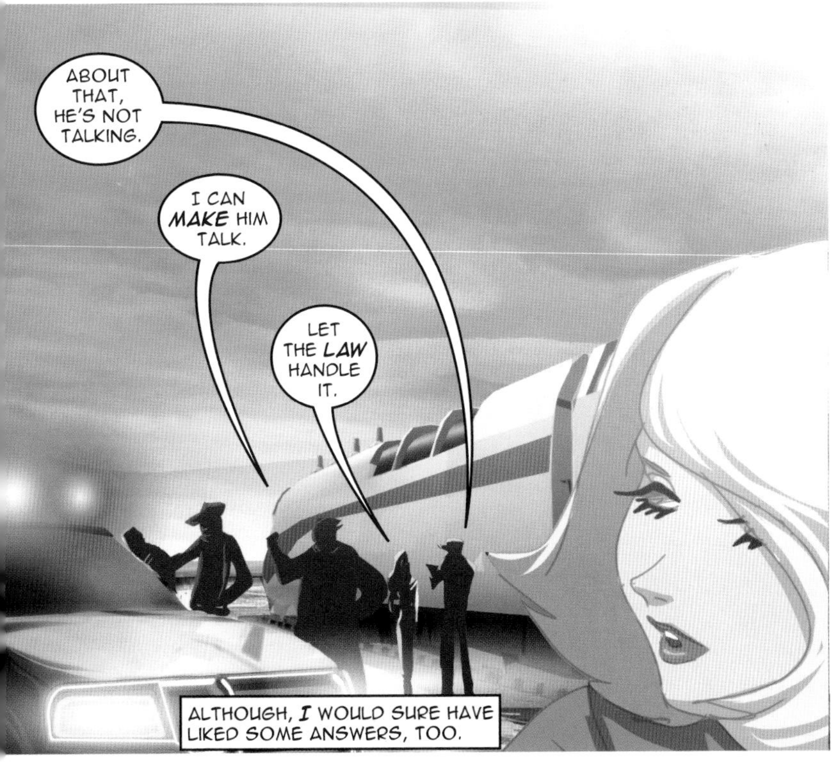
ABOUT THAT, HE'S NOT TALKING.
I CAN *MAKE* HIM TALK.
LET THE *LAW* HANDLE IT.
ALTHOUGH, *I* WOULD SURE HAVE LIKED SOME ANSWERS, TOO.

DADDY! I INSIST YOU *SUE* CREDO FOR ALL THE EMOTIONAL DAMAGE I HAVE SUFFERED!

UH-OH. EMOTIONAL DAMAGE IS A CONDITION SHE CAN *CERTAINLY* PROVE.

AND THIS *DRESS!* IT WILL NEVER BE THE SAME. I WANT IT *REPLACED* BY CREDO!

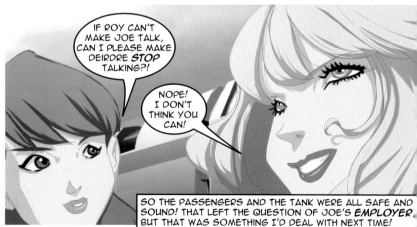

IF ROY CAN'T MAKE JOE TALK, CAN I PLEASE MAKE DEIRDRE *STOP* TALKING?!

NOPE! I DON'T THINK YOU CAN!

SO THE PASSENGERS AND THE TANK WERE ALL SAFE AND SOUND! THAT LEFT THE QUESTION OF JOE'S *EMPLOYER.* BUT THAT WAS SOMETHING I'D DEAL WITH NEXT TIME!

This Fall, take the mystery with you
on your Nintendo DS™ system!

NANCY DREW™

The Deadly Secret of Olde World Park

- **Play as Nancy Drew, the world's most recognizable teen sleuth**
- **Solve puzzles and discover clues left by a slew of suspicious characters**
- **Use the Touch Screen to play detective mini-games and access tasks, maps and inventory**
- **Unravel 15 intriguing chapters filled with challenging missions and interrogations**

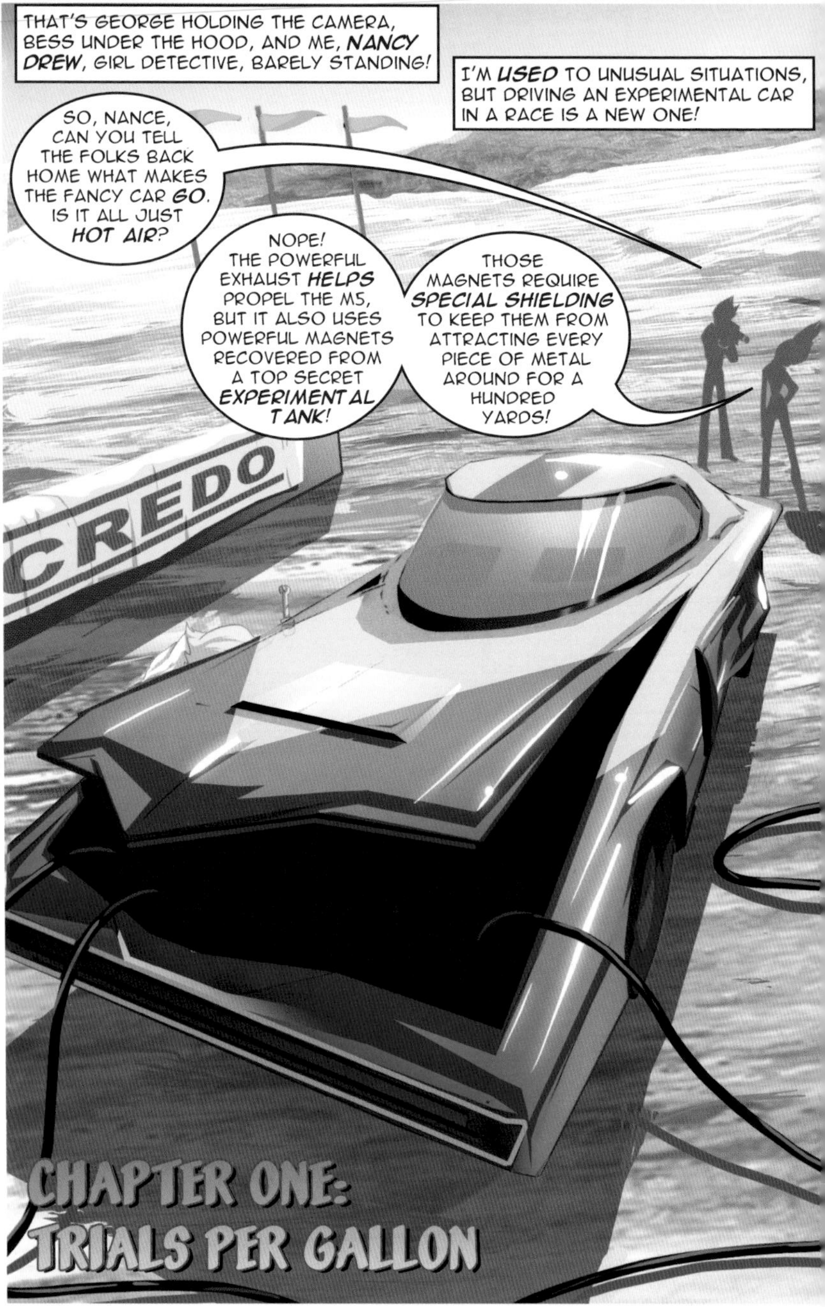
THAT'S GEORGE HOLDING THE CAMERA, BESS UNDER THE HOOD, AND ME, NANCY DREW, GIRL DETECTIVE, BARELY STANDING!
I'M USED TO UNUSUAL SITUATIONS, BUT DRIVING AN EXPERIMENTAL CAR IN A RACE IS A NEW ONE!
SO, NANCE, CAN YOU TELL THE FOLKS BACK HOME WHAT MAKES THE FANCY CAR GO. IS IT ALL JUST HOT AIR?
NOPE! THE POWERFUL EXHAUST HELPS PROPEL THE M5, BUT IT ALSO USES POWERFUL MAGNETS RECOVERED FROM A TOP SECRET EXPERIMENTAL TANK!
THOSE MAGNETS REQUIRE SPECIAL SHIELDING TO KEEP THEM FROM ATTRACTING EVERY PIECE OF METAL AROUND FOR A HUNDRED YARDS!
CREDO
CHAPTER ONE: TRIALS PER GALLON

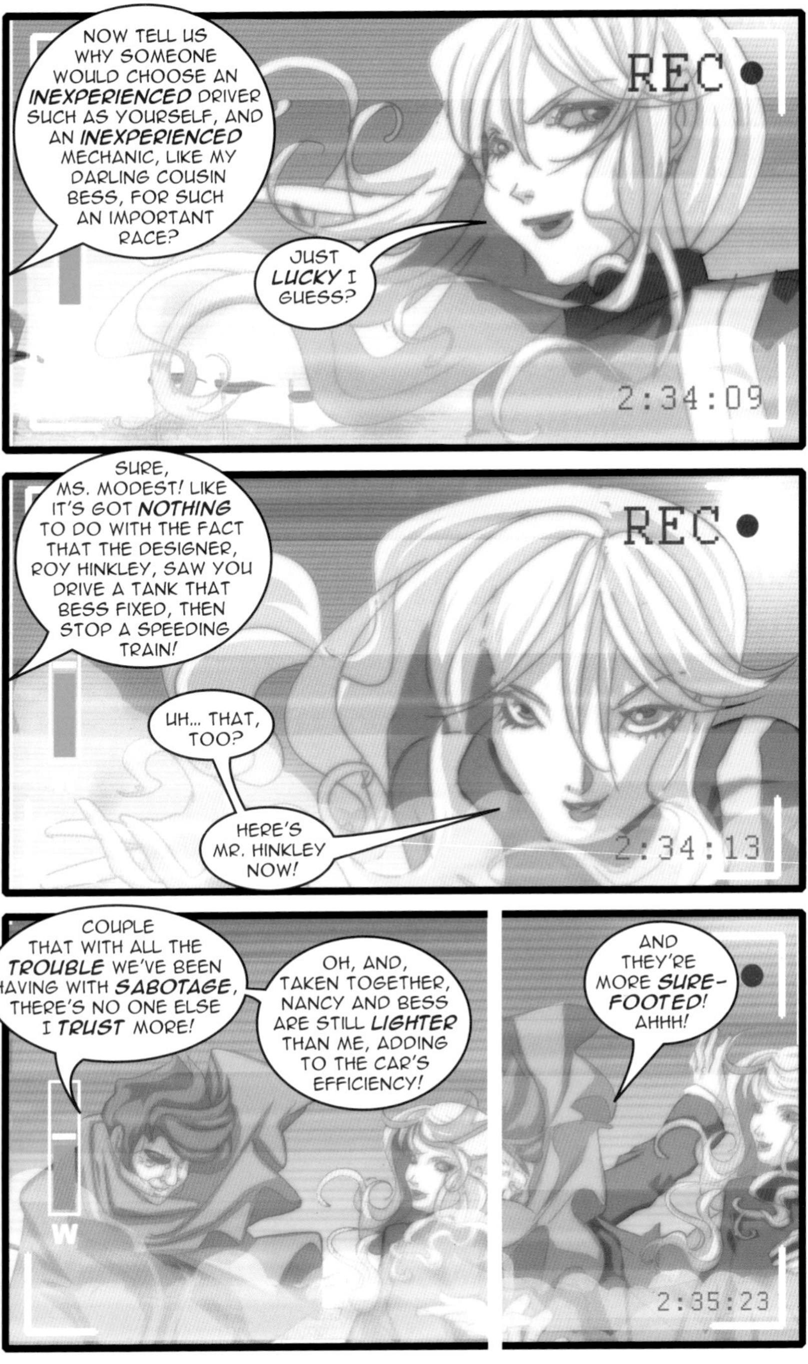
REC
NOW TELL US WHY SOMEONE WOULD CHOOSE AN INEXPERIENCED DRIVER SUCH AS YOURSELF, AND AN INEXPERIENCED MECHANIC, LIKE MY DARLING COUSIN BESS, FOR SUCH AN IMPORTANT RACE?
JUST LUCKY I GUESS?
2:34:09
REC
SURE, MS. MODEST! LIKE IT'S GOT NOTHING TO DO WITH THE FACT THAT THE DESIGNER, ROY HINKLEY, SAW YOU DRIVE A TANK THAT BESS FIXED, THEN STOP A SPEEDING TRAIN!
UH... THAT, TOO?
HERE'S MR. HINKLEY NOW!
2:34:13
COUPLE THAT WITH ALL THE TROUBLE WE'VE BEEN HAVING WITH SABOTAGE, THERE'S NO ONE ELSE I TRUST MORE!
OH, AND, TAKEN TOGETHER, NANCY AND BESS ARE STILL LIGHTER THAN ME, ADDING TO THE CAR'S EFFICIENCY!
W
AND THEY'RE MORE SURE-FOOTED! AHHH!
2:35:23

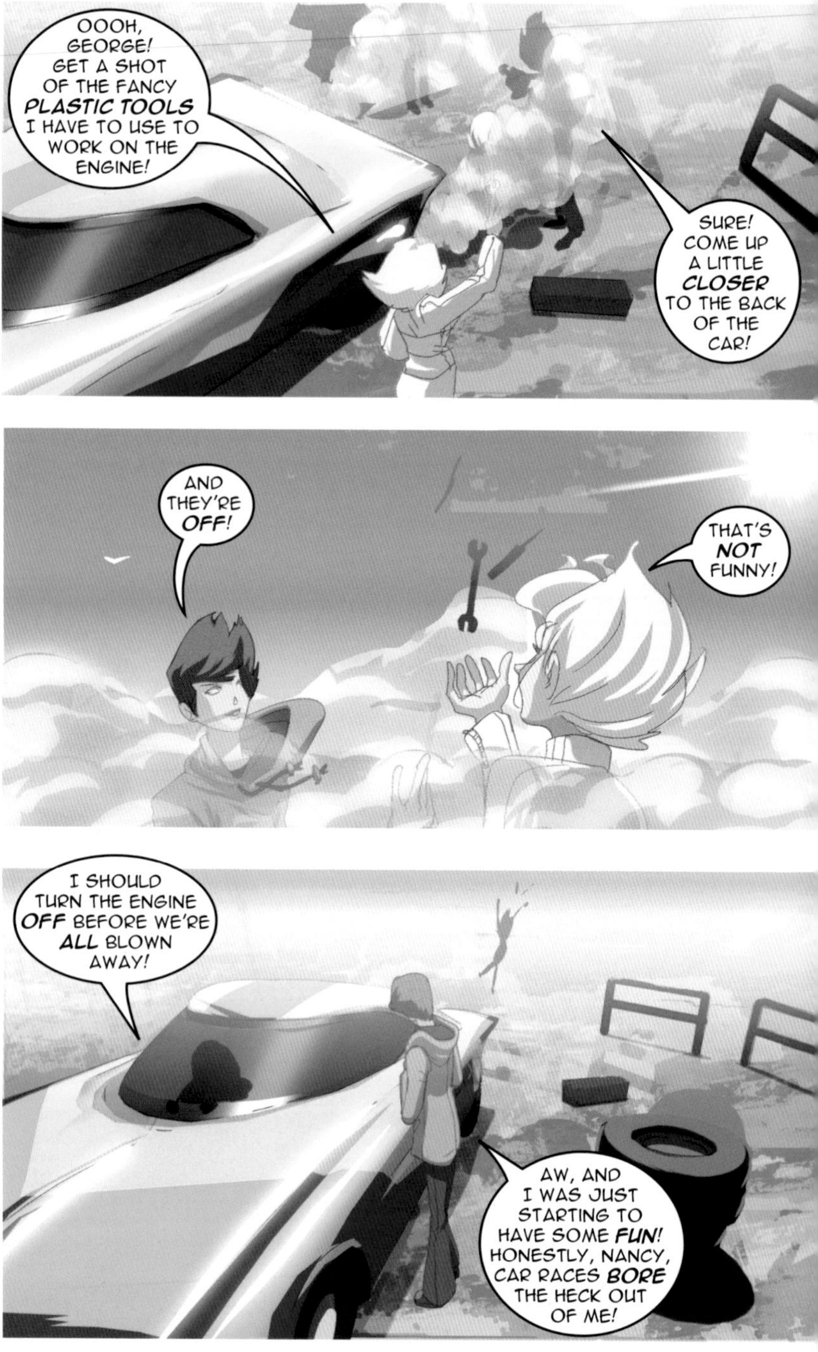
OOOH, GEORGE! GET A SHOT OF THE FANCY PLASTIC TOOLS I HAVE TO USE TO WORK ON THE ENGINE!
SURE! COME UP A LITTLE CLOSER TO THE BACK OF THE CAR!
AND THEY'RE OFF!
THAT'S NOT FUNNY!
I SHOULD TURN THE ENGINE OFF BEFORE WE'RE ALL BLOWN AWAY!
AW, AND I WAS JUST STARTING TO HAVE SOME FUN! HONESTLY, NANCY, CAR RACES BORE THE HECK OUT OF ME!

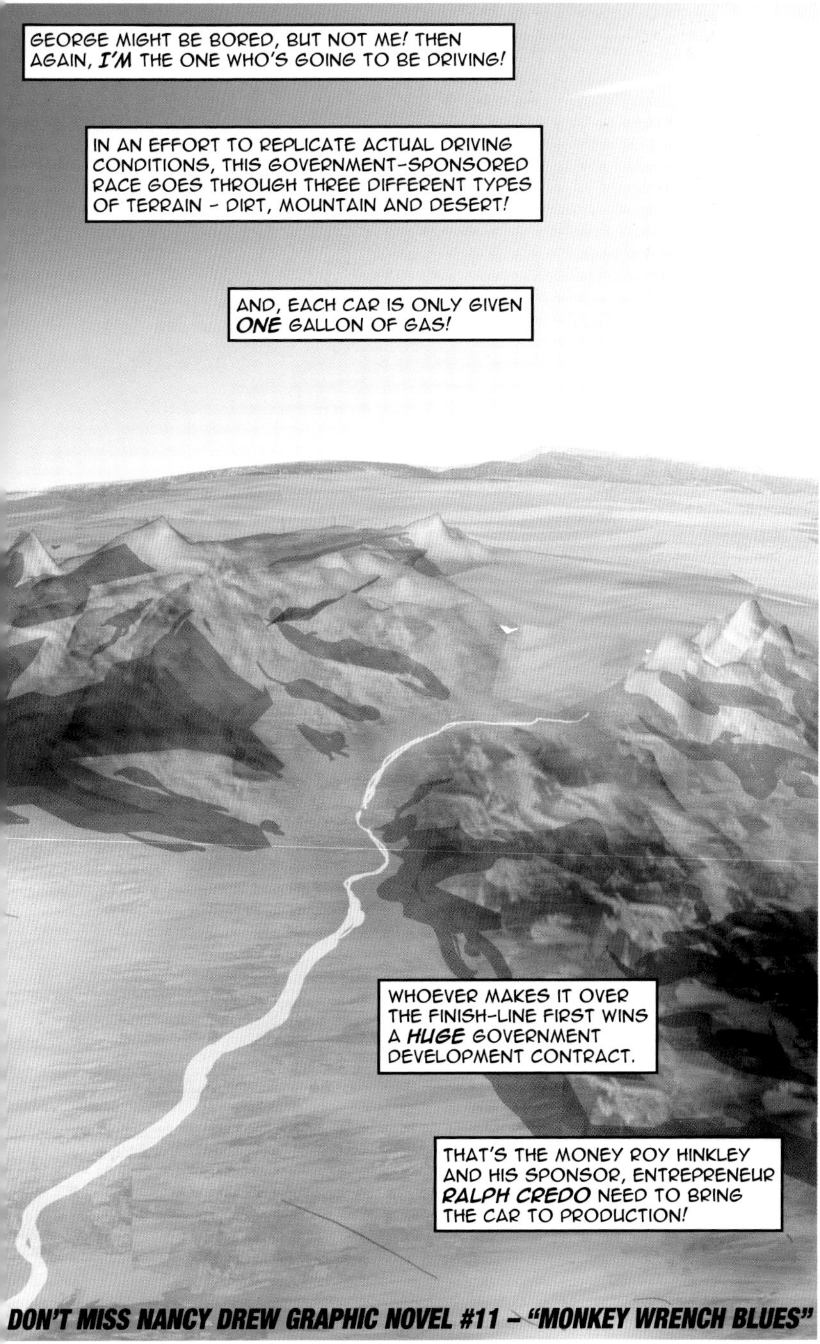
GEORGE MIGHT BE BORED, BUT NOT ME! THEN AGAIN, I'M THE ONE WHO'S GOING TO BE DRIVING!
IN AN EFFORT TO REPLICATE ACTUAL DRIVING CONDITIONS, THIS GOVERNMENT-SPONSORED RACE GOES THROUGH THREE DIFFERENT TYPES OF TERRAIN - DIRT, MOUNTAIN AND DESERT!
AND, EACH CAR IS ONLY GIVEN ONE GALLON OF GAS!
WHOEVER MAKES IT OVER THE FINISH-LINE FIRST WINS A HUGE GOVERNMENT DEVELOPMENT CONTRACT.
THAT'S THE MONEY ROY HINKLEY AND HIS SPONSOR, ENTREPRENEUR RALPH CREDO NEED TO BRING THE CAR TO PRODUCTION!
DON'T MISS NANCY DREW GRAPHIC NOVEL #11 – "MONKEY WRENCH BLUES"

THE **HARDY BOYS**®

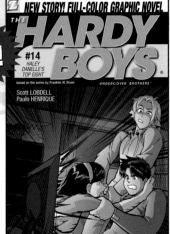

Eye a mystery . . .

Read NANCY DREW

girl detective™

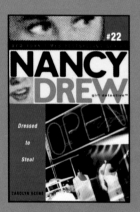

Dressed to Steal
New in February 2007

Hot young designer Alicia Adams is opening a boutique in her hometown of River Heights, and the press is all over the event. Opening day turns out to be more popular than expected—a surging crowd leads to the store window being smashed! Alicia's most expensive dress is destroyed, and her whole store is vandalized. Nancy may not be a fashion expert, but this is one case she's ready to size up!

Have you solved all of Nancy's latest cases?

Pit of Vipers

The Orchid Thief

Getting Burned

Close Encounters

Comin in Apr

Troubled Waters

Visit www.SimonSaysSleuth.com for more Nancy Drew books

Aladdin Paperbacks • Simon & Schuster Children's Publishing • A CBS Company
Nancy Drew © Simon & Schuster, Inc.

WATCH OUT FOR PAPERCUTZ™

Guess what? If you're reading this, that means you may be a Papercutz person. Don't panic -- that's a good thing. It means you're not only enjoying the latest, greatest Hardy Boys graphic novel, but you're part of a special club that's on the cutting edge of pop culture entertainment.

Let's back up a little. If you're just joining the Papercutz party, allow me to indroduce myself. I'm Jim Salicrup, Papercutz Editor-in-Chief. It's my happy responsibility to produce the best graphic novels for people of all ages. Graphic novels, as I'm sure you're hip enough to know, are simply comicbooks disguised as regular books. Or as some people say "real books."

Graphic novels also happen to be the latest thing to take the publishing world by storm. Just a few years ago, only comic-book publishers produced graphic novels, but now just about every big-time publisher there is wants to get in on the act. And you know, we think that's terrific. The more publishers giving opportunities to writers and artists to create all-new graphic novels, the greater the chances are that we'll get to see some amazing new graphic novels from new writers and artists.

On the other hand, with so many graphic novels being produced at such a rapid rate -- more now than ever before -- it's easy to be completely overwhelmed by it all. How can anyone know which graphic novels to choose, with so many to pick from? Well, we have one helpful suggestion. If you like the graphic novel you're reading now, chances are you may enjoy other Papercutz graphic novels. In the following pages, you'll find some sample pages from TALES FROM THE CRYPT, which features several scary stories within each volume, and CLASSICS ILLUSTRATED, which features comicbook adaptations of many of the world's greatest novels, such as The Wind in the Willows, Great Expectations, The Invisible Man, and many more.

So, check us out. If you like what you see, you may just be a Papercutz person. And, as we said, that's a good thing.

Thanks,

THE OLD EDITOR
Caricature by Rick Parker

Greetings, Fiends!

It's your ol' pal the CRYPT-KEEPER here, giving a guided TERRIFYING TOUR through the SCARIEST GRAPHIC NOVEL ever! It's TALES FROM THE CRYPT #4 "CRYPT-KEEPING IT REAL."

You'll not only find page after page of PULSE-POUNDING CHILLS, but me and my fellow GhouLunatics decided to get all COMPUTER AGE-Y on you! Wait till you see the stories we found on the INTERRED-NET site known as YOU-TOOMB! The SHOCKS and SUS-PENSE come at you FAST and FURIOUS!

But that's not all! Just gaze upon the CREEPY COVER on the next page, if you DARE! That poor guy made the UNFORTUNATE MISTAKE of appearing on a REALITY TV SHOW that was perhaps a little TOO REAL! The show is called "JUMPING THE SHARK" and you can see a quick preview starting right after the next PUTRID PAGE!

THE CRYPT-KEEPER

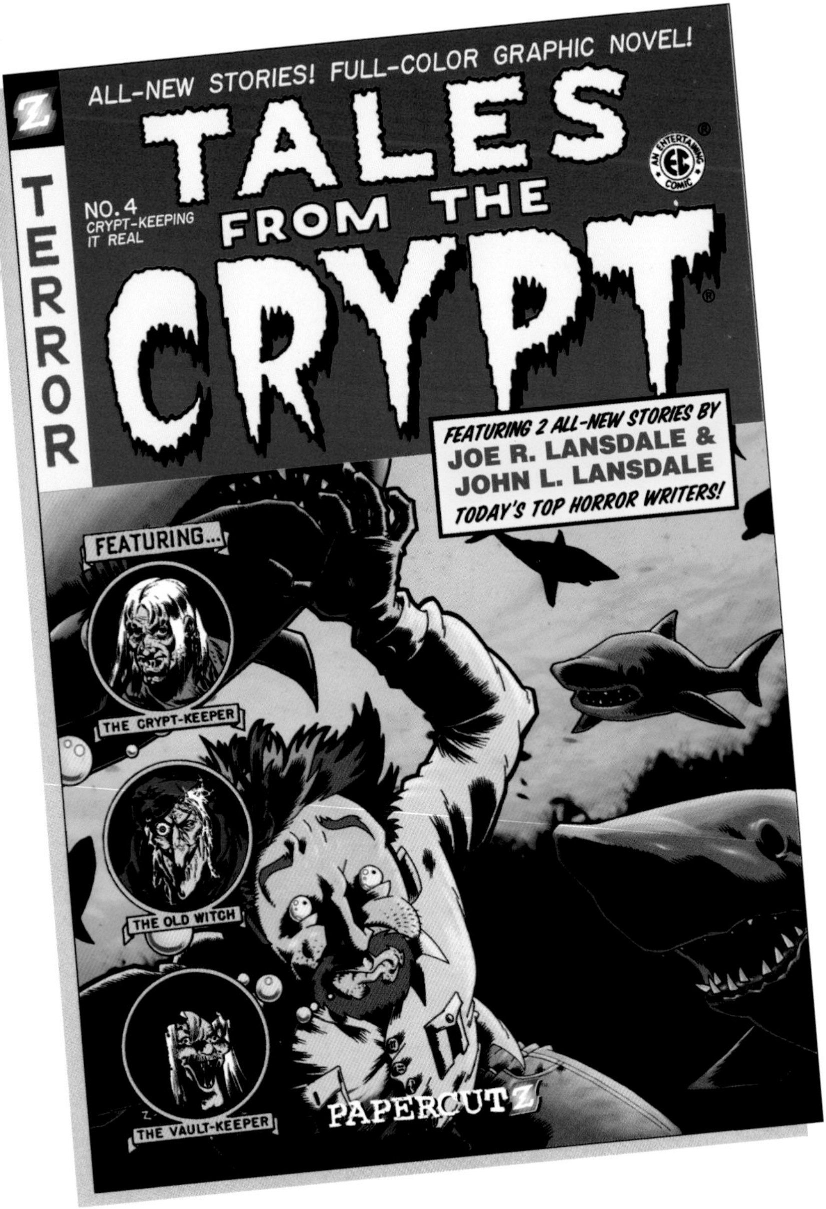
ALL-NEW STORIES! FULL-COLOR GRAPHIC NOVEL!
TERROR
TALES FROM THE CRYPT
NO. 4
CRYPT-KEEPING IT REAL
AN ENTERTAINING EC COMIC
FEATURING 2 ALL-NEW STORIES BY
JOE R. LANSDALE &
JOHN L. LANSDALE
TODAY'S TOP HORROR WRITERS!
FEATURING...
THE CRYPT-KEEPER
THE OLD WITCH
THE VAULT-KEEPER
PAPERCUTZ

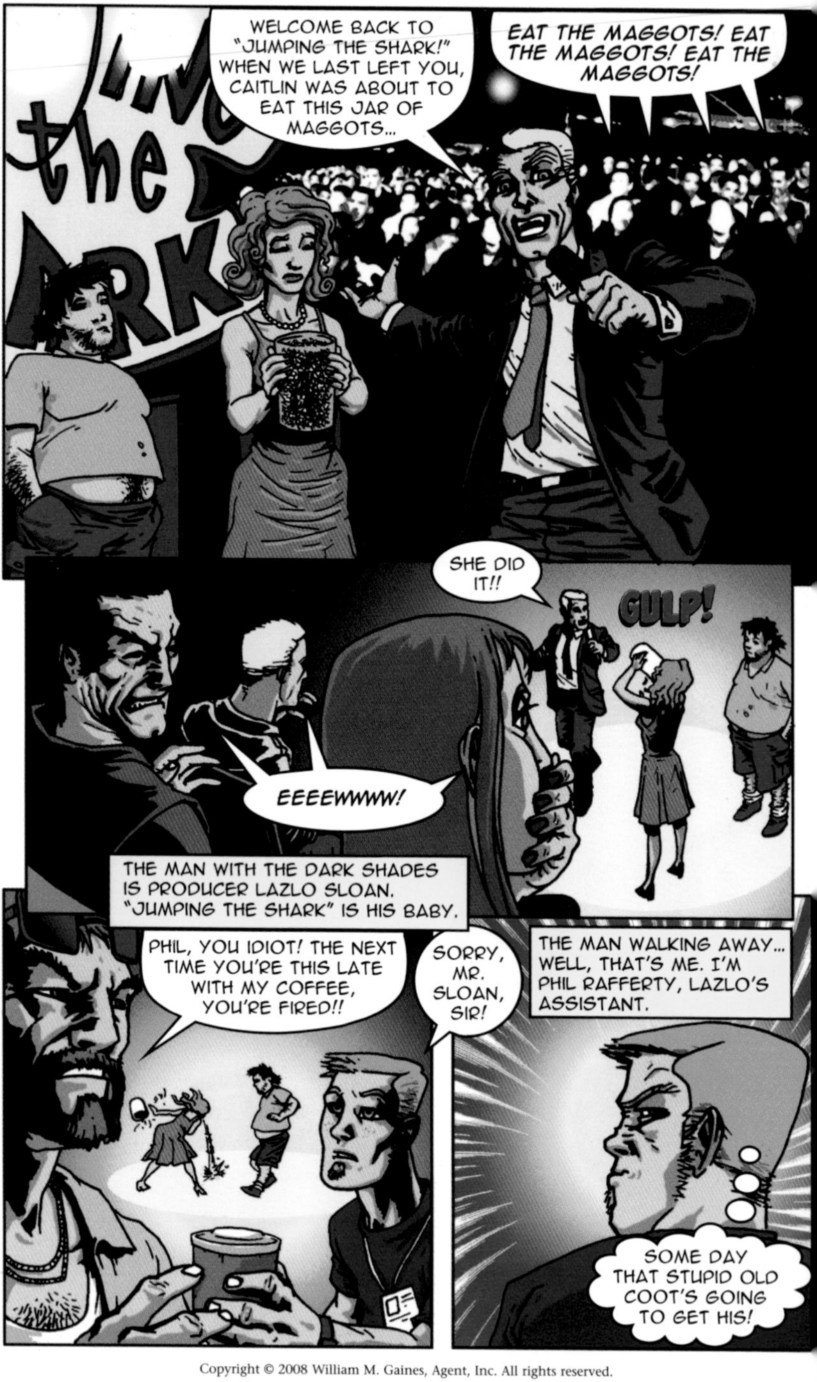
WELCOME BACK TO "JUMPING THE SHARK!" WHEN WE LAST LEFT YOU, CAITLIN WAS ABOUT TO EAT THIS JAR OF MAGGOTS...
EAT THE MAGGOTS! EAT THE MAGGOTS! EAT THE MAGGOTS!
SHE DID IT!!
GULP!
EEEEWWWW!
THE MAN WITH THE DARK SHADES IS PRODUCER LAZLO SLOAN. "JUMPING THE SHARK" IS HIS BABY.
PHIL, YOU IDIOT! THE NEXT TIME YOU'RE THIS LATE WITH MY COFFEE, YOU'RE FIRED!!
SORRY, MR. SLOAN, SIR!
THE MAN WALKING AWAY... WELL, THAT'S ME. I'M PHIL RAFFERTY, LAZLO'S ASSISTANT.
SOME DAY THAT STUPID OLD COOT'S GOING TO GET HIS!

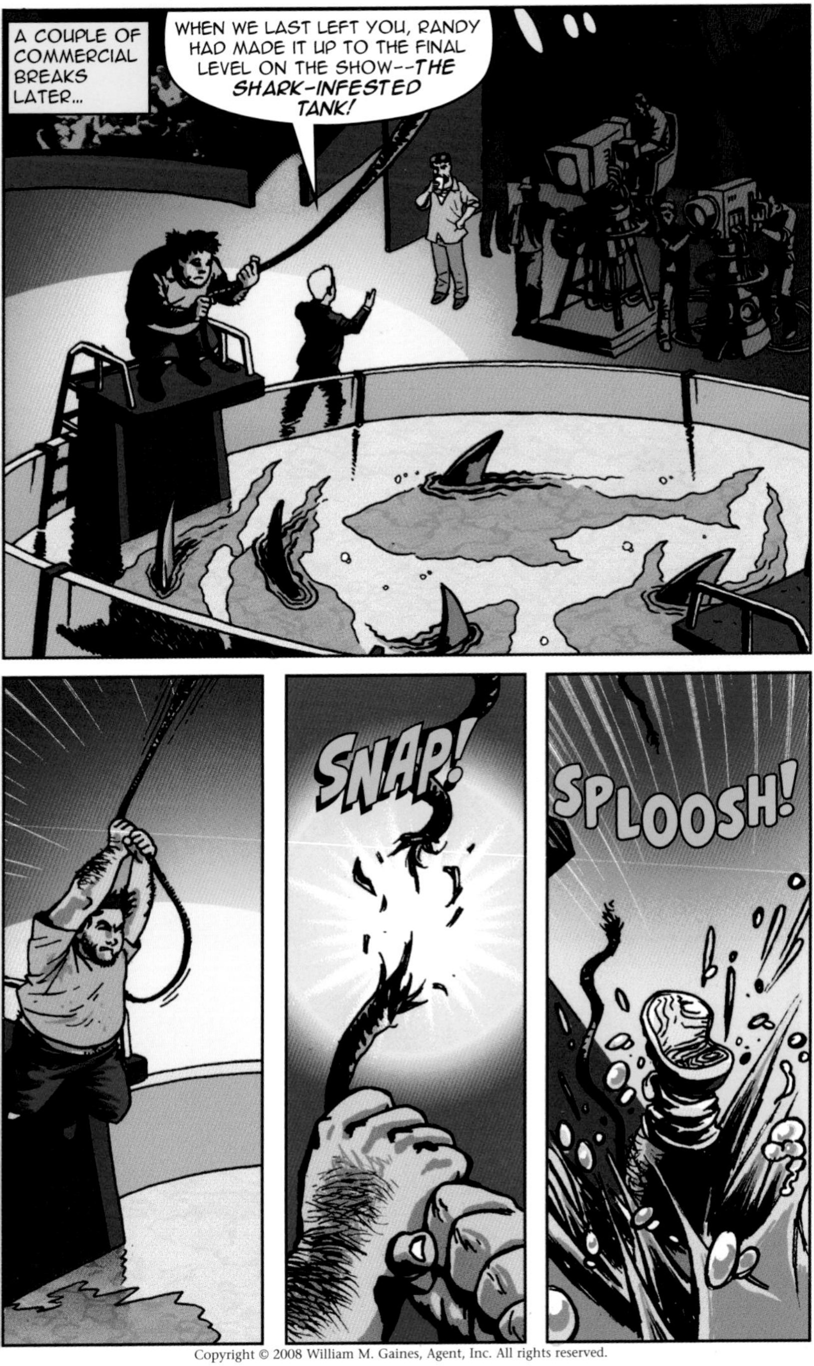
A COUPLE OF COMMERCIAL BREAKS LATER...
WHEN WE LAST LEFT YOU, RANDY HAD MADE IT UP TO THE FINAL LEVEL ON THE SHOW--*THE SHARK-INFESTED TANK!*
SNAP!
SPLOOSH!

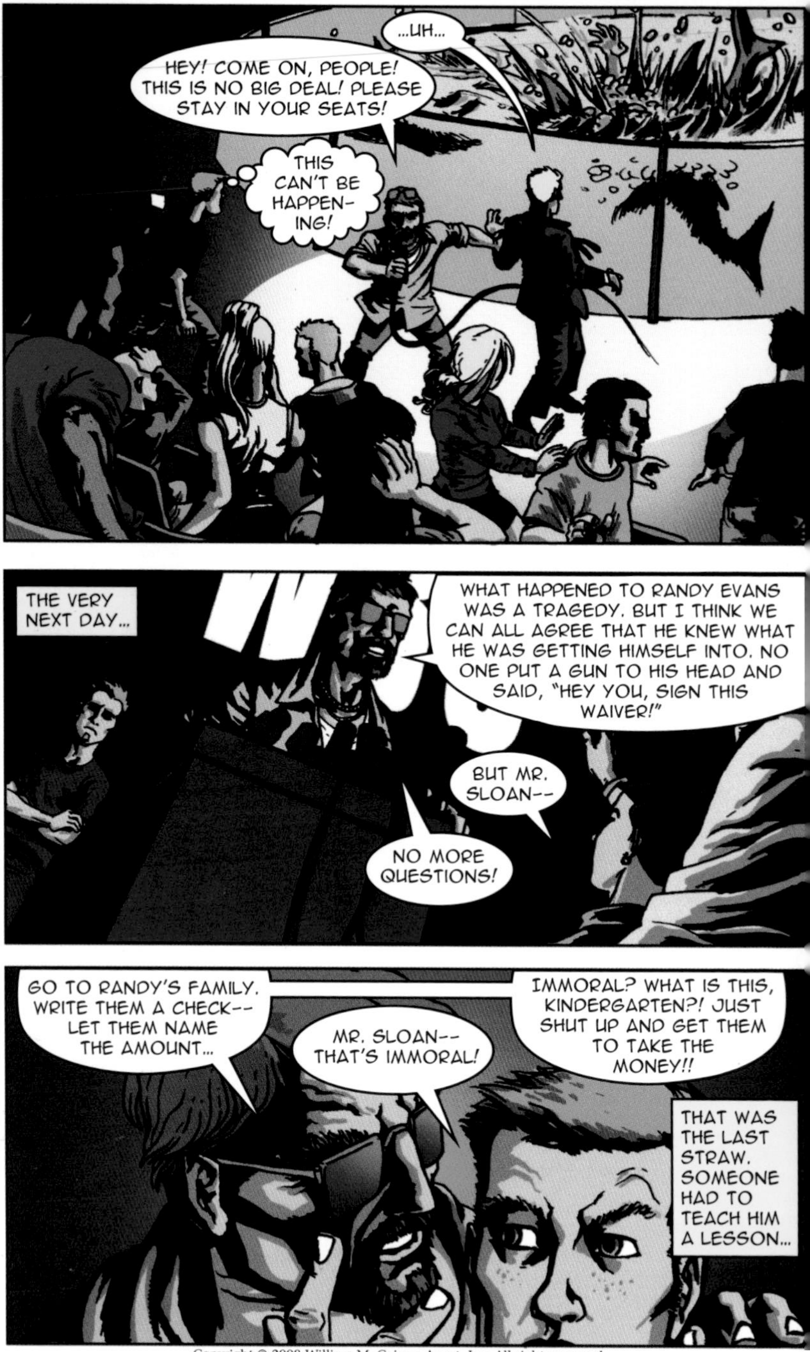
HEY! COME ON, PEOPLE! THIS IS NO BIG DEAL! PLEASE STAY IN YOUR SEATS!
...UH...
THIS CAN'T BE HAPPEN-ING!
THE VERY NEXT DAY...
WHAT HAPPENED TO RANDY EVANS WAS A TRAGEDY. BUT I THINK WE CAN ALL AGREE THAT HE KNEW WHAT HE WAS GETTING HIMSELF INTO. NO ONE PUT A GUN TO HIS HEAD AND SAID, "HEY YOU, SIGN THIS WAIVER!"
BUT MR. SLOAN--
NO MORE QUESTIONS!
GO TO RANDY'S FAMILY. WRITE THEM A CHECK-- LET THEM NAME THE AMOUNT...
MR. SLOAN-- THAT'S IMMORAL!
IMMORAL? WHAT IS THIS, KINDERGARTEN?! JUST SHUT UP AND GET THEM TO TAKE THE MONEY!!
THAT WAS THE LAST STRAW. SOMEONE HAD TO TEACH HIM A LESSON...

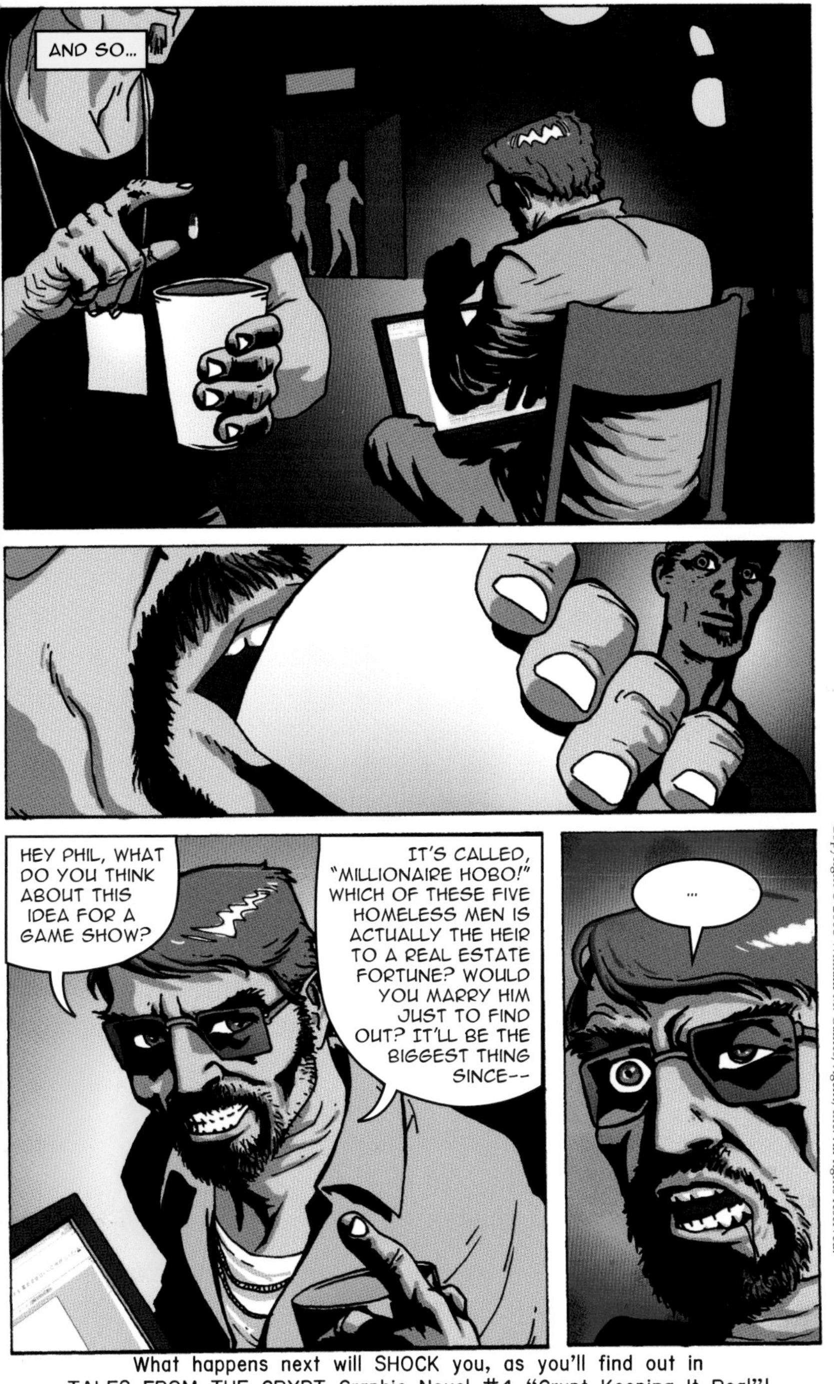
AND SO...
HEY PHIL, WHAT DO YOU THINK ABOUT THIS IDEA FOR A GAME SHOW?
IT'S CALLED, "MILLIONAIRE HOBO!" WHICH OF THESE FIVE HOMELESS MEN IS ACTUALLY THE HEIR TO A REAL ESTATE FORTUNE? WOULD YOU MARRY HIM JUST TO FIND OUT? IT'LL BE THE BIGGEST THING SINCE--
...

What happens next will SHOCK you, as you'll find out in TALES FROM THE CRYPT Graphic Novel #4 "Crypt-Keeping It Real"!

But in the meantime here's a quick peek at "MOONLIGHT SONATA" also in CRYPT #4...

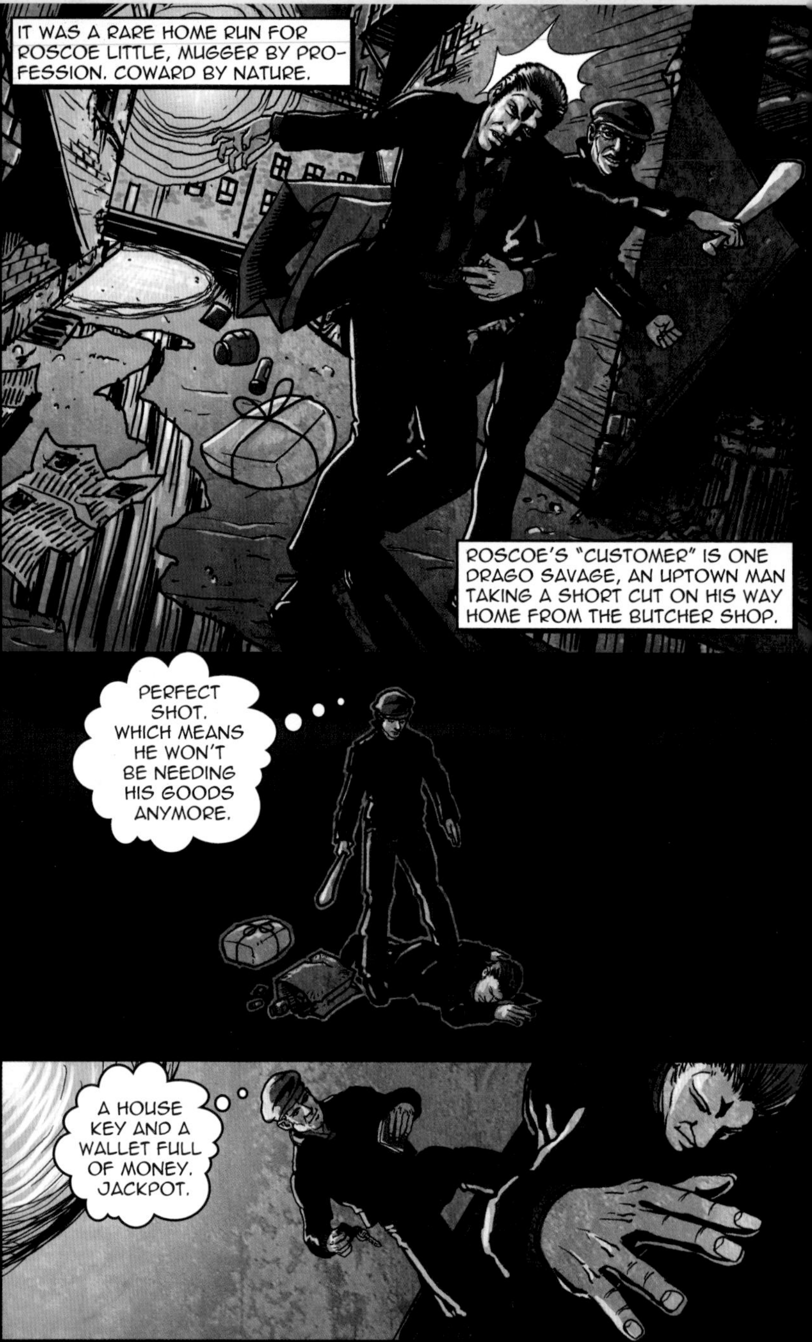
IT WAS A RARE HOME RUN FOR ROSCOE LITTLE, MUGGER BY PRO-FESSION. COWARD BY NATURE.
ROSCOE'S "CUSTOMER" IS ONE DRAGO SAVAGE, AN UPTOWN MAN TAKING A SHORT CUT ON HIS WAY HOME FROM THE BUTCHER SHOP.
PERFECT SHOT. WHICH MEANS HE WON'T BE NEEDING HIS GOODS ANYMORE.
A HOUSE KEY AND A WALLET FULL OF MONEY. JACKPOT.

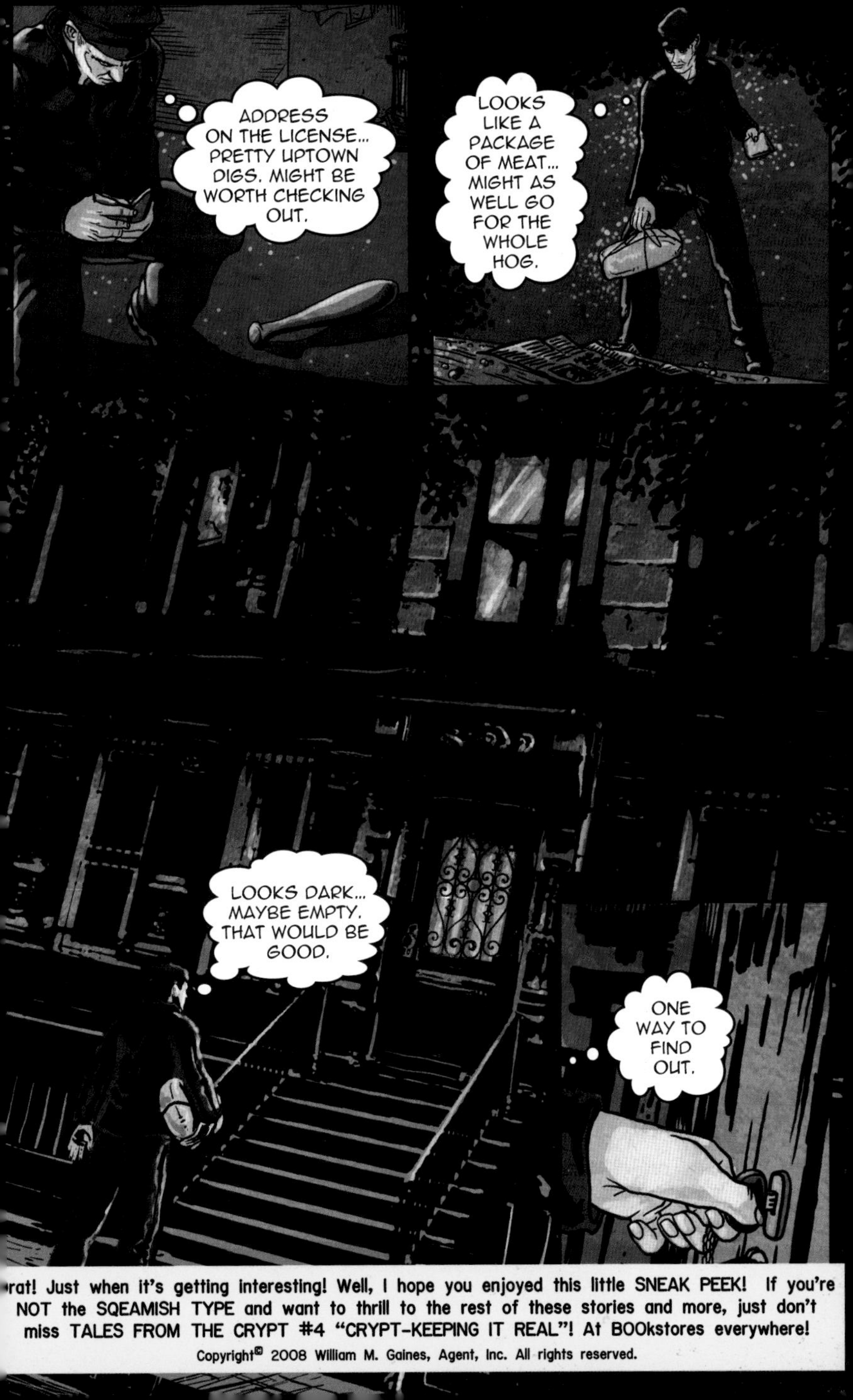
ADDRESS ON THE LICENSE... PRETTY UPTOWN DIGS. MIGHT BE WORTH CHECKING OUT.
LOOKS LIKE A PACKAGE OF MEAT... MIGHT AS WELL GO FOR THE WHOLE HOG.
LOOKS DARK... MAYBE EMPTY. THAT WOULD BE GOOD.
ONE WAY TO FIND OUT.

rat! Just when it's getting interesting! Well, I hope you enjoyed this little SNEAK PEEK! If you're NOT the SQEAMISH TYPE and want to thrill to the rest of these stories and more, just don't miss TALES FROM THE CRYPT #4 "CRYPT-KEEPING IT REAL"! At BOOkstores everywhere!

CLASSICS *Illustrated*

Featuring Stories by the World's Greatest Authors

Returns in two new series from Papercutz!

The original, best-selling series of comics adaptations of the world's greatest literature, CLASSICS ILLUSTRATED, returns in two new formats--the original, featuring abridged adaptations of classic novels, and CLASSICS ILLUSTRATED DELUXE, featuring longer, more expansive adaptations-from graphic novel publisher Papercutz. "We're very proud to say that Papercutz has received such an enthusiastic reception from librarians and school teachers for its NANCY DREW and HARDY BOYS graphic novels as well as THE LIFE OF POPE JOHN PAUL II...*IN COMICS!*, that it only seemed logical for us to bring back the original CLASSICS ILLUSTRATED comicbook series beloved by parents, educators, and librarians," explained Papercutz Publisher, Terry Nantier. "We can't thank the enlightened librarians and teachers who have supported Papercutz enough. And we're thrilled that they're so excited about CLASSICS ILLUSTRATED."

Upcoming titles include The Invisible Man, Tales from the Brothers Grimm, and Frankenstein.

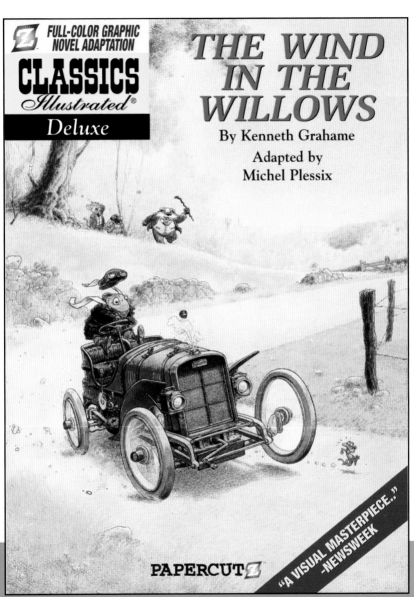

FULL-COLOR GRAPHIC NOVEL ADAPTATION

CLASSICS Illustrated®
Deluxe

THE WIND IN THE WILLOWS

By Kenneth Grahame

Adapted by
Michel Plessix

PAPERCUTZ

"A VISUAL MASTERPIECE.."
-NEWSWEEK

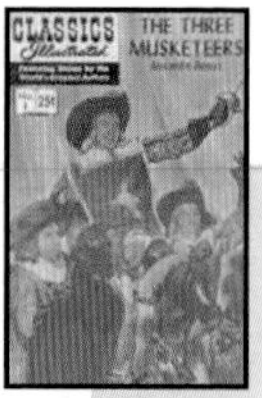
CLASSICS Illustrated
THE THREE MUSKETEERS
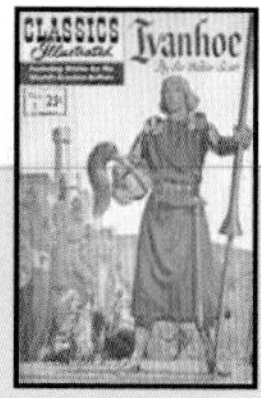
CLASSICS Illustrated
Ivanhoe
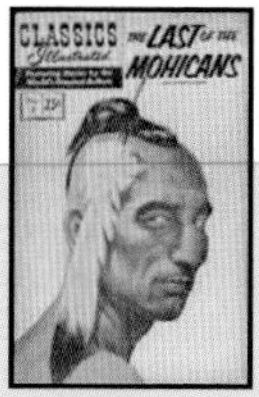
CLASSICS Illustrated
THE LAST OF THE MOHICANS
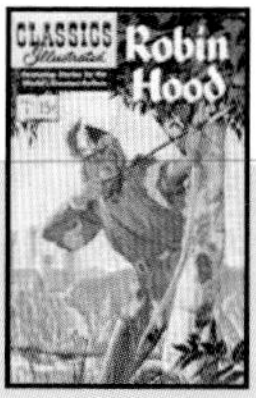
CLASSICS Illustrated
Robin Hood
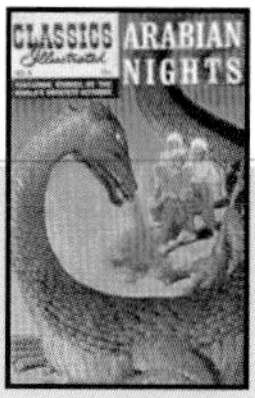
CLASSICS Illustrated
ARABIAN NIGHTS
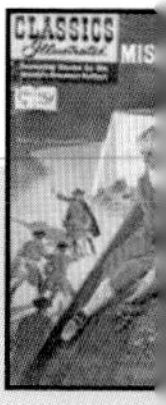
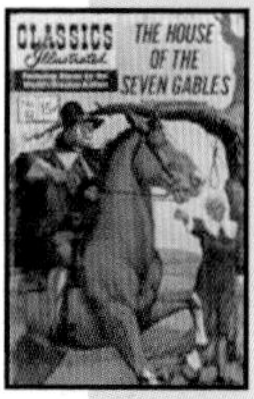
CLASSICS Illustrated
THE HOUSE OF THE SEVEN GABLES
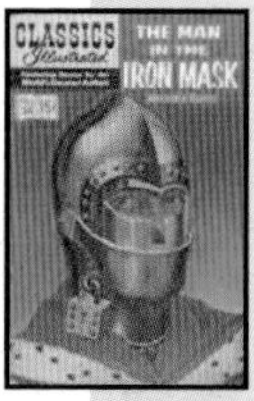
CLASSICS Illustrated
THE MAN IN THE IRON MASK
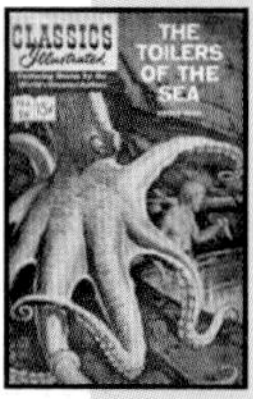
CLASSICS Illustrated
THE TOILERS OF THE SEA
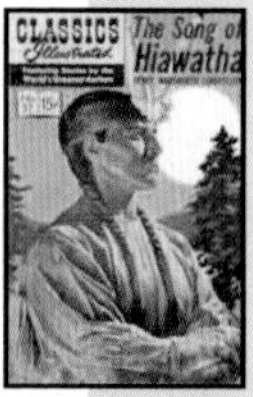
CLASSICS Illustrated

A Short History of CLASSICS ILLUSTRATED...

William B. Jones Jr. is the author of Classics Illustrated: A Cultural History, which offers a comprehensive overview of the original comic-book series and the writers, artists, editors, and publishers behind-the-scenes. With Mr. Jones Jr.'s kind permission, here's a very short overview of the history of CLASSICS ILLUSTRATED adapted from his 2005 essay on Albert Kanter.

CLASSICS ILLUSTRATED was the creation of Albert Lewis Kanter, a visionary publisher, who from 1941 to 1971, introduced young readers worldwide to the realms of literature, history, folklore, mythology, and science in over 200 titles in such comicbook series as CLASSICS ILLUSTRATED and CLASSICS ILLUSTRATED JUNIOR. Kanter, inspired by the success of the first comicbooks published in the early 30s and late 40s, believed he

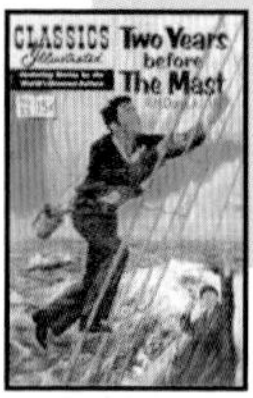
CLASSICS Illustrated
Two Years before The Mast
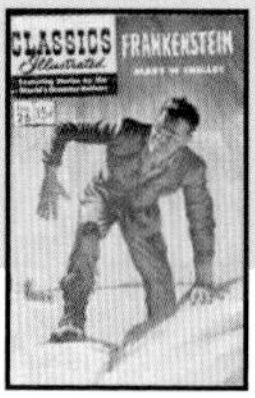
CLASSICS Illustrated
FRANKENSTEIN
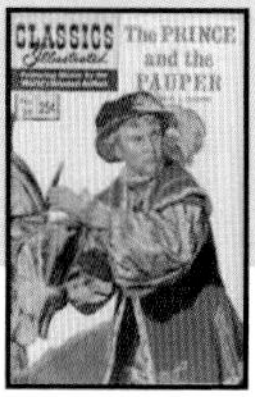
CLASSICS Illustrated
The PRINCE and the PAUPER
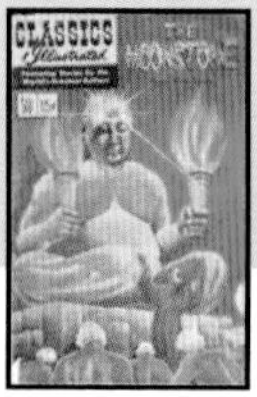
CLASSICS Illustrated
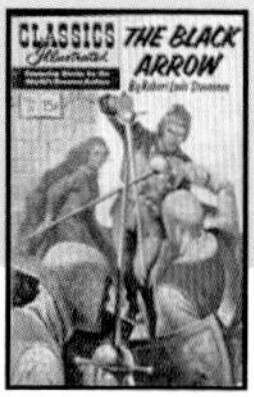
CLASSICS Illustrated
THE BLACK ARROW
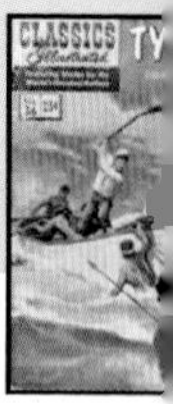

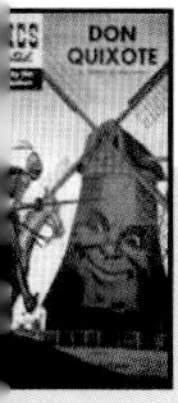
DON QUIXOTE
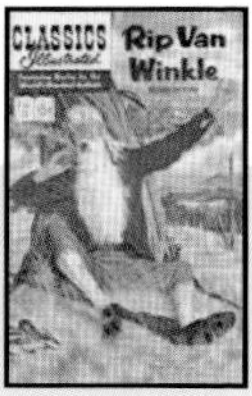
CLASSICS Illustrated
Rip Van Winkle
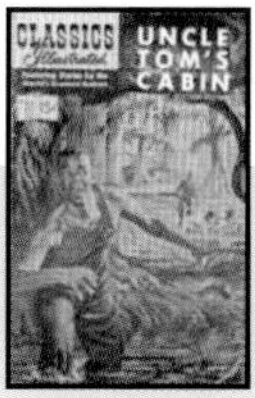
CLASSICS Illustrated
UNCLE TOM'S CABIN
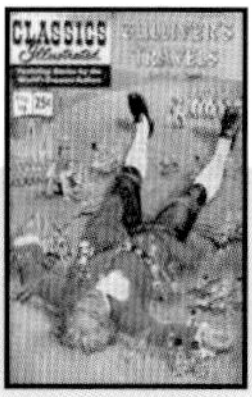
CLASSICS Illustrated
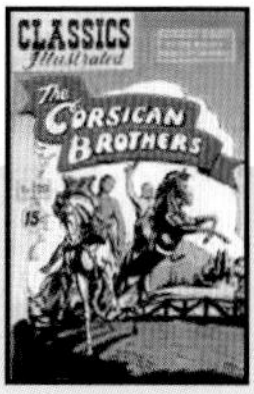
CLASSICS Illustrated
The Corsican Brothers
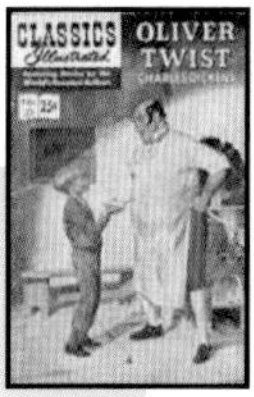
CLASSICS Illustrated
OLIVER TWIST

could use the same medium to introduce young readers to the world of great literature. CLASSIC COMICS (later changed to CLASSICS ILLUSTRATED in 1947) was launched in 1941, and soon the comicbook adaptations of Shakespeare, Stevenson, Twain, Verne, and other authors, were being used in schools and endorsed by educators.

CLASSICS ILLUSTRATED was translated and distributed in countries such as Canada, Great Britain, the Netherlands, Greece, Brazil, Mexico, and Australia. The genial publisher was hailed abroad as "Papa Klassiker." By the beginning of the 1960s, CLASSICS ILLUSTRATED was the largest childrens publication in the world. The original CLASSICS ILLUSTRATED series adapted into comics 169 titles; among these were Frankenstein, 20,000 Leagues Under the Sea, Treasure Island, Julius Caesar, and Faust.

Albert L. Kanter died, March 17, 1973, leaving behind a rich legacy for the millions of readers whose imaginations were awakened by CLASSICS ILLUSTRATED.

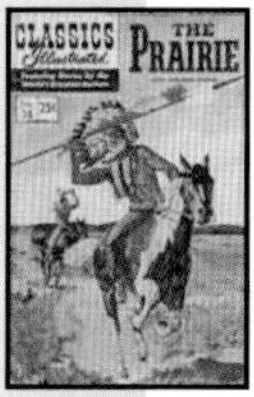
CLASSICS Illustrated
THE PRAIRIE
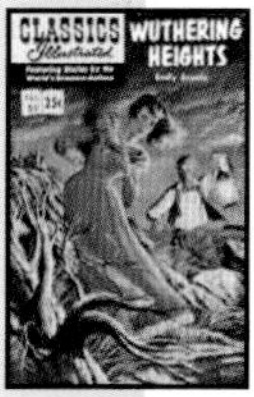
CLASSICS Illustrated
WUTHERING HEIGHTS
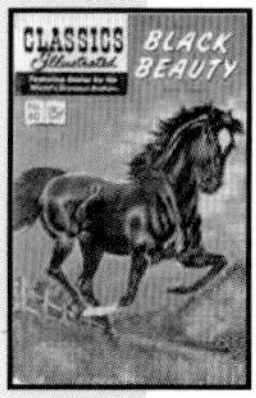
CLASSICS Illustrated
BLACK BEAUTY
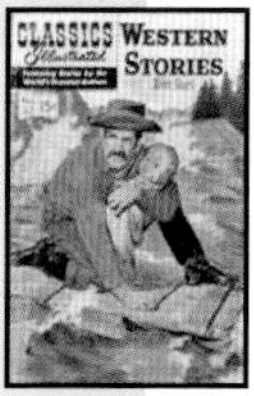
CLASSICS Illustrated
WESTERN STORIES
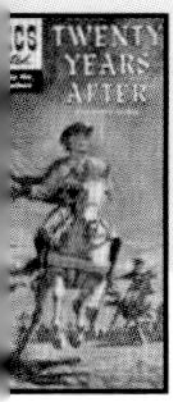
TWENTY YEARS AFTER
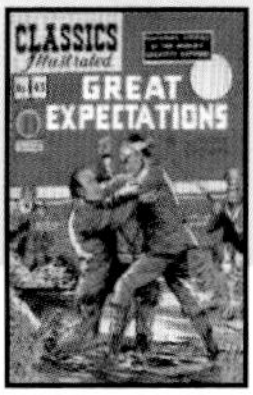
CLASSICS Illustrated
GREAT EXPECTATIONS
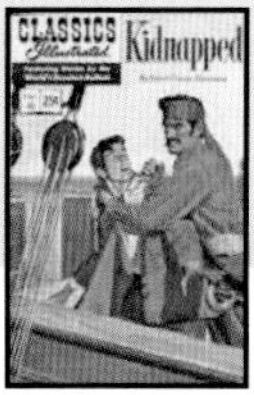
CLASSICS Illustrated
Kidnapped
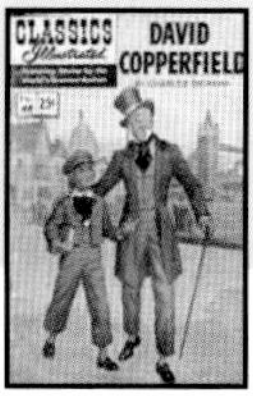
CLASSICS Illustrated
DAVID COPPERFIELD
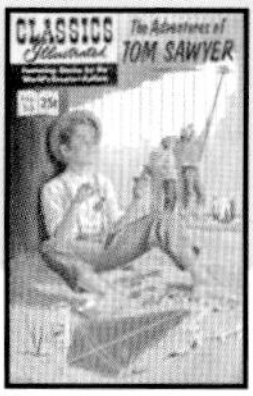
CLASSICS Illustrated
The Adventures of TOM SAWYER
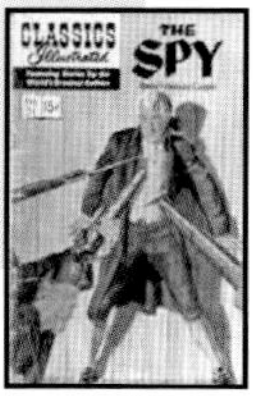
CLASSICS Illustrated
THE SPY

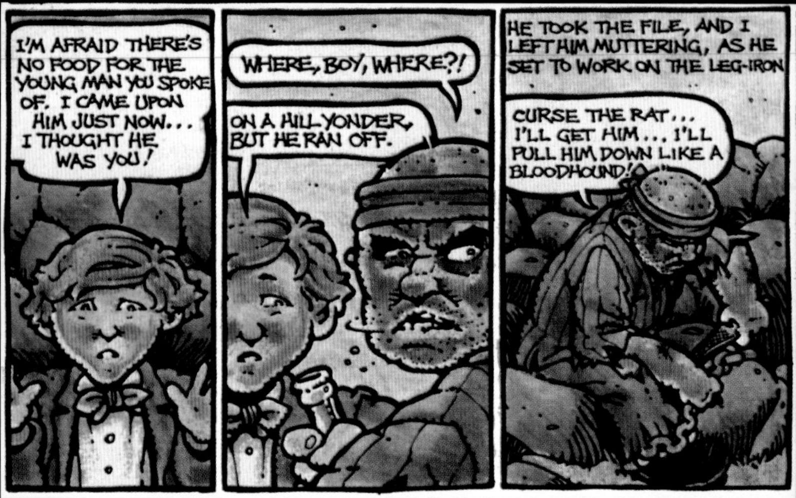
I'M AFRAID THERE'S NO FOOD FOR THE YOUNG MAN YOU SPOKE OF. I CAME UPON HIM JUST NOW... I THOUGHT HE WAS YOU!
WHERE, BOY, WHERE?!
ON A HILL YONDER, BUT HE RAN OFF.
HE TOOK THE FILE, AND I LEFT HIM MUTTERING, AS HE SET TO WORK ON THE LEG-IRON
CURSE THE RAT... I'LL GET HIM... I'LL PULL HIM DOWN LIKE A BLOODHOUND!

CLASSICS ILLUSTRATED was re-launched in 1990 in graphic novel/book form by the Berkley Publishing Group and First Publishing, Inc. featuring all-new adaptations by such top graphic novelists as Rick Geary, Bill Sienkiewicz, Kyle Baker, Gahan Wilson, and others. "First had the right idea, they just came out about 15 years too soon. Now bookstores are ready for graphic novels such as these," Jim explains. Many of these excellent adaptations have been acquired by Papercutz and will make up the new series of CLASSICS ILLUSTRATED titles.

The first volume of the new CLASSICS ILLUSTRATED series presents graphic novelist Rick Geary's adaptation of "Great Expectations" by Charles Dickens. The bittersweet tale of one boy's adolescence, and of the choices he makes to shape his destiny. Into an engrossing mystery, Dickens weaves a heartfelt inquiry into morals and virtues-as the orphan Pip, the convict Magwitch, the beautiful Estella, the bitter Miss Havisham, the goodhearted Biddy, the kind Joe and other memorable characters entwine in a battle of human nature. Rick Geary's delightful illustrations capture the newfound awe and frustrations of young Pip as he comes of age, and begins to understand the opportunities that life presents.

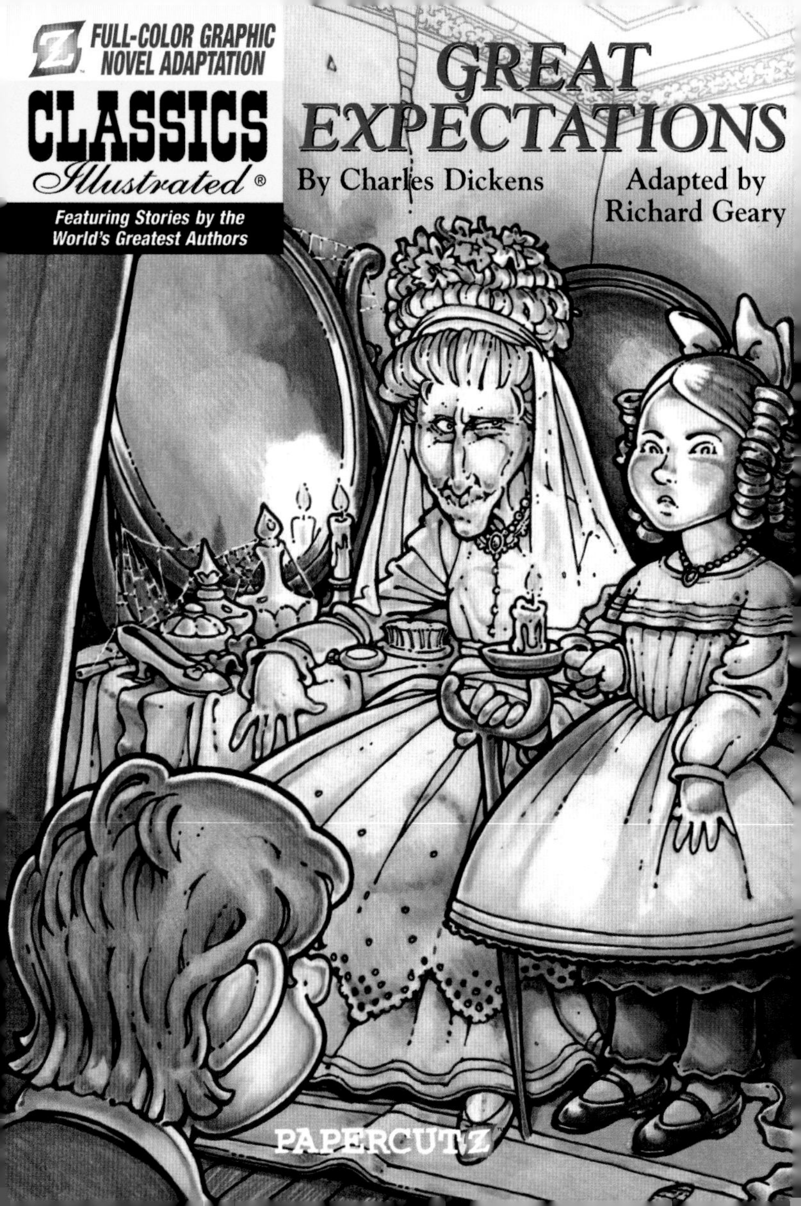
FULL-COLOR GRAPHIC
NOVEL ADAPTATION
CLASSICS
Illustrated®
Featuring Stories by the
World's Greatest Authors
GREAT
EXPECTATIONS
By Charles Dickens
Adapted by
Richard Geary
PAPERCUTZ

Here is a page of CLASSICS ILLUSTRATED #1 "Great Expectations" by Charles Dickens, as adapted by Rick Geary.

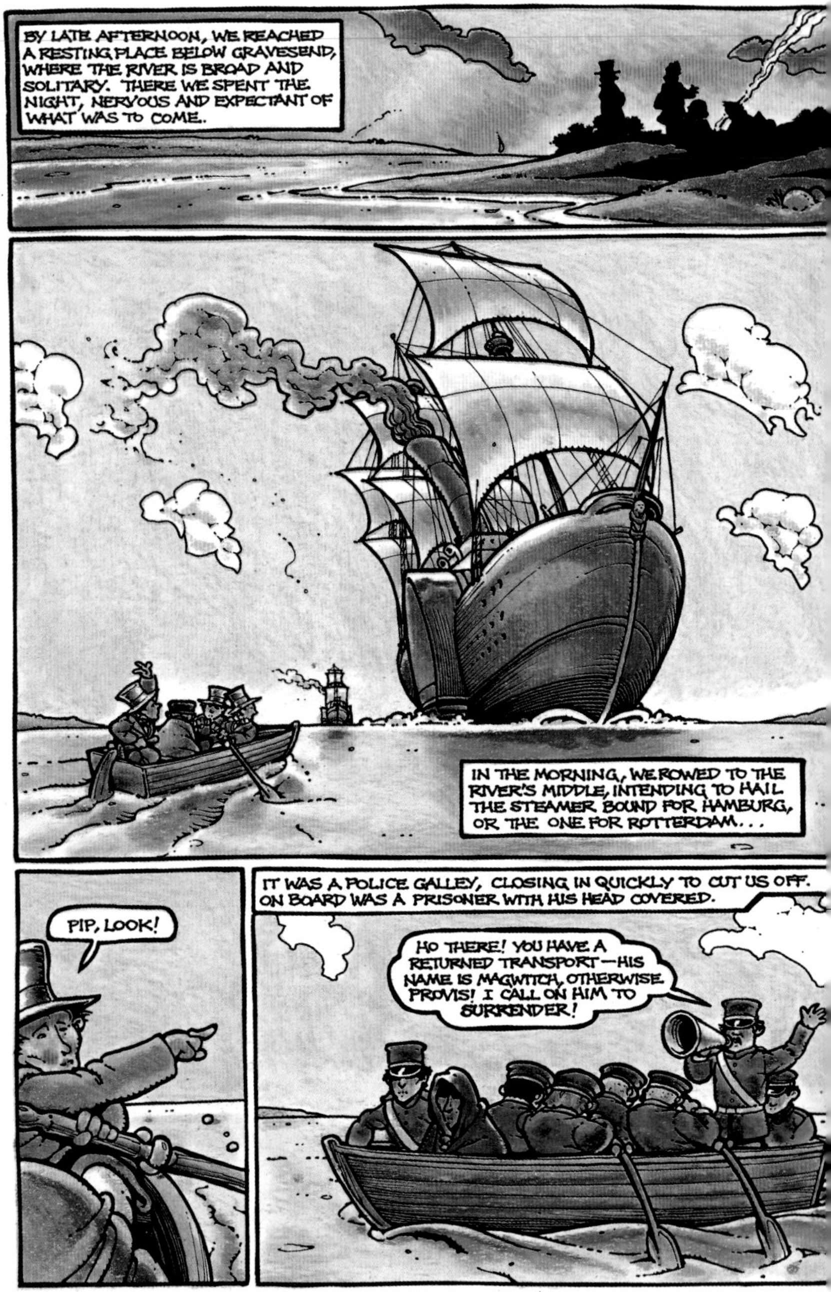
BY LATE AFTERNOON, WE REACHED A RESTING PLACE BELOW GRAVESEND, WHERE THE RIVER IS BROAD AND SOLITARY. THERE WE SPENT THE NIGHT, NERVOUS AND EXPECTANT OF WHAT WAS TO COME.
IN THE MORNING, WE ROWED TO THE RIVER'S MIDDLE, INTENDING TO HAIL THE STEAMER BOUND FOR HAMBURG, OR THE ONE FOR ROTTERDAM...
PIP, LOOK!
IT WAS A POLICE GALLEY, CLOSING IN QUICKLY TO CUT US OFF. ON BOARD WAS A PRISONER WITH HIS HEAD COVERED.
HO THERE! YOU HAVE A RETURNED TRANSPORT—HIS NAME IS MAGWITCH, OTHERWISE PROVIS! I CALL ON HIM TO SURRENDER!